McLEAN'S HEART

a novel

ALSO BY PATTI DOTY

Runaway
Finding Home

McLEAN'S HEART

a novel

PATTI DOTY

Lucky Bat Books

A Lucky Bat Book
McLean's Heart
Copyright © 2018 by Patti Doty

ISBN-10: 1-943588-75-9
ISBN-13: 978-1-943588-75-6

Cover Artist: Nuno Moreira
Published by Lucky Bat Books
10 9 8 7 6 5 4 3 2 1
Discover more from this author at pattidoty.com

For Miss Bordewich

CHAPTER 1

HEAD RESTING ON BOTH HANDS, ELBOWS planted on the two-top claiming more than their allotted space, Chris McLean stared into his steaming coffee—drink or drown, his expression proclaimed—and rued his vow. One slug of Maker's Mark would go down just fine. No harm, no foul. A second would remind him that he didn't have to make any decisions today. A third might fill the void.

May 27—twenty-nine days since the MI. Nothing left but surveying the wreck he had become, wondering if there was anything left to salvage.

"Shite," he grumbled under his breath, "just take me out and shoot me." On this bright, sunny morning, he was nothing more than the dottle in his father's pipe, good for nothing but a trip to the ashtray.

"Excuse me?" a small voice at his right shoulder interrupted. "May I sit here? There's no other place, and I really need my tea."

Looking around, Chris saw that the other tables were, in fact, occupied, and he suppressed a groan. On a road trip to nowhere and too exhausted to continue, he'd slipped into this California backwoods after midnight to find two hotels—one chock full of fishermen and hikers, the second with an accidental vacancy, thanks to some poor soul's emergency appendectomy. The proprietor, roused from a face-rumpling sleep, had generously changed sheets, provided clean towels, and suggested that business could wait for morning. Grateful, Chris had slept through breakfast, then handed over his credit card and now wished he'd skipped coffee, too. The last thing he wanted was company.

Before he could respond, a petite woman entered his field of vision, her tote bag depressing one shoulder, her super-sized gray purse dangling from an elbow, and a cup and saucer trembling in her hand.

The manners drilled into him by his Irish mother forced him to his feet.

Tan liquid sloshed as her cup wavered. He reached to rescue it.

Cup and saucer eluded his hand and crashed to the table, spreading hot tea and bits of flowered china over the open pages of the journal he'd meant to read.

"Dang," the woman said in a matter-of-fact tone.

She dropped into the opposite seat, her bag bumped the table, and Chris's glass wobbled and surrendered. Commingled, tea and water raced for the floor. The woman pulled tissues from her purse and, in a manner as matter-of-fact as her tone, went about staunching the flow.

Amused now, Chris resumed his seat and applied his own napkin to the task.

Minutes later, the woman looked at him over a pile of sopping paper and held out her hand. "Sorry about that," she said. "My name's Grace—clearly a misnomer."

Chapter 2
McLean

McLEAN WIPED HIS HAND ON HIS pant leg before extending it. "Chris McLean." Honesty kept him from adding, "Happy to meet you."

The woman, Grace, gestured at the sodden mess on the table between them. "Sorry about that. I'm used to it, but most people aren't."

She sounded so rueful he couldn't suppress a smile. "No worries. Shall I get you another cup?"

"If you wouldn't mind." She dug in her purse, scattering its contents, and unearthed a wallet.

He stood, waved the money away. "No need."

When he returned minutes later, the teacup small in his hand, his soggy *Journal of Thoracic and Cardiovascular Surgery* lay spread across an adjacent chair. On this morning when he'd been sure he'd never smile again, he set the new cup on the damp vinyl table top and smiled for a second time.

Grace grasped the cup in both hands, raised it to her mouth, and took what appeared to be a lifesaving swig.

"Ahh." Another swallow, daintier this time, and she smiled at him. "Thanks. I missed breakfast this morning, and I'm worthless without my caffeine."

"Here you go." A super-sized sweet roll appeared between them. The server, a boy of about sixteen with scattered papules and pustules and five or six dark whiskers posing as a soul patch, added a stack of napkins, a knife, and two forks to the table's confusion. "Anything else?"

When McLean shook his head, the boy scooped up the wet napkins and china chunks as though he did it every day and ignored Grace's sorrys and thank yous.

"Well, *he* earns a big tip," she said, watching him go, then nodding toward the pastry. "Yours?"

"Ours. Seems we both missed breakfast."

Now he expected her to gabble on, ask questions, tell her life story or demand his. That had been his experience with aged-out sorority girls. She had the look—dark brown hair arranged loosely at the nape of her neck, no roots visible; faint pink at her cheeks and lips; short fingernails white-tipped and shiny; a soft pink sweater with its arms tied around her neck in the manner of an old-fashioned Yale man. A well-to-do woman with an uneventful life.

Instead, she tipped her head to one side, a little brown bird eager for table crumbs, and said, "Thanks, I needed this." She fumbled the knife twice before she got a firm grip and divided the pastry into two pieces. "There, I cut so you pick."

Chris chuckled. That had been his family's rule, too; the one with the knife didn't get to choose, thus averting many an argument that started with, "No fair, you cut yourself the biggest piece." He nodded, moved the smaller segment toward his side of the plate, and forked a piece into his mouth.

Again the head tilt, but no comment.

They ate and drank. The boy brought a pot of tea, topped off McLean's coffee. The silence was not uncomfortable.

When only crumbs remained, the woman cleared her throat and spoke. "Thank you again. That was kind. Keeps me from fainting on the hike."

Here it comes, he thought, the stupid getting-to-know-you conversation. The need to escape rose like saliva in his mouth, but before he could act, the memory of his Irish mother poked like a sharp stick. "It won't hurt you to be nice," she'd have said. "Besides, what else do you have to do?"

Ouch.

He settled back in the chair and raised an inquisitive eyebrow. "Hike?"

"Guided, a walk in the woods, really. Ranger who knows the plants and the animals, especially birds, if he's to be believed. I have a friend who's a birder, and when I'm with her it's so interesting." She shrugged. "Since I'm here, it seemed a good way to spend an afternoon."

She began to rise, and he grabbed his coffee mug.

She laughed, looked at him for a moment, and sat back down. "I'm here for a little change of scenery," she said. "Why are you here?"

CHAPTER 3
GRACE

DANG IT. GRACE REGRETTED THE WORDS almost before they left her mouth, but it was in her to help, and this man seemed to need something. *Why me?* Her therapist had been adamant. "It's not your job to save the world," Dr. Jack Haskins had insisted just before he'd sent her off to be a stranger and get some work done. And the work *had* gone well, two sets of lyrics at least in recognizable form. Better than she'd done since Cal died.

About time. And about time to thank this man and leave.

She'd tried.

"Thank you again. That was kind," she'd said and stood, then noted his left hand rubbing his chest, a post-CABG gesture she'd recognized from her shifts in cardiac rehab. His other hand had instinctively reached to protect his coffee mug.

His hands: broad and hairy, the spatulate fingernails clipped close and immaculate, the movements precise. Imagination fluttered. *Not even,* she told herself as she sighed and sat back down. She couldn't retrieve the words now, even if she wanted. Hands clasped to still her fidget, she waited.

It took a few beats before he responded. "Nothing much," he said. "Just passing through." His hand continued up and down the center of his chest, threatening the buttons on his red plaid shirt.

Yes. CABG—coronary artery bypass graft—and recent. He hurt, body and mind.

She could accept his words at face value, thank him again, and leave. The guide would be at the hotel any minute. No one would think badly of her.

His shoulders slumped. His hand worked harder. His gaze remained riveted on the table, and his jaw muscle twitched. *A torture victim might look like this*, she imagined. Something kept her still.

"I just had surgery."

The sentence emerged, one word at a time dragged out of him, the information—admission of weakness, maybe—not surrendered easily. "I was told to rest and relax. Here I am." The clipped tone spoke of a man used to having the final say in any conversation.

She'd dealt with surgeons all her life. His hands and his manner screamed, "I'm a surgeon, don't mess with me," even as he resisted her question. *Leave, Grace, leave while you can*, her inner self clamored.

"'Rest and relax' is often a good prescription," her outer self said, resisting the urge to ask why he wasn't still in rehab. "That's all interesting, but really, why are you here?"

She watched his face—surprise, irritation, anger, and something else, all quickly hidden under the professional mask of a man used to guarding his feelings.

But when his eyes met hers she saw it: raw despair.

He shook his head. "You know, I really don't know."

CHAPTER 4
McLean

FLUSTERED AT THE WOMAN'S IMPERTINENT QUESTION and his own too-revealing answers, Chris kept talking, describing the decision to take a road trip, the impulse buy of the apple red Mustang convertible now parked in front of the McCloud Hotel, and the winding road that ended here. He hoped it sounded more like an adventure than the exodus it had been.

Grace nodded. "Okay, I get it." Without another word she gathered her belongings, strewing and retrieving bits with practiced inefficiency.

He stood when she stepped away from the table, then sat back down, relieved and ready to see her backside. He started when she pressed her lips to his cheek.

"Thank you for sharing your table," Grace said. "I'll see you at dinner tonight."

Threat or promise? He turned and watched as she threaded careful passage through endangered souvenir racks, scattered postcards trembling in her wake.

Hmmm.

He ordered another pastry and accepted more coffee then pondered the morning's events—pleasant thoughts after a month of dark ones, the touch of her lips rain after a long drought. Then, sated and somnolent, Chris left money on the still-damp table and stepped into the May sunshine.

The little town didn't quite bustle, but the few people on Main Street nodded and smiled at the big stranger with the jaunty step and the wide grin, a wet magazine dangling from his fingers.

Humming under his breath, McLean marched back to the hotel to ensure his dinner reservations matched hers, having assumed she wasn't bedding down with the sporting types. That matter resolved, he fanned open the journal as the woman had done and settled into a porch chair with the hotel library's dog-eared *Moby Dick*.

The breeze off snow-capped mountains cooled his exertion-flushed cheeks, and his flicker of well-being faded. *Shite. Two blocks. What bloody good's a man if he can't even walk two blocks?*

More than once he dozed, each time waking with a jerk. "Old man naps," he grumbled, just before the sentences ran together and he slid into yet another.

Finally the journal's pages were sufficiently dry. Ensconced in a chair uncomfortable enough to keep him awake, he skimmed the text, then heaved the *Journal of Thoracic and Cardiovascular Surgery* off the porch with a snarl of disgust and a string of invectives hurled at the absent author whose surgical technique demanded the hands of a supremely talented midget.

Exhausted by his tantrum, Chris McLean crumpled back into the chair and rubbed his eyes with the big hands that would never again repair a tiny heart.

The bedside alarm chirped, and McLean woke from a shadowy dream that left his heart pounding and fear bitter in his mouth and with no memory of setting the alarm, let alone getting himself to his room, taking off his shoes, and crawling under the covers. And a six-hour nap? *God, just take me out and shoot me.*

Hunger and a full bladder forced him from the bed.

At exactly seven o'clock, hair still damp from the shower, cheeks rosy from the razor, well-worn leather belt cinched in two notches, Chris presented himself to the host.

"Chris McLean."

"Good evening, Doctor, your friend is already here."

The host—in fact the now-unrumpled proprietor, Curtis Jones, natty in dark slacks and a crisp, blue-striped shirt—gestured toward a small table by the front window. Grace waved and started to rise, then switched her attention to a glass teetering on its slender stem.

Foreseeing the future, McLean shouldered the host aside and reached the table in three long strides, but by the time he arrived the glass was steady, and only two red drops, reminders of potential disaster, glistened on the white tablecloth.

"Good save."

A smile lit her face. "Lots of practice."

Unreasonably happy to have generated the smile, McLean sat, his still-considerable bulk filling the chair. Now that the wine was safe for the moment, he turned his connoisseur's eye toward the woman. White linen pants, plain white tee covering small breasts, pink sweater artfully draped over narrow shoulders—a bakery confection, or a little girl playing dress-up. That drew his own smile.

Her gray eyes held a question.

A rangy young man clad in black slacks and white shirt interrupted. "Good evening, sir. My name is Matthew and I'll be your server tonight." His outdoorsy complexion and slicked back ponytail seemed at odds with his professional attire, a perfect fit for an upscale restaurant hidden away in a rustic village. He slid a menu and a wine list in front of McLean. "May I bring you a drink? The lady has already ordered."

Both men looked at the gleaming red wine, breath held as Grace raised the glass in acknowledgement.

Having never purchased wine by the glass, McLean warily regarded the list: California wines, of course, with labels he didn't recognize—Ferrari Carano fumé blanc, Rombauer Chardonnay, Kendall-Jackson merlot, Caravan cabernet, and a very high-priced Duckhorn merlot. His mouth filled with saliva and memory—chianti, merlot, cabernet, hints of peach, apricot or plum, of rain and deep, dark earth, a mellow slide into oblivion. He swallowed hard and dropped the list as though it had fangs.

"One drink a day," Rich Bennet, the surgeon who'd saved his life, had prescribed. "Preferably red wine, preferably with the evening meal."

Fool, McLean thought, then and now, *doesn't recognize a binger when he treats one.* His best friend DeMello, well aware of his secret, had extracted a promise.

Nodding at Grace's glass, he said, "I'll have what the lady's having."

GRACE SIPPED HER WINE AS CHRIS perused the menu and made his selection.

Matthew delivered his wine. "Here you go, sir, a glass of the Kendall-Jackson merlot."

Chris swirled the red liquid and admired its legs, then sniffed and sipped, murmured in appreciation, and set the glass down—ploys to keep from behaving like a shipwrecked sailor and taking it all in one lifesaving gulp.

"Nice," he said.

When he looked up from the wine ritual, Grace was regarding him with twinkling eyes, and he wondered what she found amusing.

Before he could ask, she said, "What were you thinking?

"What?"

"What were you thinking when you first sat down? Besides rescuing my wine, I mean."

He remembered, thought she might not appreciate being compared to a cake. "I was thinking that you looked lovely."

"Oh." She flushed as though not expecting a compliment. "Well, thank you."

Their salads arrived, then the mains—hers, a quinoa-crusted salmon with mango salsa and curry sauce; his, sautéed pork medallions with a mustard-herb sauce. Food that could headline any five-star restaurant in the District.

"How was the rest of your day?" Grace asked between bites.

"Not bad. Seems I've become the artful napper."

Her laughter unfurled and drew him in.

After that, conversation flowed, easy and light—his favorite foods, the birds she'd seen on her hike, the book he'd begun before the nap took over, a movie she'd heard was funny—a back-and-forth banter that held snippets of truth. The level in his glass dipped slowly as he savored each sip, recognized the razor edge on which he balanced, and remembered the promise he'd made.

Grace spooned up the last morsel of her crème brûlée. Laughing at the tale she'd just spun, McLean doctored his decaf and fought the craving for his habitual after-dinner brandy.

Matthew appeared at the table and cleared his throat. "Perhaps you'd like to finish your coffee in the library?"

McLean looked around: dining area empty, candles extinguished, tables already set for breakfast. He hadn't noticed. Grace had been talking as if no one had ever listened, and he realized she might think the same of him.

She glanced at her watch, heavy on a slender wrist. "Oh my heavens, it's nine-thirty." She hurried to stand. Dishes rattled. McLean steadied the jiggling table, surprised himself at the easy passage of time.

She apologized.

He tucked a twenty under his cup.

Then they were standing at the staircase, his hand on the bannister. Grace stood on the second step, eye to eye. She lay her hand over his and his flesh tingled. "Thank you for a lovely evening, Harrison. Perhaps you'll join me in the woods tomorrow."

She disappeared up the stairs before he could process the sound of his never-used first name on her lips.

Hmmm.

Still craving the brandy he had refused, Harrison Christian McLean stepped outside, settled into a garden chair, and looked up. Darkness, as black as his life had become, welcomed him, and his heart thumped a warning just before one star and then two and then a multitude exposed themselves to his hungry eyes. His chest tightened and his heart thrummed an unfamiliar message. As the crisp mountain air closed around him, Chris sighed and thought about the woman whose name was a misnomer.

CHAPTER 5
GRACE

GRACE FIDDLED WITH THE HEAVY KEY until the old lock released and she stumbled into her third-story room—slanted walls, wainscoted and papered in fading flowers; dormer windows that welcomed the starlight; a double bed dressed in lace; an old-fashioned dressing table with a bottom-shaped bench; and enough privacy that her guitar plucking could pass unnoticed. At least that had been her hope, and so far no one had complained.

Leaving the lights off, she placed the key beside her purse and lit a candle. A flowery scent—plumeria, gardenia, jasmine—filled the small room as she undressed and hung her clothes in the wardrobe. Clad only in a brightly colored silk wrapper, a guilty pleasure that had replaced a threadbare flannel robe, Grace settled onto the bench.

In the articulated mirror, other Graces looked back, flickering and unreal in the candlelight. "What am I doing?" she asked her images. "What was I thinking?"

Elizabeth Grace Dart was at the McCloud Hotel to work, specifically to get over herself and write the new songs she would need when she returned to Maui. The Hawaiian Cowboys—Jaimie, Derek, Rick—were waiting. It was their band's way that they wanted an original song for each performance, or at the very least one per season, and that was her value to them. That she could belt out a tune like Juice Newton or Linda Ronstadt or, on a good day, Dolly Parton, was just icing on the cake. No one seemed to care that she didn't sound, or look, a bit like Taylor Swift.

She grinned, her present thoughts focused more on man than music. Dr. Harrison Christian McLean had looked at her hungrily, as though she were a cake he wanted to devour.

He'd looked at his wine in the same way. She thought he didn't know how much of himself showed.

The mirror-image eyes narrowed. *Not good. Complications.* A wounded soul had no place on her agenda.

Her therapist, the only one who knew her whole story, would concur.

A few weeks in the McCloud Hotel in the minuscule California town of the same name had been his idea; he'd been convinced that the isolation would force her butt to the chair, her pencil to the paper, her fingers to guitar strings silent since her husband's death thirteen months ago. So far it had worked—the backbones of two songs nestled in her bag, ready for the guys to sing them to life.

But he *was* big. She'd never been with a big man.

She grimaced. The mirror images grimaced back, reminding her that she'd only been with one man, and that man was small, wiry, stingy, and . . . now dead. She broke eye contact. Surely it was okay, more than a year after Cal's quick and horrific descent into pancreatic cancer and oblivion, to think about another man. Or maybe not. Maybe never.

Sensations barely recognized squeezed into tiny places long ignored. She jumped to her feet. The table wobbled and the candle trembled and her hand shook as she steadied it.

Enough.

The silk wrapper swished against smooth calves and her bare feet whispered on the ancient wooden floor as Grace walked across the room, picked up her guitar, and settled into the window seat overlooking the garden.

She was aware of his presence before she saw him, burrowed deep in the garden's cushioned chair, eyes raised to the stars. She strummed lightly, fingers still tender as they rebuilt calluses lost to time and neglect, and her lips found the new refrain, "resting in the arms of a big man."

Chapter 6
McLean

A HAUNTING MELODY, THEN DEEP AND REFRESHING sleep, dreams unremembered. Chris McLean woke just in time to make it to breakfast.

He seated himself by the window and looked around. Only the corner table was occupied by a young couple holding hands and whispering as they lingered over coffee. No Grace. The surge of disappointment surprised him, and in his mind a black dog crouched, ready.

Stop it. Hands clenched, eyes closed, Chris concentrated on his breath. In and out, in and out, just as Quinn had taught him, and at snail speed the darkness receded. When he opened his eyes, Matthew hovered, his steaming coffee pot poised to pour.

"Morning, doc. What'll it be this morning?"

Hoping the man would assume he'd been meditating, or even praying, Chris nodded yes to the coffee and placed his order. Before he'd finished doctoring his coffee, breakfast arrived, and he tucked into a meal even better than last night's dinner. As he relished the quiche and enjoyed the coffee, he reminded himself that he'd been eating alone for years, enjoyed it, even preferred it.

Rot.

He took his third cup of coffee into the hotel garden, pulled out his phone, and punched in a familiar number. Around him bees worked spring flowers whose names he didn't know. Quinn DeMello answered on the third ring, out of breath and laughing.

"About time. I was ready to send out the Mounties."

Despite the humor, he knew there was a furrow between her brows and concern in her turquoise eyes. He squeezed his own shut to blot the visual—that he would cause this woman pain almost killed him.

"Don't worry," he said. "Only the good die young."

She laughed, and he felt better. He filled her in on his travels, mentioned Grace whose name was a misnomer, then felt guilty as Quinn laughed at the absent woman's expense.

Life had suddenly become very complicated.

As though it were an afterthought, DeMello coughed away the laugh and said, "Have you been taking your meds?"

Silence. Beta blockers, ACE inhibitors, statins, blood thinners, an almost-full bottle of oxy—his thoughts went to the pharmaceuticals stashed deep in his old duffel.

"Damn it, McLean, you've got to take your pills. I know you hate it. I know you're embarrassed to be human like the rest of us, but—"

"I've been taking the damn things," he interrupted. "Nobody said I have to like it."

DeMello chuckled. "Okay, 'nuff said."

She paused, and he thought she was going to bring up his promise. Instead she said, "This McCloud place seems just the ticket for a little R and R . . . but I think there's something you're not telling me."

He groaned. To be this transparent made him crazy, so he flicked aside self-pity, doubt, and despair and lied. "Nope, just a quaint little town with bees and flowers and hiking trails and a restaurant that serves better food than any place in Reno."

She seemed to take him at his word, let their conversation drift into tidbits of family life and gossip about the Wildflower Inn B&B. There was no reproach in her voice, but he felt another twinge of guilt just the same. She had dumped him there in the care of her sisters-in-law after he'd escaped the cardiac rehab unit. And she'd been angry when he left. She was right. He hadn't been ready for the world, maybe still wasn't.

Then children clamored to say hello. The girls chattered about chickens and Will reminded him not to forget *Human Anatomy for Children*, the book Papa Chris had promised after *Inside Your Outside* was deemed too babyish.

When Quinn regained the phone, she said, "Get a life, McLean, but don't forget you're expected here in September for their first day of school." Her "love you" kissed his ear as the call ended.

He pocketed the phone and leaned back against the cushions. Quinn DeMello, love of his life, fulfillment of all fantasies, and for the last five years, the wife of Owen Johnson, a man he'd come to care for and admire. Family member by fiat—Papa Chris to Megan, Makena, and Will. Complicated, indeed.

He squeezed his eyes shut, thinking, remembering: He'd been in Unionville, Nevada, ghost town and home of the bed and breakfast, celebrating the triplets' fifth birthday, when the heart attack felled him. He had little recollection of the first frantic moments, none at all of the agony his friends had suffered as they struggled to keep him alive until the helicopter arrived and whisked him away. The days following his bypass had been tough—who'd ever predict a heart surgeon lying on an operating table? But worse than the pain and the surgery had been this realization: The DeMello-Johnson family loved him, but they were not his. He'd known this when he'd struggled to consciousness from the pit of anesthesia; it was time to start over, begin anew.

Then he thought about Grace. *Hmmm.*

"Dr. McLean." Curtis Jones's voice cruised into his musing. "Sorry to bother you."

"No worries, just resting my eyes."

"I have a message from Mrs. Dart," the proprietor said instead of "yeah, right," and handed Chris a note.

Must be Grace. Mrs? Hmmm.

Pink paper folded twice, words in black ink: "Harrison, I've planned a hike and a picnic for this afternoon. Please join me if you'd like. If not, no worries." Old-fashioned but legible longhand. Signed simply, "Grace."

He looked up at Jones.

"She'll be picking up the picnic at one o'clock. Gotta tell ya, it'll be good."

Chris wasn't sure from the man's expression whether the proprietor meant the lunch or the woman, so he nodded and said thank you and returned to his room for a post-prandial nap.

McLean was sitting in the lobby at 12:48 when Grace descended the stairs. He thought he saw both surprise and pleasure on her face, but she just said, "Good, you're here," and disappeared into the kitchen. In a few minutes she emerged, hefty-looking backpack in place. "Ready?"

He stood. "Let me take the pack."

She shook her head. "I've got it. I make it a point to only take what I can carry."

He wondered what that meant, but she hustled out the door and he followed, no chance to quiz her unless he wanted to talk to a khaki-clad back.

A few minutes and a steady pace took them into the woods that surrounded the town. Civilization dropped away. Tall pines lined the trail. A cool breeze tickled the sweat already flowing down his back, and he was aware of his heart thundering in his chest.

Can I keep up? Can I keep breathing?

He'd never doubted before.

He forced his attention to the path. One step at a time, one foot after the other. One breath in, one breath out. Soon the path evened, and he could let his gaze shift to the figure in front of him—butt cheeks soft in the hiking shorts, legs firm and slender, feet small even in the boots that looked like they weighed more than she did.

A flash of well-being and he grinned. *I may be dying, but I can still appreciate the view.*

Grace moved with confidence and ease, no clumsiness now, and he followed her over pine needles and dirt, their steps producing dusty puffs that coated boots and socks and finally legs as well. The route wound gently uphill.

They proceeded in that manner for almost an hour, the silence broken only by an occasional, "watch the rock here" or "look, that's a mountain jay," their progress interrupted by her need to adjust the pack, remove a rock from her boot, and examine a yellow lump that turned out to be a snail. The heat dissipated into a cocoon of cool, pine-scented air.

Nostalgia—memories of boyhood tramps with his brothers, the camping vacation when his girls were tiny, the road trip with his mother to Acadia National Park just months before she died—roused tears he didn't understand.

Grace walked on. His vision blurry, Chris followed. Then stillness prevailed, and his mind stilled too.

Grumbling stomach and dry mouth brought him back to himself just as the woods opened to a vista of verdant green and the faraway rustle of water.

"Here." She let the pack slip from her back and knelt beside it on a bed of needles. "We'll eat here."

For just a moment, Chris felt refreshed. Then the ache in his sternum and the pounding in his chest reminded him, and, suppressing a groan, he dropped down beside her, thanking God that the woman was a slow hiker and he hadn't needed a breather.

Then Grace smiled and tossed him a bottle of water. "Good job," she said as she uncapped her own bottle, and he knew she'd purposely set a pace that suited him. Before he could comment, she tipped her head back and drank deeply, drawing his attention to a thin, well-healed scar at her throat, a tiny flutter as her heart rate settled, and tight skin that might have been the product of a good plastics man.

She caught the direction of his gaze. "Thyroid," she said. "Fifteen years ago. Cancer, no recurrence." Her eyes danced. "And good genes."

She knew what he'd been thinking. He flushed, once again transparent and still not liking it. He could almost hear his own voice telling patients not to worry, that surgery, especially cardiac surgery, might leave them more emotional, more vulnerable than they had previously been.

But me?

He frowned and focused on her running commentary: the land, the trees, the birds she couldn't name and wished she could. By the time she'd dispensed the contents of the pack—sparkling cranberry juice, chicken salad sandwiches, apples, and brie—he'd caught his breath and pulled himself back together.

When she tipped her head at him with that *your turn* look in her eyes, he was ready.

"Where did you get my name?"

She didn't blink. "Hotel register, of course."

Hmmm. Was it on his credit card? He didn't remember. Harrison was his father, long dead, a small man with a love of family and poetry and beer.

Grace fluttered her hands. "Conversation's a two-way street, Harrison."

He let it go for the moment. "Right. Surgeon. Some Red Cross volunteer work on the side." Her murmurs kept him talking—new to this part of the country, not much of a hiker, not used to sitting around doing nothing—leaving out the parts that included tramping through Mount St. Helens's volcanic dust or climbing into the rubble of Mexico City's earthquake or watching airplanes take down tall buildings, let alone questioning himself once the trajectory of his life had been set.

And now reset?

He munched the apple and grew quiet.

Her raised eyebrow warned, "I know there's more to the story," but she only said, "More later, maybe," and tossed him a Snickers. "Hope you're not allergic to peanuts." She tore open the wrapper of her own doubled-sized bar and bit into the chocolate-caramel-nutty goodness.

Off the hook, he did the same.

On the way down, the detritus of their picnic stowed in the pack, she rewarded him with a few factoids of her own life: almost sixty, retired nurse, widow, mother, grandmother. As they parted at the hotel stairs, McLean realized that while she'd kept up a steady flow of words, he really didn't know any of the important things about Mrs. Grace Dart, RN, retired, widow.

Surprised, he knew he wanted to.

Chapter 7
Grace

GRACE DANCED UP THE STAIRS, CHORDS and phrases colliding, twisting, particles in a superconductor. Never before had she so needed her guitar, afraid that the music in her head might disappear. Her key didn't want to fit the lock. Then the lock refused to release. With frenzied fingers she jiggled and jabbed until it cooperated, and she fell into the room in her haste to reach the instrument. Fingers dancing on the strings. Lyrics tumbling out as though writing themselves. Seamlessly setting music to the words from her heart.

Minutes passed. Hours. The sun finished its run and disappeared into the western night, its journey unmarked by the woman in the little dormer room. The moon rode high in the sky when Grace tossed the pencil stub to the floor and thrust chicken-scratched pages over her head, triumphant. *Yes!*

The room crackled, lightning-struck. Then: *Caesura! Stop!*

Grace sat breathless as the air seemed to still and the dust motes to pause in their moonlight dance. Moments, a lifetime.

A huff of surprise, tattered papers gathered to her breast, Elizabeth Grace Dart tumbled into sleep.

She woke to a knock on her door.

"Breakfast, Mrs. Dart."

Breakfast? Grace raised her head and looked at her watch. Eight o'clock. In the morning? In fuzzy slow motion, memories unfurled—strumming, humming, scribbling—fuzzy, as though they were not her own. Doubting, she glanced at the pages still clutched in her hand.

Her handwriting, black words and notes with little tails following one another across wrinkled staff paper. Could it be real?

Thump. Another thump. The doorknob rattled. Matthew's voice said, "Mrs. Dart, you in there? Coffee's gettin' cold."

"Sorry, sorry. I'm coming." She scrambled up, and dust puffed from the hiking clothes she still wore. *At least I'm dressed,* she thought and waded stocking-footed through piles of discarded paper to open the door.

"Matthew, good morning."

The young server's eyes widened as he scanned her unconventional morning garb and the litter that carpeted the floor, but he just edged past her without a word, deposited the tray on her desk, and began arranging the dishes.

Hurry, hurry. Grace jigged foot to foot as Matthew, with agonizing precision, removed the covers and displayed her breakfast—one egg over easy, wheat bread lightly toasted, chunks of banana and strawberry overflowing a bowl's fluted edge. As he poured steaming coffee, the pages in her grip trembled to be read.

Hurry. Hurry. Inside, words struggled to escape—big man, big man, resting in the arms. *Did I imagine it? What did I write? Was memory true?*

When he unfolded the napkin and held it out to her, Grace feared the boy might be planning to stay and make sure she cleaned her plate.

"All good, Matthew, it's all good," she said before impatience could slip its bonds. At his look of confusion, she accepted the napkin, hugged his skinny arm, and tucked a twenty-dollar bill in his hand. He was blushing and grinning as she pushed him out the door.

Alone, suddenly boneless, Grace dropped into the chair and examined the crinkled pages still tight in her hand. Once, twice, humming a little toward the end. Then, quietly, she began to sing. Words and music filled the room, the refrain almost whispered. "I am loved as I am with a love that is true. Now I'm resting in the arms of a big man." When the last notes faded she dropped her head and let the tears flow.

It's good. It's real. It's mine.

CHAPTER 8
McLean

Exhausted, Chris McLean forced himself to shower off the trail dust before he collapsed onto the bed and fell instantly, deeply asleep. He woke before the alarm. He'd missed dinner, slept through a dreamless night. Now sun peeked through the window as he stretched under the covers, enjoying the protest of muscles that had survived a good workout. Clearheaded, content, and hungry—a good beginning for a life that had, until yesterday, lacked promise. Under a hot morning shower, he assessed his body: heartbeat steady, chest less tender, shoulders and arms moving through a fuller range of motion, his face wearing a smile.

Yep, promises to be a good day.

In the breakfast room, he settled once again at the table he'd shared with Grace and looked around. No Grace, but pecan waffles, two eggs, and four strips of bacon, crisp and hot and brimming with saturated fat, helped keep the day in perspective.

Curtis Jones refilled his coffee.

"Mrs. Dart?" McLean asked.

"Takes breakfast in her room," the proprietor answered, apparently unconcerned about sharing another guest's business. "Matthew says something must have happened last night 'cause she was in fine fettle this morning."

Hmmm.

Disappointment stirred the dregs of depression.

Enough of that, man. You don't know this woman and you don't need complications.

Rejecting his own good advice, Chris pictured her slender arms, the scar on her neck, the pulse fluttering at her throat. Vulnerable, not one-night-stand material, even if he was ready. Wondering if he'd ever be ready, he drained his coffee and forced himself out into the spring morning.

Yesterday's trail was easier now with practice and a twelve-hour sleep under his belt. This early, the shade was deep and the air cold, the vista point still breathtaking. No Grace.

He returned to the hotel. No Grace.

He took the stairs two at a time, then halted on the second-floor landing, breathing hard and shaking his head.

Stop, man. What the hell are you thinking?

He started up the second flight. He'd been alone before, most of his life actually. A good life, for sure, but he'd always been a working man—

He stopped abruptly. If he hadn't been so cognizant of the heart's anatomy, he would have sworn his plunged straight into his shoes. *I'm not a working man anymore.* One thought accompanied the plunge: *No sort of man at all.*

Get a life, he ordered himself, echoing DeMello's words, relieved that only a deserted stairway witnessed his foolishness. A shrug, one glance upward, before he clattered back down the stairs and climbed into the little red Mustang.

It was impossible for a man to wallow in dark thoughts even if he tried when the wind whipped around him and his impulse-buy convertible responded to his lightest touch, when the sun warmed his shoulders and eagles soared and then dove into pristine mountain lakes. Sometime during his ride Chris made a plan.

He would invite the dratted woman to drive out with him tomorrow, show her the sights he'd discovered—Burney Falls State Park, the town of Shasta with its tourist shops, its bookstore full of locals and their dogs, its café that served the best burger and fries he'd ever devoured. They would have lunch at the foot of Mount Shasta, and he'd get some questions answered. In a word, resume control.

Three hours later, feeling more himself than he had in months, Chris dressed in clean khakis and his last pressed shirt and entered the dining area as the lobby clock chimed seven.

Grace sat at the little table by the window. Tonight her slacks and tee were gray, but the pink sweater still embraced her shoulders. Even from across the room, he could see a difference. Luminous.

He hesitated.

She saw him. A flush whooshed up her neck and colored her cheeks.

Hmmm.

Then she smiled and gestured him to her. Like a moth to a pink-clad flame, Chris McLean walked to the table.

Over wine and another gourmet meal, they continued their conversation. Grace told him about her sons, grown men, Jed a lawyer in California with a wife she didn't know well and two granddaughters she adored, the younger son Jacob in Washington, DC, with a life partner, Raul, who called her "Mamacita."

McLean, less guarded now for reasons he didn't quite understand, described his Foggy Bottom home and his work at George Washington University, omitting his fear that he could never return. And then, though she didn't ask, he told her about Genevieve, for whom he'd been an asshole husband, and the two daughters and their children who loved him but didn't need him much. "I earned it, you know. I wasn't there when they did need a father. How can I complain now?"

She reached across the table, dragging a pink sleeve through the dregs of gravy on her plate and laying her hand over his. No words of absolution, yet he felt lighter as he dabbled his napkin in his water glass and helped her clean the sweater.

Again they parted at the stairway after another tactful reminder from their host. Wearing her kiss on his cheek, Chris was halfway to his room when he realized he hadn't invited her for tomorrow's ride.

He turned back, but the hallway was dark and quiet. No matter—a note with her breakfast tray would fix things. Humming off key, he strolled to his room, climbed out of his clothes, and fell asleep as his head touched the pillow.

CHAPTER 9
GRACE

THE SCRATCHINESS OF HARRISON MCLEAN'S UNSHAVEN cheek still tickled her lips as Grace danced up the steep stairs to her cozy room under the eaves. She could hardly remember the last time she'd kissed anyone, and here she'd laid her lips on this stranger more than once in the past two days. As her mother would have said, "What is this world coming to?"

She giggled. The man was just too goldarn sexy.

Even though the first kiss had been an impulse of kindness, her usual habit of soothing the wounded, tonight's had been about spending time with this particular man, this big man who made her laugh, and who, through no fault of his own, had become the hero of the best song she'd ever written.

Big hands, big body, big laugh. A hero in his own life, even though he still doubted. She winced, remembering his hand scrubbing at the center of his chest, just the once, as he talked about his work. As clearly as words, the gesture proclaimed his fears. With a shiver, she forced Nurse Grace thoughts aside.

Chanting under her breath, "tomorrow, not tomorrow," in the way of young girls plucking daisy petals to determine the course of true love, she reached the narrow landing and slid the skeleton key into the lock. She didn't need daisies. She knew she'd see him tomorrow.

For once, the lock cooperated, and her bedroom door opened smoothly. In the darkness, her phone, left to charge when she'd gone off to eat, glowed with messages.

One sigh and fantasies disappeared as though they'd never been. The McCloud Hotel was her sanctuary. Now the world intruded.

Should have left this darn thing in Reno, she thought, frowning as she scrolled. Seven from Martin, all deleted unread. One from Jed, **URGENT** in caps. Two more, the same. Sighing again, she dialed her son's number and counted the rings.

Finally, he answered. "Mom, Mom. You've got to do something about this guy."

Her head full of Harrison McLean, it took a minute to readjust. "Hello to you, too. What guy would that be?"

"Mom, don't be so dense. You know I mean that Grimes nutcase."

Guilt stabbed. She hadn't told her sons about Martin Grimes. Didn't want to worry them. Didn't want to think about it.

Before she could ask how he knew, Jed continued, "He wheedled my number out of somebody at home and called here demanding to know where you are. Demanding, Mom! Demanding! You should have told me about this before. He's a stalker, Mom. Call Dad's lawyer and get a restraining order."

"Honey, calm down. He's just a poor, sad man who thinks he's in love with me." Embarrassing, talking about love with a child, even an adult one. "I've told him I'm not for him, and he'll get over it. Those things just take time."

"Be real." Her elder son put on his courtroom voice. "Guys like him don't just 'get over it.' You pick up strays like a dog picks up fleas." He paused at her chuckle; both remembered the stray dogs and cats, the wounded bunnies and birds, even the occasional stray child. Then Jed resumed, a chill in his voice. "Strays, Mom, and this is a bad one. Call Jonathan, get a restraining order. Tomorrow." He switched to a little boy voice. "Please, Mommy, just listen to me for once."

With a smile for the son so like his father, Grace promised to think about it, asked about Caroline and the girls, said goodnight.

And then she tucked herself into the window seat and secured trembling hands between her thighs.

Jed's right. Martin's trouble, and it's my fault for not seeing it earlier. Now I've got to do something before he draws my family into this craziness.

Last night's musical triumph, the simple pleasure of a meal with a very appealing man, the pride of finally making it on her own, all faded to gray as she thought about the man who said he loved her.

An accountant in Reno, nice enough looking in a nondescript kind of way, upper lip a little long, chin a bit small for his face, but all in all not bad. She'd consulted him about a tax matter just after Cal's death, and he'd invited her for coffee.

His first email was just what would be expected of an old-school professional, and she'd smiled, even preened a little, when she read it, memorizing the words.

"Dear Grace," he'd written in proper Times New Roman, "I enjoyed meeting you today. If you don't mind my saying so, it felt like a long-lost connection. I am looking forward to coffee on Friday."

They'd met at Bibo's Coffee House on the Friday. Grace remembered that hour. It had felt more like a date, she'd thought at the time, than the friendly chat she had anticipated. "Nah," she'd told herself on the way home as she scrubbed away his cheek kiss. "I just don't remember what a date feels like."

His second email beat her home.

"Dear Grace, What a delightful hour. Seems like we've known each other forever. I hope to see you again soon." Benign. Sweet. Kind of nice for a man to be interested, even if she wasn't.

Trouble. In his mind, their soul connection was fact from the moment she'd stepped into his office. Subsequent texts, emails, phone calls—all with fulsome compliments, movie and dinner invitations, constant reminders of that imagined connection—filled her devices.

In all fairness, she thought now as she sat in her beautiful room waiting for her hands to steady and her mind to clear, *I acted like a normal person.* Declining invitations, making excuses, finally declaring that she would never love again.

Nothing she said penetrated his we're-destined-to-be-together veneer.

The last text she'd read had stirred her anger.

Dear Grace, I understand your reluctance to date but surely you realize our connection. A magnetic force draws us together. Such strong emotion cannot be one-sided. Deal with your issues, my darling, and come to me.

How dare you. Natural compassion worn thin, she'd started deleting his messages unread.

Moonlight streamed through the dormer windows as Grace pulled her knees against her chest, hugged her arms around them, and rocked. *Darn him, darn him, darn him.*

Gradually her mind cleared. She released her knees and uncurled. He was a sad man, but he had no right to bother her family. She filled her lungs with cold mountain air, felt strength return, blew air out, did it again, sat up straight. *Time to go home and put an end to this mess.*

But first . . .

She stood, each muscle and joint, tendon and ligament protesting as she rose to her full five feet and four inches. *Just like the Tin Woodman*, she thought. *I've lost my oil can, too.*

Blinking at the sudden dampness in her eyes, Grace sat at the desk, pulled a sheet of pink paper from the drawer, and began to write.

Chapter 10
McLean

CHRIS MCLEAN SANG IN HIS MORNING shower, left his scruffy beard in place, and buttoned up his next-to-last clean polo shirt. He found a sheet of McCloud Hotel letterhead in the desk drawer and wrote out his invitation, printing carefully to counter the illegible-physician-handwriting rumor, although he could read his writing just fine. Automatically, he scribbled the whole H. Christian McLean, M.D. signature, wondered if he should start over, and decided it was fine the way it was. In point of fact, everything was fine.

He folded the paper twice, as Grace had done with her pink missive, tucked it into his shirt pocket, and stepped into the hall. The chirp of a morning bird accompanied him toward the fragrance of very good coffee.

If I were a bird, I'd be chirping now too, he thought, and didn't care if people saw him grinning like an idiot. No earthquake, no tsunami, no chest pain. No tiny heart struggling to beat. The sun had come up. He was alive. And he would soon be driving out with a very fine woman.

A very fine day.

In that mood, he sauntered into the breakfast room. Early rising guests were seated around in ones and twos. He nodded at those he'd seen before as he made his way to the table by the window.

Our table. His heart performed a little jig, even as he grimaced at his own foolishness.

Dust motes danced in the sunshine as it streamed into the room and perked up the cool morning air. He slid into his accustomed seat, waited until the proprietor, who seemed to be on duty twenty-four-seven, poured his first cup of coffee and then handed him the note. "For Mrs. Dart, with her breakfast tray if you don't mind."

Jones shook his head. "Not here."

"What do you mean, she's not here?"

The room grew suddenly still.

Chris modulated his voice. "I know she's not *here*. She takes breakfast in her room."

The other man shook his head, reminding McLean of Nate, the lugubrious proprietor of La Traviata, an Italian restaurant laced with memories of 9/11 rescue work. The image of the wounded Pentagon, an airplane nose-deep in its side, rose in his mind, and his whole body tensed.

Jones seemed to notice and hurried into an explanation—never good business to make a guest unhappy. "She left early this morning, don't know why. She had a reservation through the weekend. Lucky since we're always booked up for this weekend, pre-holiday and all. But she left you a note." He plucked a pink scrunch of paper from his pocket. "Here."

He placed the note in Chris's slack hand and hurried to the next table, and the room resumed its breakfast-conversation hum. Chris smoothed the wrinkles, inhaled the scent of a flower he couldn't identify, and placed the note on the linen tablecloth, not sure he wanted to know what it said. This Grace thing had gotten totally out of hand.

Fuck black coffee, he thought as he doctored the brew Jones had placed before him with real cream and two big scoops of real sugar, then drank it slowly and let the caffeine do its job. He poured a large glass of orange juice and downed it. Guests moved in and out of his vision, but all he could see was the slip of pink paper lying just beyond the tines of his fork. When breakfast arrived he looked at it, pushed the plate away, and picked up the note.

Harrison,
I'm sorry not to say goodbye but I must leave quickly. I did so enjoy our hike and our meals together. I realize your life is unsettled right now. I have a small place in Hawai'i on the island of Maui. It has an extra bedroom which will be available after the last Friday of June. If you would like to visit me we could continue our chats.

Grace

A phone number scrawled like an afterthought across the bottom of the page.
Hmmm?

Chapter 11
Grace

At first light, Grace departed McCloud and headed toward Reno—two hundred and six miles, many of them tree-lined and beautiful. Her heart wasn't in it. Her foot kept straying from the gas pedal, and she'd notice only when another vehicle honked impatiently before it blasted past her on the winding two-lane road.

She did not want to go home.

The McCloud Hotel, a jewel in the forest, had inspired her, just as Dr. Haskins had predicted. The hotel and the man, she acknowledged with insight—an inspiration no one could have predicted.

There *was* another sanctuary. She smiled as she envisioned the second-floor apartment with its louvered windows full open to the wind and the monkey pod tree and the sea. *My heart's home—and my only secret.*

Now that was threatened.

And by my own actions, she thought with a rueful smile. *My own totally crazy actions.*

By now, Harrison McLean knew. Or at least he knew there was an apartment and an island and an invitation. A shivery thrill coursed her body. Would he come? What would happen if he did? She grimaced. Her marriage had been in its tenth year before she had realized she would always be a substitute wife. If her own husband didn't want her, why would any other man be different? But still . . . would he come?

The eighteen-wheeler roaring past recalled her foot to its task and her thoughts to the business at hand.

THREE AND A HALF HOURS LATER, Grace turned onto Jefferson Drive, a street so familiar she paid no attention to the shiny new sedan parked near the mailboxes. This was a neighborhood of big trees and mature landscaping, older homes and new money. Cadillacs and Audis and an occasional Lexus SUV were common sights.

Reluctant to re-enter this life, Grace let her little brown Corolla idle in the drive as she stared at the house she'd lived in all her married life. Two stories, practical, brown-shingled siding, big windows allowing street views of the living room—it was quite a nice house.

She hated it.

She and Calvin Dart had said their vows in the Reno City Hall the day she graduated. Starched white nursing hat on her head and a plain gold band on her finger—registered nurse and married woman on the same day.

"Good planning," Cal had said. "That way we only need one party."

Her parents had been there, and her brother Courtney, who was younger and still at the university. Franklin, eldest of the four siblings, already off on his adventures, and Florence, married and estranged from the family, had been absent. She hadn't minded. It wasn't really a proper wedding with a white dress and a church and someone singing the "Ave Maria" from the choir loft. Cal had already had one of those. And he and his first wife had also built this house, big enough for a basketball team. But Leona and the child she carried had died leaving her husband bereft, childless, and in possession of a four-bedroom home in this very nice part of Reno.

She hated it.

Always there'd been the promise of a home that was hers, as soon as they could afford it, but then Jed arrived and two years later Jacob, and it was clear they would never afford a different house. So she'd filled it with birthday parties and backyard sleepovers and graduation parties and wedding receptions and, finally, going-away parties.

Now she was stuck with a second mortgage that had been taken out without her knowledge just before Cal was diagnosed, and an underwater house that held only dust and unopened bills and reminders of her husband in the last difficult days.

A sharp rap on the car window jerked her into the present. She looked out.

Oh, yes . . . it also had Martin Grimes.

Frowning, she rolled the window down halfway. "Martin, what are you doing here?"

His mouth moved in an I-know-you're-glad-to-see-me smirk. "I had a feeling you'd be home soon so I came right over. But you were just sitting here, and I thought something might be wrong." He fiddled with the door handle. "Your door is locked, Grace. Please open it and get out so I can welcome you home properly."

Grace paused as a shiver ran up her back. Then she laughed at her momentary fear. Too much Jed influence. *It's just Martin.*

She turned off the motor, opened the door, and climbed out of the sedan, eluding his attempt to hug her.

This *had* gone too far. Jed was right about that. She held up her hand to ward Martin off and he halted, almost nose to nose, the pungent scent of his aftershave threatening her senses.

He muttered something she couldn't decipher.

"Martin." She stamped her foot. "Martin, stop this foolishness and listen to me."

He stepped back, one, two, and considered her. He stood a few inches taller than her, a slender man in a very nice suit, hair trimmed neatly at his neck, washed-out brown eyes holding a puzzled expression. "What's wrong, Grace? I missed you. Didn't you miss me?"

He stepped forward.

She stepped back.

"Let's go inside," he said. "The neighbors are watching. We can talk."

In that instant she knew she didn't want him in her house. Something was just not right. During her long ago rotation in Saint Mary's psych ward, she'd had feelings like these. She shook her head. "I'm tired, Martin. It was a long, difficult week. Why don't you go on back to work and we'll talk later."

Before she could move, he stepped forward and kissed her mouth, hard, then stepped back. "Okay, Grace, go in and get some rest. We'll talk later." He turned and marched across the street, got into the shiny black Cadillac, and was gone.

Hand scrubbing at her mouth, struggling to catch her breath, Grace leaned against the Corolla's warm door and listened to her heart thunder in her chest.

Dear God, what do I do now?

Chapter 12
McLean

Never indecisive, Chris McLean couldn't decide what to do.

Promise be damned. He raised his hand to get Matthew's attention.

The young man, also on twenty-four-seven duty, snatched up the coffee carafe from the warming tray and hurried over.

"Hey, Matthew. Is there a liquor store in your town?" He didn't inquire about his favorite Maker's Mark; anything in a bottle would do.

"'Fraid not, Dr. McLean. The General Store has beer and some wine, but it's not a proper liquor store. Closest to that would be in Shasta City."

Foiled. "Thanks, man, I'll check that out later." He held up his coffee cup for a refill and carried it to the garden, ignoring the bees and the perfume of the early flowers and the chill air that caressed his face. With an audible groan, he settled into a chair still damp with morning dew.

What next?

He was a physician; he knew what he should do. He should avoid stress, take his meds, and build up his strength, figure out what to do about the surgical practice waiting for him, and get through enough days that alcohol wasn't his first and last thought.

Hmmm.

For the past two days, Grace Dart had been his first and last thought.

What he really wanted was to chase down the dratted woman and find out what the devil she'd intended with that invitation of hers. Who would ask a complete stranger to her home? For all she knew, he could be a serial killer or—

He snorted, interrupting *that* train of thought. She knew his name. She'd probably Googled him and knew more about H. Christian McLean than he did himself. And, for that matter, what did he know about her? Only that she had a quiet voice and a gentle touch and soft gray eyes that held a promise. What kind of a name was Dart, anyway? It didn't fit her. And he didn't even know where to find her . . . except for Hawaii, in June, as it were.

He returned to the lobby to fix that.

FOUR HOURS LATER, ARMED WITH THE number of a post office box in Reno and a printout of her perfect record as a registered nurse, he loaded up the Mustang and got as far as the stop sign before he realized he still hadn't decided which way to turn. Clearly, if she had wanted him in Reno, she wouldn't have invited him to Hawaii. Clearly, he had no need to complicate his life. And saliva filled his mouth at the thought of that bottle of Maker's Mark just sixty minutes away. Left or right?

The apple red Mustang swung right, surged onto CA 89, the Mount Shasta-Mount Lassen highway, and settled into a fifty-mile-an-hour pace between an eighteen-wheeler and an RV large enough to house a swimming pool. He was in no hurry, no hurry at all.

TWO DAYS DRIVING HIGHWAY 1, THE Mustang clinging to the curves like a tight-fitting glove. Two days exploring San Francisco, walking the beach and the hills. Now Chris McLean was running up a gargantuan bill at Nordstrom while a personal shopper named Carlos, tut-tutting over legs that had rarely seen the sun, strongly advised shorts, Tommy Bahama shirts, and walking sandals.

Just as Chris was wishing he hadn't bypassed Shasta City and the liquor store and the Maker's Mark, Carlos returned to the dressing room with another armload.

"What's this?"

"Swimming attire, sir."

"Don't need 'em. Don't swim."

"It's Hawaii, sir. Swimming pools and ocean. Everyone swims."

To McLean's eye, the two items that finally joined the pile looked more like 1880s swimwear than the fashionable board shorts Carlos declared them to be.

What the hell, he was now ready for anything.

His purchases safely squeezed into a new twenty-two-inch Victorinox bag with a handle and wheels, the battered leather duffel having finally proven too small, he put the Mustang's top down, settled his UNR Wolf Pack ball cap (last year's Christmas gift from the triplets) firmly over a new haircut, and headed east. As San Francisco, the Bay Bridge, and the Pacific Ocean faded behind him, Chris McLean questioned his sanity, then shrugged and kept on driving. He would park the beast at DeMello's and fly from Reno-Tahoe International.

Four hours and fifteen minutes later he pulled onto the gravel drive of the DeMello-Johnson home, a ranch-style house with its three garages, barn, and duck pond sprawled over two acres, perfect for their growing family. Chris took a moment to appreciate the quiet as the Mustang's eight-cylinder motor grew silent. He hoped he could maintain the good sense to keep his mouth shut.

Quinn's shout shattered his reverie. "Owen, he's here!"

She yanked the car door open, grabbed McLean, and tried to pull him from the vehicle. They were both laughing before he was fully extricated and in her embrace. Then she was pushing him back and looking him over.

"Wow, you're skinny." Worry creased her brow. She stepped in, wrapped her arms around his middle, and then stepped back again. "I've never gotten my arms around you before. Are you okay?"

This was the woman he had loved and lost. For her, he would lie. "It's all good," he said, hoping his voice held conviction. "No steak, no booze, and way too much exercise." He grinned and sucked in his belly, felt each breath stretch the tender, knotted scar that desecrated his chest. No mention of nightmare-broken sleep, of sweat-drenched battles with the alcohol god, of the fear that his life was over or, worse, that it was not.

Quinn fussed, ignored his words, cast worried glances at his narrower chest, thinner waist, and face browned from the sun.

"Leave off, babe, the man says he's fine—believe him." Owen Johnson strolled down from the house, dishtowel over one shoulder, and thrust a hand toward McLean. "Welcome back, Chris. Good to see you still alive. Come on in, food's almost ready, and I just opened a fine bottle of merlot." Ignoring his wife's cautionary glare, Owen slung one arm around her, the other around the man who had been his rival, and shepherded them toward the house.

After his solitary days on the road, the chaos over dinner almost did McLean in. He had his one glass of fine merlot and picked at a delightful dinner while three five-year-olds vied for his attention. Their cousin Sophie, the epicanthic fold of her eyelids giving her black eyes a look of wisdom far beyond her three years, tugged at his shirt until she, too, secured a place on his lap. Nothing would do but for him to peruse *Human Anatomy for Children*, which he'd brought for Will, and then read *The Little Mermaid* twice before they would allow Auntie V and Uncle Harold to sweep them up for bath and bedtime.

"Wow." Chris dropped into a big armchair in the great room and wiped imaginary sweat from his brow. "You exercise like this every night?"

Laughing, Quinn delivered his decaf. "Doctor's orders," she said when he frowned at the plain black brew, and then she dropped onto the couch beside her husband. "Some days it's worse. Vivian and Harold and Sophie are staying this weekend. The adoption ceremony's on Tuesday." She scrunched into a more comfortable position and sipped her tea. "The whole crew will be here. Owen says he's leaving town."

McLean knew the story—Owen's sister and her new husband had fought a long, hard battle to adopt the little Chinese girl. He himself had written letters to people who might help. Now the long battle had come to a welcome conclusion—but at the moment he could not keep his eyes off DeMello's long legs, slender and tan, as she tucked them under herself on the sofa. His body responded, and he shifted in his own chair. This was the reason he couldn't stay too long. He loved DeMello—attitude and legs and a body that promised anything a man could ever want—but he loved the children with a ferocity that staggered him, and he loved Owen Johnson as he would love a son.

He forced his eyes up, saw Owen's wry grin that seemed to say, "I know, man, but what can you do?" Chris sipped his coffee and again wished for Maker's Mark.

Quinn was still talking. "So, McLean, I know you're off to visit some folks you know." She ticked his destinations off on her fingers. "Phoenix to visit an old colleague; Mexico City, that Juarez lady you put through medical school."

McLean nodded. After he'd decided to follow Grace to Maui (why he'd made that cockamamie decision, he still wasn't sure), he'd added in stops to visit people he hadn't seen in years. *Why not?* he'd reasoned, *lots of time to kill.* Thinking someone should know where he was, just in case, he'd sent DeMello a copy of his itinerary.

With a plan in motion, he'd found himself almost excited about the adventure, especially about seeing Anita Juarez.

Anita was a cardiac surgeon in Mexico City, but he'd known her since he'd dug her out of Mexico City's earthquake rubble—a tiny child with jet-black hair and hopeless eyes, three years old, dirty, dehydrated, and alone. Somehow Quinn had eked the story out of him—that he'd sent money for the child's care even when he'd had none for his own food, even as he'd struggled through medical school and residency and the early years with his own family. Only his ex-wife Genevieve had known, and she only because she'd found a cancelled check and accused him of keeping another woman. Now Nita mended tiny hearts and traveled with Doctors Without Borders and loved her Dr. Chris like the father she'd lost.

"Kauai and then Maui?" Quinn asked, eyes skeptical, head tilted. "I get Kauai, you did hurricane relief there, but why Maui?"

McLean thought about Grace tilting her head like a little brown bird just before she asked him yet another impertinent question.

"You're smiling, McLean. I knew it. It's that woman, isn't it? That Grace-the-misnomer person you met in the mountains?"

He flushed.

He knew she saw.

He explained. By the time he was done, they were both standing, Owen quiet on the sofa, eyes steady on the red liquid in his glass.

Quinn fixed McLean with a fierce frown. He waited. He hadn't realized until this moment how much he wanted her blessing—wasn't sure he'd get it. She drew in a breath, a smile split her face, and she laid her head on his shoulder. His arms went around her, drawing her close, and her words were muffled in his shirt. "All good, all good, it's all good. But damn it, McLean, I told you to get a life, not a wife."

Chapter 13
Grace

Grace blinked her eyes open as the 737 taxied toward its Hawaii home. Not that she was afraid to fly, but she always closed her eyes and crossed her fingers for landing, just in case. Around her, the other passengers on the long flight from LAX to Kahului stirred and began gathering their belongings.

Home. She sighed, fatigue and delight commingling. *Finally home.*

It had taken just seven days to get her Nevada affairs in order. Two College Guys helped pack up her personal stuff and whisked most of it off to storage. St. Vincent's Catholic Thrift happily hauled away the extra. Merry Maids cleaned, shined, and polished until the rooms sparkled. That was the point, Grace knew—clean and empty so prospective buyers could use their imaginations. At least, that's what Coral Pearson, real estate agent and friend of a friend, told her. Coral had provided such competent advice that Grace's anxiety had withered, and by this morning, when she'd signed on the last dotted line, only relief remained.

The house had been Cal's; it needed to go. Her sons didn't want it, and neither had protested when she told them she was going to put it on the market, although she suspected they thought she meant sometime in the future, not right away.

Did they know how much she disliked the house, how much she'd come to dislike their father before the months of his illness had made him dependent upon her care and she could no longer feel anything but pity and sympathy and horror at his suffering?

She shook her head. *It's done. Doesn't matter now.*

Setting dark thoughts aside, Grace rose to her feet and reached up to retrieve her carry-ons. A large arm reached over her head, and memories of another big man flooded her as a very large and helpful traveler handed down her red bag and, with a look of surprise, her guitar case and placed them in the aisle.

"Thank you."

She banned Harrison McLean and the impulsive invitation—*sounds like a title for Harry Potter*—from her thoughts and waited for the cabin doors to open.

Oᴜᴛ ᴏғ ᴛʜᴇ ᴘʟᴀɴᴇ ᴀɴᴅ ᴇɴᴠᴇʟᴏᴘᴇᴅ in the warm island air, Grace secured her pink sweater around her shoulders, made capris out of her travel pants, and headed for baggage claim. Two more bags—big ones—would be waiting. Everything she needed for her new life. She just hoped she could cram them into her car.

"Lizzie! Eliza! Aloha!" A familiar voice boomed from below.

"Jaime." Her smile was so big it hurt her face as the very slow escalator carried her down and into the embrace of a super-sized man with dark skin and a smile like a toothpaste ad.

She squealed as he grabbed both her cases in one hand, wrapped his free arm around her, and spun her off the floor in a joy-filled circle. Releasing herself to the moment, Grace threw back her head and laughed.

I'm home. Elizabeth Grace is finally home.

They came to rest at carousel three where American Airlines luggage always appeared. Before the big man could restore her to her feet, Grace Dart, the woman known to herself and Maui as Eliza King, planted a kiss on his cheek and gave herself up to joy.

"I love you, Jaime Hokoana." She spun in her own crazy circle. "And I love this airport and the air and the guys and . . ." Her voice trailed into the flowers of his shirt as Jaime pulled her to his chest in a hug that said it all.

In Maui, Eliza King wrote songs and sang with a group called The Hawaiian Cowboys: Jaime Hokoana on lead guitar, Derek Heller on bass, Rick Enoki brilliant on drums. Their high school garage band had gotten back together for their twentieth class reunion and had had so much fun that they'd just kept playing. Soon enough, they'd been invited to play at the Fourth of July celebration on Lahaina's Front Street, and their local popularity soared. They wanted more, but nothing had happened until the day this *haole* woman brought them her lyrics and her voice and the offer of a partnership if the song was good enough.

Eliza jigged in place, waiting for her bags, thinking. Somehow her new name and her newfound home allowed her to be the woman she wanted to be; she could almost forget clumsy, sad-eyed, mainland Grace. Here she could be herself.

Jaime kept her secrets. She could trust him with her life. But—troubling thoughts: *Harrison McLean, Martin Grimes, two sons who don't know my dual identity. It's time to make things right.*

She listened with half an ear as Jaime chattered—the guys, the wife, the kids. Details of a life that had gone on without her in the months she'd been held hostage stateside, and the ensuing year when she'd been unable to do anything except worry and weep.

He noticed. "You are troubled?"

"Nothing. It will all be right now."

"The songs, you have them?"

"Of course." She grinned, no *of course* about it, and held up two fingers. "Two." Even to Jaime she was not quite ready to reveal "In His Arms."

"Good," he said, his smile flashing, his voice matter of fact. He'd expected no other answer. Then he put her aside and hefted a big red bag as though it were filled with feathers. "All?"

"Nope, another."

"Two?" His eyes questioned, then cleared. "Oh yeah, you're finally moving in. Also good." He retrieved the second bag and appraised them. "Sister, I'm glad you're here, but these are not going to fit in Gretchen."

MINUTES LATER, THEY STOOD BESIDE THE cream-colored Mini Cooper known as Gretchen. She had been waiting patiently in a rental car lot, driven once in a while to keep her in good working order. Eliza loved Gretchen, but now she uttered a rueful laugh. "Once again, you are right, my best friend." She put on a pretty pout. "But surely you can make this happen."

"But surely." He grinned and waved toward the Ford 4x4 idling beside Gretchen. The driver's door sprang open and a woman as small and blond as Jaime was large and dark popped out and wrapped Grace in a hug that matched her husband's.

"Aloha, my dear friend Eliza. Your bags will fit in my vehicle, and we will go together to your new home. It waits for you."

Rosie Hokoana's welcome was warm, but her eyes glistened with apprehension. Born Rosamund Wilson in a small town in Minnesota, Rosie had come to Maui for spring break. One look at the island, one look at Jaime Hokoana, and she would never leave. Instead, she finished college at the University of Hawaii, Maui, and became a real estate agent. Now a broker, Rosie sold homes, she didn't remodel them—until Eliza's.

Eliza knew fear when she saw it. "Oh, Rosie, don't be worried," she said and pulled the smaller woman back into a hug. "I know it's wonderful. No other person in the world could have done what you've done for me." Singing, "Don't worry. Be happy," she rocked them back and forth until Rosie laughed and hugged her back.

With a last squeeze, Eliza disengaged and picked up her guitar case. "Okay, my friends, let's go. I'm ready for the grand tour."

With Jaime and Rosie in the truck following her, Eliza drove toward her new home.

Rosie had discovered the second-floor apartment, rundown and virtually abandoned by its mainland owners. It is a mess, she'd texted Eliza, but its windows open to the wind and the ocean, and I can make it beautiful.

Do it, Eliza, raw from her husband's death and doubting her own future, had texted back before her small store of courage disappeared. The sale of her first song made the down payment.

No one off island knew.

Eliza wrinkled her nose. *Too many secrets. That has to change . . . but not tonight.*

With one hand and a laugh, she scattered the pins and bands that imprisoned her hair in its tight coil, and within moments, a riot of curls crowned her head. Free. Free herself, Eliza sang to the moonlit night. Her heart thundered with joy as the wind anointed her island self and the tiny convertible covered the miles from Kahului and the airport to Kihei.

Heart beating even faster, she pulled into the drive of the Waipuilani Apartments. She'd had the virtual tour; now it was time for the real thing.

I'm scared, she realized and wondered why.

There was nothing special about the L-shaped, two-story building in front of her, eighteen units all quietly asleep just past midnight. In the hulking darkness, she discerned an outside walkway, an enclosed stairwell, a nightlight, but Gretchen nuzzled into parking space eight as though she'd been there a million times. A little bit reassured, Eliza sucked in a deep breath—plumeria, gardenia, jasmine—and hopped out of the car. Jaime hoisted her bags from the truck and she followed him up the stairs. Rosie, silent, trailed behind.

On the landing, Rosie handed her the keys. "House keys, pool keys, gate keys, mailbox keys. Yours, Eliza. You first."

With another deep breath and a scold at her own nervousness, Eliza ignored her pounding heart, slid the key into the lock, and turned it. The door opened hard. She put her shoulder to it and shoved. The room beyond was dark, empty. Her breath caught. Then she blinked, and her eyes adjusted, and moon reflecting on water filled her vision.

Oh, yes. This is more than all right. This is perfect.

CHAPTER 14
McLean

ROW OF WINDMILLS MARKED THE RIDGE of the hill. The airplane's shadow swept across the island's scrub-dotted earth. Inside, Chris McLean stretched and gathered his things. Inured to emergency travel in whatever vehicle was available, he had now discovered the comfort of business class. So many airline miles given away. In the future, if there was one, he'd keep a few for upgrades. But extra legroom and wider seats didn't answer his questions: *Why haven't I heard from her? What the hell am I doing here?*

He'd spent the minutes between Kauai and Maui in unwanted introspection, thoughts bouncing like overstimulated five-year-olds. Who was she anyway, this Grace Dart who invited a stranger to an island? Sounded like an Agatha Christie mystery. Was he the hero or the victim? And who was she? Do-gooder nurse? Widow seeking spice? Woman in need of security? Unkind thoughts. He had enjoyed the time they'd spent together, but an aged-out sorority girl, no matter how attractive, was really not his type. Whatever—he'd find out soon enough, spend a few sunny days, and get back to reality.

That is, if I ever hear from her.

Frustrated, he pushed Grace and his unanswered texts to the back of his mind. Phoenix had been pleasantly hot and his old friend from medical school welcoming and witty. His body twisted with arthritis, Arthur O'Connell had long ago retired from active practice and now was Emeritus at Arizona State, his brilliant mind still producing quality papers and mentoring the students in his care. The men had stayed up late reliving long-forgotten events and laughing at the boys they had been. With Arthur, present reality had been easily set aside.

The time in Mexico City had been all a man could hope for. A car and driver met him at the airport and whisked him to the hospital and Nita's smiling embrace and then a whirlwind of surprise consultations.

I'm old, he'd thought as the cadre of students clustered around him at each bedside, *old and tired.* Feeling neither competent nor capable, he'd listened as a student presented the case, looked over the supporting material—neat sheaves of EKGs and scans and blood tests in the universal language of medicine— and, with a borrowed stethoscope, examined the patient. Then, in the way of teachers everywhere, he let his questions challenge the thinking of these young men and women eager to learn.

Four hours later, he collapsed, laughing, into an overstuffed chair in Nita's spacious fifth-floor apartment overlooking the sprawl of Mexico City.

Nita looked down at him, and he could see the love in her eyes. "You did good, Dr. Chris. I didn't think I would ever be able to spring you from their questions. Now they will look at me with new respect, knowing that all I am is from you."

In the days that followed, he lectured, did rounds with students, and explored a Mexico City rebuilt and thriving since the long-ago earthquake that had given him Nita and his rescue work. On the last day of his visit, trusting Nita would intervene if he faltered, he gloved and gowned and, for the first time since his infarction, held a beating heart in his hand.

The glow of that experience still on him, he'd arrived in Kauai to a warm welcome from the Red Cross community and a proud tour of Kauai's restoration. But when he was alone in the Kaua'i Marriott Resort in Lihue, the blackness he'd been dodging finally caught him. By the time he boarded the Maui-bound plane, depression weighed heavy.

As he descended into Maui's warm air, McLean sensed a change. Inside, something unfamiliar shimmered. His step quickened as he hurried to pick up his rental car. He would check into his hotel, discover whatever Maui had to offer, let the black dog feed somewhere else.

Time to stop wallowing and move on.

Driving away from the airport, he caught himself humming an old show tune, something with the words "my special island," and he recognized his feeling: hope.

CHAPTER 15
ELIZA

ELIZABETH GRACE DART, NÉE KING, WOKE to raucous birdsong. *I'm here. I'm Eliza. This is mine.*

Pale pink walls, bamboo furniture, traditional Hawaiian quilt now folded neatly at the foot of the bed—her bedroom had welcomed her, and sleep had descended easy and deep. Now the lazy ceiling fan stirred the morning air and brought the scent of plumeria from the tree outside her window. White curtains fluttered in the breeze.

She pushed aside the crisp white sheet, slipped into her silk wrapper, and padded on bare feet to view the rest of her new home. No trace of the dilapidated ruin she'd seen in the pictures Rosie had sent. Under her friend's capable direction, the crew of Hokoana Construction had stripped the apartment bare and turned it into a place of simplicity and comfort: walls the color of soft sand, countertops of stippled granite, cabinets of pale wood, and stainless steel appliances that gleamed in the morning light. Long distance and grateful for faxes and texts and email, Eliza had chosen it all. Rosie had made it happen. Now it was hers.

Uttering a cry of sheer joy, she stood at the window and surveyed her domain.

Days later, drenched in sweat, Eliza grabbed a bottle of water and rolled it against her forehead before swallowing a glorious gulp. Rehearsals were exhausting. Around her the guys fiddled with their instruments, their grins letting her know how much they liked her new work. Panting, she lay back on the floor of Jaime's garage, and her thoughts strayed.

Martin Grimes, undaunted by her demand to leave her alone, continued his pursuit. Most messages she ignored, but a few days ago she'd opened one. *Just to make sure he's winding down,* she'd fooled herself. "Grace, my dear," it read, "such coy avoidance is not becoming at our age. Each day you delay is one less day of the time we're meant to spend together. I encourage you to change your ways promptly." Filled with sudden unease, she'd huffed and deleted it, and, ignoring everything else, she'd turned off her phone.

The worry was harder to turn off.

Now, lying on the cool concrete surrounded by friends who had become family, she pushed worry away, made space inside, and let well-being sweep away mainland troubles. Money and bills, the not-quite-issued restraining order, and even the impulsive invitation to a man she didn't really know could be dealt with later. It did cross her mind to wonder why she hadn't heard from him, but in this moment she would relax and believe and work like hell to ready herself for her debut.

"Ready for tomorrow, Lizzy?" Rosie settled beside her and handed her another bottle of water.

Eliza knew the guys worried about her, Jaime most of all, and that Rosie had been sent to snoop. In the four years of their partnership, the men had come to know and care for the haole woman who came to their island. Off-island, she disappeared. They had shrugged and accepted this until the mainland husband died. Family helped family, and she was family. They couldn't help her if they didn't know her. This was not okay.

Eliza understood, but her silence had been so absolute, her secret life so imperative, that she found it hard even now to break free. For three weeks she had slaved with Jaime to put music to her lyrics. They had all put in long hours until the new songs and the old ones were polished and ready. Time to shed secrets, she knew, just as soon as she told her sons.

Enough fussing.

"Ready as I'll ever be, Rosie my friend." She grinned. "The guys seem happy with the new songs."

"Oh, yes, the new ones are wonderful. You'll do them tomorrow?"

Eliza's heart stuttered. Eliza K and her Hawaiian Cowboys would headline Kihei's Fourth Friday. Each community hosted a town party one Friday a month. Kehei's was tomorrow. When she'd been on island earlier, her performances had been low-key: a graduation party, a local dance, background music for other things. Tomorrow they were the featured attraction. The Kihei world would be watching. The Hawaiian Cowboys were ready. She hoped she wouldn't let them down.

"Nope, just one," she answered Rosie's question. Their playlist was eclectic. The guys liked the Beach Boys with a little Jimmy Buffett and reggae and Kenny Chesney thrown in for good measure. Eliza liked Dolly Parton and Emmy Lou Harris, but Juice Newton was her favorite. She never felt as good as when she belted out "love's been a little bit hard on me."

"We'll save the second for later in case I can't come up with anything new."

Rosie huffed in disbelief.

Joyful tears threatened. Her friends believed in her even when she doubted. Eliza chugged the second bottle of water, scrubbed at her eyes, and then jumped to her feet as Jaime's guitar riff called them back to practice.

"And don't worry, Rosie. I love my new home. I'm happy with the music. I'm scared about tomorrow and that's normal. It's all good."

All good, she thought as she picked up her tambourine and strutted into the music, *but how do I explain it to my boys?*

Chapter 16
McLean

Depression lifted, Chris McLean explored the island of romance, falling under its spell even as he kept his eyes peeled for a glimpse of Grace. He had arrived before the appointed day, but you'd think she would at least respond to his texts. He'd tried calling but her voicemail was always full, and he was beginning to believe he had imagined the interlude at the McCloud Hotel. *Detox hallucinations*, he thought, half serious.

Get a life.

The Maui Beach Hotel faced into the sunrise, so he was up and ready early each day. He drove through Hailuku and hiked to the Iao, experiencing for himself the mountain's spiritual nature. Upcountry, he found, was a step backward in time, with rodeos and cowboys and chickens that roamed the streets alongside upscale art galleries and boutiques and jewelry stores. And he had a marvelous lunch at Mama's Fish House.

When his heart pounded and his breath came too fast, when his thoughts strayed toward the operating room far away or the bottle of Maker's Mark available at the nearest store, when he wondered if he would ever again be useful, desirable, loved, he did the impossible—he used another DeMello trick and chanted, "I'll think about it tomorrow," under his breath until his mind returned to the business at hand.

On Thursday, that business was the road to Hana, where he shared the curves and single lane bridges with what must have been half the world's population. Up and back with a short detour to the Seven Sacred Pools and a nap on the black sand beach consumed eleven hours of one day, and his sleep that night was deep and dreamless.

He woke on Friday tingling with anticipation. Tomorrow he was invited to "continue our conversations"—if the dratted woman materialized, that is. Never known for premonitions or intuition, and feeling foolish for even being in Maui, Chris McLean continued to tingle.

Showered and sporting a vacation beard, ready for whatever the day would bring, McLean entered the dining room and found his way to his regular booth overlooking the harbor. In the distance, the sun shone through fluffs of white clouds and the sea rose and fell on its journey to the beach.

A dark-skinned woman of ample proportions ambled to his table, a wide smile on her young face. "Morning, doc, my name's Nene. I've been off a few days but now I'm back, and I'll be your server today. Coffee?"

He lowered his eyes to hide his smile. He didn't know how, but by the end of his first day here, all the staff knew he was a physician. At home he was *Doctor* or at the very least *sir*, but the "doc" that slipped from Nene's lips held only friendly respect. He decided he liked being just plain doc.

He didn't need the menu. "Thanks, Nene, I'll have plenty of coffee and then scrambled eggs and dry toast."

She filled his mug and jotted down his order, making a face at its paucity of calories, and he almost felt like he needed to explain.

His food arrived. It did look pretty sparse on the white plate.

"Where you off to today?" Nene asked as she refilled his mug.

"No plans. I think I've been everyplace. Any suggestions?"

She favored him with a chiding head tilt and a knowing smile. "You haven't been anyplace yet. You've missed West Maui."

He didn't bother to ask how she knew where he'd been. "Okay, tell me where."

"My family's from Kihei Town. You can end up there." She considered a moment. "Goodness, yes, that's perfect. Fourth Friday."

"What's Fourth Friday?"

"A *pau hana* night. Wailuku Town First Friday, Lahaina Town Second Friday, Makawao Third Friday, and Kihei Town Fourth Friday."

For a minute he thought she was speaking another language. "Sounds interesting but still not getting it. *Pau hana?*" He struggled with pronunciation.

She laughed. "With only seven consonants, you gotta say every vowel," she said, coached him until the Hawaiian words and the town names satisfied her, then continued. "*Pau hana* means town party—outdoor music, food, booths with stuff to buy, lots of booths actually, and many food trucks." Her lips pressed together in an *mmmm* sound. "You gotta go tonight. Go early to eat and then stay for the music. My cousin's band starts at eight—Jaime Hokoana. He's lead guitar for Eliza K and the Hawaiian Cowboys. They're really good. But go up the coast first, Lahaina and Ka'anapali, beautiful beaches. And have

65

lunch at The Gazebo, it's really good, too, if you have patience to stand in line for one hour."

She cocked her head at him, assessing. "Yes, you have patience. You can do it. And tell my little sister hi. Lisa. She's the hostess there."

Amused at Nene's infectious enthusiasm and intrigued by the town party concept, he agreed to follow her plan. He'd seen the sights; a little local culture would do him good. Several cups of coffee later, McLean gathered up guide book, sunscreen, and hat and headed across the island.

Away from the ocean breeze, the air clung hot and sticky, and he kept the windows rolled up and the AC on high. To his left, white smoke blossomed from two smokestacks. Sugar cane rose high in the surrounding fields—the last sugar cane processing plant on the islands, he'd been told, the production of sugar being cheaper in other countries. Besides, no one liked the smoke from the burning cane. He wondered what would take its place. There was a museum near the plant but he didn't stop. Today he had an agenda, and he needed to be in Kihei by six.

The rented sedan zoomed past Maaelea Harbor and the Ocean Center, around curves with startling views of the sea, under a canopy of monkey pod trees, and through Lahaina. He'd catch it on the way back, maybe go to the aquarium, too, and think about a luau for another night. He laughed as he repeated the word *luau*, congratulating himself as he pronounced all the vowels.

The beaches were as beautiful as Nene had promised, and after he said hi to sister Lisa and consumed a second breakfast—macadamia nut pancakes with a whipped topping that more than compensated for his earlier caloric paucity—he spent an hour on the beach at Kapalua Bay. As he'd told Carlos, he wasn't much of a swimmer, but the buoyancy of the water held him weightless, and the turtle's head poking up by his shoulder provided a heart-stopping experience. Besides, he had to get some wear out of the ridiculous swim trunks the personal shopper had foisted on him.

The sun won its battle with his sunscreen, and his shoulders and the top of his head were smarting as he rinsed the salt and sand from his body and found a place to change back into street clothes.

Lahaina's Front Street teemed with tourists and souvenir shops, but he noted several promising restaurants and an ad for the Old Lahaina Luau. He didn't know if he would be taking Grace out to dinner; he didn't know where on the island she lived. Damn it, if she thought about him at all she was probably laughing her head off right now. He didn't know one thing about her and here he was, poor soul, ready to play the fool.

In this dark mood, he left Lahaina behind. At least Fourth Friday should be interesting.

Chapter 17
Eliza

Friday morning. Vibrating with anticipation for the upcoming show, Eliza picked up her iPhone, which had been off for days so she wouldn't have to endure Martin's words populating the screen faster than she could delete them.

Visible through the bank of windows facing sun and sea, palm trees rippled and white waves ruffled toward the sand. Pigeons scanned the grass for leftovers while mynahs strutted and protested in their loud voices. She smiled. In Hawaii, she knew the birds by name. In the distance, tennis rackets and balls collided with resounding thunks. Determined to call her sons and at least let them know where she was, she took a deep breath and turned the phone on.

The man's message popped into view.

Oh my.

Grace, I look forward to continuing our chats. Will arrive Maui June 21, staying at Maui Beach Hotel. See you anytime you say after the last Friday. Chris McLean aka Harrison.

The last Friday. That would be today. Oh my goodness.

Quick fingers flew over the tiny keys—I'll meet you at your hotel noon Saturday. G—and hit send before she could think too hard. With a knot in her stomach, she scrolled and deleted and then called her son.

"You did what? You're where? With who?" Jed's voice rose an octave from his calm, cool lawyer persona. This was all outraged child. "Mom, have you lost your mind?"

She held the phone away from her ear and counted to ten. Sometimes her elder son sounded a little too much like his father. "Enough, Jed, enough. I bought an apartment in Hawaii. I'm selling the Reno house because none of us want to live there. I already told you boys that. And I met a nice man who just had a heart attack and needs a quiet place to recuperate." All true, all incomplete; she *was* still the mother.

While Jed stewed over what to say that would return his mother to her senses, Eliza thought about her boys: Jed, christened Jedediah, a real estate attorney with a booming practice, a home on Catalina Island, and a psychiatrist wife who thought the mother-in-law needed constant care; and Jacob, a bassoonist with the Washington, DC, symphony orchestra. Jeddy and Jakie they'd been until they towered over her and demanded to be Jed and Jacob, claiming the names of the men they were becoming.

She frowned. Somehow she'd gotten into the habit of dreading their displeasure as she had feared their father's. The mother they knew was Grace, the nurse who took care of people. Her face scrunched as she thought about the mother she'd been— kind, helpful, always there, always afraid to say boo. *Wonder what they'll think of Eliza K.*

Jed cleared his throat.

She cleared hers. *Bring it on, my boy. I can handle it now.*

"Send me the papers, Mom." Firm, reasonable. "I'm sure I can get you out of whatever mess you've gotten yourself into, and I need the name of the real estate agent in Reno. And how do you know that guy isn't a—"

A genuine laugh escaped, and she interrupted. "An ax murderer, or a serial killer? Why, you silly boy, I Googled him."

HER FATHER HAD OFTEN REFERRED TO being "rode hard and put away wet." By the time she got off the phone, she knew exactly what that meant. No way was she sending papers to Jed, and she'd managed not to give him Harrison's name either. All she needed was her son sending out Hawaii 5-0, or its Maui equivalent, to investigate a—a what? New friend? Potential lover? Another sad soul for her to rescue? And she hadn't told him the half of it—too soon to disclose the name change, the songs, the band, and the new life she was creating. Old habits die hard. More knots in her stomach. Jed would be on the phone right now informing his younger brother that their mother was clearly demented. She could just imagine Caroline whispering "diagnosable" in his ear.

Then Jacob would call, or he'd make Raul do it. They both knew Raul could twist her around his little finger just by calling her Mamacita and smiling his wicked smile. She grinned and turned her phone off. She'd call him later. No time for that now. She had a job to do.

Hours later, soothed and steadied by a long, salty swim and a snooze on the beach, then a cool shower and a coconut oil treatment that had her hair shining and dark and so curly she hardly recognized herself, Eliza straightened the skirt that swirled around her ankles, made sure the shirt clung in all the right places, and pulled on red cowboy boots. Raspberry lip gloss in her pocket for touch-ups—she tended to chew it off between numbers—and she was ready.

Downstairs, with the truck's AC on high, Rosie waited to give her a ride—no sense wilting before she even got on stage. She'd walk the mile home from the Azeka Mall when they were done, time alone then for processing, but for now, no more thinking. It would be good, or not, and then she'd deal.

Food trucks lined both sides of Piikea Avenue, cordoned off for the event, and people of all ages and shapes and sizes lined up for fish tacos and pork skewers and shave ice. A loudspeaker blared near the bounce house, and the white roofs of the booths were like beacons under the setting sun. Her spirits rose and she thrummed with happiness: Maui people, Maui culture, Maui home.

The truck slid to a halt behind the flatbed trailer which served as a makeshift stage for this parking lot event. Jaime and Derek were setting up. Terror rose in Eliza's throat.

Dear God, what was I thinking? Willy K headlined last month and I think I can follow him? The guys will hate me. "Argg."

Rosie looked up at Eliza's gurgle and laughed. "Stage fright. Jaime has it all the time. Go find a corner to throw up and you'll be fine." She shoved Eliza toward the door. "Out. No puking in my truck."

Her laugh was still audible as Eliza leaned against the fender and vomited.

Rosie was right. She did feel better as she sipped cold water from the bottle Rick Enoki, blond surfer looks belying his Japanese surname, handed her with a sympathetic grimace.

Applause as the local hula group waved and bowed and left the stage. Jaime and Derek did a final check on the equipment:

speakers, monitors, enough outlets for their electronics, stands for acoustic and electric guitars. Everything was ready. One by one, the guys spoke encouraging words—they'd done this before, knew she hadn't, recognized nerves when they saw them.

Deep sigh.

They'd gone through their playlist in the early afternoon. She didn't sing every song, and halfway through the performance Rick had a wild drum solo, but with humming and singing the choruses and keeping time on her tambourine, she would be on stage the entire hour.

One more deep sigh and then it was eight o'clock, and Big Ray, local radio station celebrity and emcee for the evening, finished talking about whatever and began their introduction.

"Tonight, ladies and gentlemen, we have a special treat. We all know Jaime Hokoana's band." He paused for applause. "Tonight we'll meet their new vocalist. Come on, folks, let's give it up for Eliza K and the Hawaiian Cowboys."

The guys walked on, plugged in, and tuned up to the scattered applause and stirrings of a full house: white folding chairs occupied, grass littered with bodies, folks propped up against light posts and plumeria trees. At the end of June, summer and tourist season in full swing, everyone was ready for a good time.

Jaime strummed the first bar, leaned in to his mic, and announced, "Here comes the treat of your life, Ms. Eliza K."

No turning back now.

The first words of "Queen of Hearts" were already filling the air as Eliza, tambourine tapping against her side, skirts swirling and sequins twinkling, strutted onto the stage.

CHAPTER 18
McLean

CHRIS McLEAN LOCATED THE AZEKA MALL, divided in half by a street teeming with cars and bodies all moving at half speed. Having misjudged the travel time, he was already later than he'd planned. Now he wasted another half hour looking for parking before he found a space on a side street five blocks away. Sweat was trickling under his shirt by the time he fought his way through the crowd to a truck selling bottled water, bought two bottles, and emptied them both.

No time for food if he wanted to catch Nene's cousin and his famous band. Rehydrated, he purchased a third bottle for good measure and, rolling it against his overheated neck, made his way toward the bright lights that must indicate the stage, if such existed in Kihei Town.

At the left edge of an impressive crowd, Chris found an unoccupied tree and settled against it just in time to hear a brown man wearing Levi's and a flowered shirt big enough to cover a bed announce, "Here comes the treat of your life, Ms. Eliza K," and a tiny woman flitted like a firefly onto the stage.

Swirling skirts, stamping red boots, jewels twinkling at wrists and ears, and a voice as smooth and rich as melted chocolate. The tambourine tapped and rattled as Eliza K twirled and belted out the words to an old Juice Newton tune, playing to the crowd on her left. Half the audience was already dancing, the other half clapping, some even singing along.

McLean's own foot was keeping time when the big man, obviously lead guitar, obviously the cousin, riffed, and the bassist upped the pace. Into the refrain, the woman flounced right, her chestnut curls alive around a delicate face and gleaming eyes.

Chris stared, caught in the music and the words and the woman's magic. At that moment, all else forgotten, he wanted only to hold her in his arms. Entranced, he took a step forward.

She must have noticed because she looked right at him.

Eyes met, gray eyes. *Grace?*

Her voice faltered, and she missed the beat.

The cousin started forward and she waved him away, picked up the melody, and moved back across the stage as though there had been no interruption at all.

McLean's heart stuttered and he sank into a squat, legs suddenly unreliable. *Grace? My aged-out sorority girl? What the hell is going on?*

She didn't look his way again.

Heat whooshed up his neck, flamed his cheeks. What had he expected? A too-good-to-be-true invitation from a complete stranger. She'd felt sorry for him. And now, of all times, his body sitting up and taking notice. What a pathetic wreck.

Anger and lust warred. He wanted to shake her, ask what game she was playing, what she wanted with him. He should stalk away and be done with this. His heart thundered and his body yearned, and he couldn't drag his eyes from this sprite whose voice poured out words of love.

The band performed "Lookin' for Love," "Missing You," and something fresh and fun that he was sure he'd never heard before, and when the big man with the Kenny Rogers voice held Grace in his arms as they sang "Islands in the Stream," he wanted to push the guy aside and take his place.

Sometime during the performance, a young voice had whispered, "Hey, mister, you look like you could use a chair," and gestured to one she'd occupied. He sat.

Grace, miraculously transformed into a woman he didn't know, finished Linda Ronstadt's "Poor Poor Pitiful Me," executed a wide curtsy for the applauding crowd, and ran off the stage as the drum solo began.

Chris watched the sparkling creature snag a bottle of water from a woman by the stairs and head in his direction. Before he could stand, she was beside him, her gaze even with his.

He expected, *wanted*, an apology, embarrassment, chagrin. Instead, the gray eyes gleamed with mischief and her hand was cool on his cheek. "Nice beard."

His questions fled. "Nice hairdo."

Silence for a beat, then they both laughed. Her lips brushed his. "I'm glad you're here, Harrison. I suppose I do owe you an explanation."

His lips tingled: raspberry, sweat, woman.

With no logic at all, he knew this would come out right. "You don't owe me anything, Eliza Grace, but I can't wait for the explanation."

CHAPTER 19
ELIZA GRACE

SHE'D STUTTERED WHEN SHE MET HIS eyes and electricity snapped between them. Surprise and dismay—so much for secret lives. Harrison McLean looked solid, normal, safe, and oh so sexy. She'd meant only to offer a space for a wounded man to regain his balance, and here she was, drawing him into her little drama. Perhaps he'd run. She wouldn't blame him.

Amusement curved his lips as she kissed him. No words of anger, no questions, no demand for explanations.

Jaime's guitar gave up the opening bars of "It's So Easy (to Fall in Love)."

The wicked gleam in Harrison's eyes encouraged her. One more kiss, deeper and longer. Deliquescent, her body flowing into his, his mouth opening to receive her.

Wow.

Her hands fluttered to his shoulders. Just as his hands settled on her waist, the guitar's impatient repeat penetrated her fogged senses.

Golly, my cue.

"Go home," she whispered. "I'll find you tomorrow."

She strode away, already offering the "it's so easy, so easy" refrain from Juice Newton's lively song as she rattled the tambourine and attained the stage. She grinned at the question Jaime's glance held, then cleared her mind, swung into the music, and didn't look back.

"Angel of the Morning," their voices blending into the chorus, and their Fourth Friday debut concluded with applause that rocked the night.

Jaime's arm circled her as they took their final bows. "You did good, girl. We did good. But who was that fucker who was trying to eat you up?"

A schoolgirl blush climbed her neck. "Let's pack up and get a beer, my friend, and this time it's full disclosure."

They gathered later, expectant, on the grass behind her apartment. Jaime, Rosie, and the guys—she always thought of Rick and Derek this way, though they were grown men with real lives—hunkered into lawn chairs, their faces toward the moonlit ocean a hundred yards away while they swigged beers and waited for Eliza's story. She'd made it a command performance; once through was all she could manage.

"Can't," Derek had stated. "Got a girl with legs up to here just about ready." His Paul Newman eyes and dark, chiseled features gave truth to his story.

Rick just said his mama had dinner on the table. Everybody laughed. They all knew Rick's mama was celebrating her seventieth birthday at the Bellagio in Las Vegas, and cooking was the last thing on her mind.

"Short and sweet," she promised. They stayed. Now they waited.

She paced.

"Sit, sister, you're making us dizzy." Rosie's voice held impatience, sympathy, and a large measure of curiosity.

Eliza dropped to the grass by their chairs. "Okay. No questions 'til I'm done and no telling me I'm stupid."

Derek hooted. "Can't make those promises, but you got my attention." He toasted her with his sweaty bottle, drained it, and tossed it toward the pile growing on the grass. Breaking down equipment was hard and thirsty work.

"Fair. Okay. To begin, my legal name is Grace Dart, really Elizabeth Grace King Dart dba Eliza King." She waited until their exclamations subsided. "I was a nurse, a housewife, and a mother. When I started coming here, my husband thought I was doing charity work for the poor, but really I came to experiment."

Jaime's face scrunched up. "Experiment?" As her best friend and her island attorney, he knew most of the story, but not all.

"Yep. I needed to know if I could really write songs or if it was just a silly girl's dream."

She paused, thinking about the guitar she'd purchased with her babysitting money after her parents had told her guitars were for boys and paid for piano lessons instead. That guitar still shared her songwriting struggles.

She cleared her throat and pushed back the memories. "And after that," she went on, "could I write lyrics that someone would play, would listen to, might even buy?"

Rick snorted. "Well, you didn't need much experimenting to get the answer to that."

Tears rose in her eyes. She ignored them. "Thanks. But I didn't really know until Willy's people . . . well . . . you know, wanted my song. At least, at that point I had enough sense to realize that I was a babe in a very big woods. Luckily, Jaime's ad in the phone book was a full-page one. Made me brave enough to make the call."

Jaime reached out to knuckle her head.

"And he was brave enough to listen to me."

"Yeah, and look where it got me."

Laughter all around. They all knew tonight's performance had been better than good, that her new song had been well received, that they were another rung up the shaky entertainment ladder.

Rosie climbed over her husband's legs to wrap Eliza in a big hug.

This time the tears did fall. She wiped them away with the heel of her hand, accepted her second Longboard, and took a deep pull of the crisp Hawaiian beer.

"Not done yet. Now it gets complicated. See, nobody at home knows anything about this."

Attention that had been drifting snapped back. Derek's beer paused in its journey to his mouth. Only Jaime looked unsurprised.

"I couldn't tell. I was afraid I couldn't come back, not brave enough to ask for a change in my marriage."

"Or a divorce," someone's voice chimed in.

"Yeah, or a divorce. So I had this kind of James Bond double-identity thing going. Nerve-wracking, but exciting, too, and I was hooked. But then Cal, my husband, got sick, and I had to take care of him, and then he died and I was kind of paralyzed."

"That kiss didn't look paralyzed."

She wasn't sure if Jaime's voice held censure or just amusement and wasn't quite ready to ask. She sighed. "That's complication number two. He's a nice man I met while I was in California trying to write something worth singing. He's been ill, and I invited him here for some peace and quiet."

Jaime's big laugh boomed. "That's not what we call it around here, girl."

They all chortled. Apparently even Rosie had seen the kiss.

Feeling the flush creep upward again, Eliza grimaced. "That wasn't part of the plan. But hey . . ." She hummed a made-up tune, sang "when life gives you lemons," and had them all laughing.

She answered their questions and finally promised to show them the boys' baby books if they needed more details. Rosie gathered up the empties for recycling. The guys lugged the chairs around to the front and, with hugs all around, the evening ended.

Eliza was here. Eliza was theirs. Pretty much end of story.

LATER IN HER NEW BATHROOM, ALL pale peach and blue gray like the sunset, Eliza lingered in the shower and let the cool spray settle her thoughts. *I'm glad I told them. There's really no need for the secrets anymore.*

Now it was just a matter of making her name change official, telling the boys about the singing part of things, and finishing the paperwork for the restraining order. *Should I have mentioned Martin? Nah, he's off island. The restraining order will convince him to move on. Problem solved.*

Eliza pulled a sleep shirt over her head and slipped under her crisp white sheets. *Tomorrow I'll decide what to do with my big man.*

She fell asleep with a smile on her lips.

Chapter 20
McLean

Lights twinkled up the hillsides to the north, small communities going about their business—he'd been in many such places: Iran, Turkey, Vietnam, even his own backcountry and the smaller enclaves within American cities. Tonight his usual curiosity—*Who lives there? What are they doing? How do they live their lives?*— was quiescent. Instead, he drove across the island, grinning like a loon and wondering why he hadn't asked any questions, why he hadn't demanded answers, then chuckling at his own stupidity.

That kiss just fried my brain.

"Go home," the Grace, not-Grace woman had said. "I'll find you tomorrow." And he'd gone, just like that. Hadn't even waited for the finale.

Hmmm.

He relived the delicious moments—her mouth, hot and soft, promising; her body melting on his like liquid wax; his own body rising in response. At least he knew now that all his parts were in working order.

Not sure what would happen next, he pulled into the hotel's parking lot, found the restaurant still open, and ordered a steak. Sat fat be damned, some things just demanded celebration. Later, when he tumbled into bed, just before sleep found him, he realized that he hadn't had his one glass of wine for the day.

"DID YOU DO FOURTH FRIDAY?" NENE asked the next morning as she filled his coffee mug. "Did you see the band? Aren't they great? And isn't that Eliza K the best singer ever? I want to be her when I grow up."

He noted her plus size, kept his thoughts to himself, and filled her in on his day—The Gazebo, the beaches, the swim, and Fourth Friday—leaving out the best parts. Of course, sister Lisa had reported in, and Nene knew most of it already. She had ideas for today, but he told her a friend was coming by and they were doing something.

"Lady friend?"

He nodded, surprised that she didn't already have those details.

She pointed toward the lobby door. "There is a hairdresser here on Saturdays. You will want to have a trim. Tell her Nene sent you."

She hurried to assist a new arrival, leaving McLean grinning. *Guess I know how I'll be spending my morning.*

Tutti in the salon tut-tutted a bit but agreed to fit him in at ten. "While you're waiting," she said, "you might want to return to your room and put on a different shirt."

He looked down. What was wrong with his black polo shirt? It was clean. It had a logo. The personal shopper hadn't protested when he'd added it to the steadily growing pile.

She must have seen his confusion. "It is too dark, not . . . welcoming, not . . . not happy."

Hmmm.

He considered Tutti's words as he obediently headed for his room. It hadn't occurred to him that he might need a makeover, but in retrospect, all things being equal, this was no surprise. He hadn't dressed for happy in a long time.

When he returned to the salon at ten wearing the pale blue Tommy Bahama shirt with Hawaiian flowers, her smile was almost reward enough for the hour it had taken him to iron the damn thing. He could only hope that Grace—no, Eliza—liked happy Hawaiian-print shirts, size extra-large.

In the lobby at 12:10, just as he thought he'd been forgotten, McLean heard a car screech to a halt under the resort's portico. He looked up. A small figure hopped out of a cream-colored Mini Cooper convertible. The woman, Grace, adjusted the baseball cap that held her brown hair in place, straightened her narrow shoulders, and started toward the lobby door.

He rose and stepped out to meet her. God, she was tiny. He didn't remember her this small; last night she had been larger than life. No mischief today. Her eyes were wary as they met his.

"Aloha, Harrison. I'm glad you're here."

"I think I am, too, Grace, or is it Eliza?"

A little twinkle displaced the wariness. "Here I am Eliza, or even Lizzie, and you are Harrison. New to each other and even new to ourselves."

"Hello, Eliza," he said, the name already a kiss on his lips, the words ripe with promise. "Aloha."

"Ah, yes, already you speak our language." She grinned. "Come. We'll explore a little bit, and if we still like each other,

I'll tell all." A sly glance and the head tilt let him know the woman he knew as Grace was still present, name change or no. "And then you will, too."

"Can't wait," he said, instantly sorry for the sarcasm but not willing to retract it.

She turned back to the car.

He hesitated.

She saw and chuckled. "Meet Gretchen."

He looked around, saw no one. "Gretchen?" He hoped he didn't sound as confused as he felt, what with Grace who was not Grace and now an invisible Gretchen.

What a rabbit hole.

Eliza smiled and patted the Mini's hood. "My car, Gretchen. She is too wonderful to just be called *car.*" When he still hesitated, she encouraged, "Climb in. One size fits all."

It came over him in a flash, the visual—Gretchen expanding and contracting, vagina-like, to accommodate all comers—and the laughter took over before he even found it funny. Arms tight against his chest to keep from splitting open, he laughed until tears ran down his cheeks.

Eliza's brows drew together, an irritated look. "Don't worry, Harrison, you'll fit inside her. If Jaime fits, anyone will."

This shattered whatever control remained. Leaning against the fender for support, he snorted and hiccupped, and just when he thought he was done, it started over. In minutes he was gasping for breath.

Eliza's face scrunched up. "What is it, Harrison? What is so fun . . ." Her words trailed off as she got it, and color rose in her cheeks. "Gretchen . . . expands and contracts . . . inside her . . . Jaimie . . ." By the time she'd thought it through, she was leaning against the fender beside him, her laughter even bigger than his.

Finally, when normal breathing had resumed, she mopped her eyes with her fists and assumed a superior tone. "I just meant, Harrison, that Jaime also can ride in Gretchen."

Once again, laughter convulsed them both.

Eventually, when they could breathe without going off, Eliza pressed one finger to her lips in a *keep quiet* sign and pointed at McLean before she climbed into the driver's seat and motioned him into the car.

He got the message. Avoiding eye contact, Chris squeezed himself into the passenger seat and barely had time to buckle up before Gretchen wheeled away from the hotel and whizzed up the street.

They were almost out of town before Eliza spoke. "If you promise to behave yourself, Harrison, I will tell you about Jaime."

"Oh, right," Chris hiccupped and struggled to keep a straight face, "Jaime, the big lead guitar guy who nuzzled your hair." *Like I wanted to*, he thought but didn't say.

She giggled. "Yes, that Jaime. He is lead guitar, but he is also my attorney and my best friend. If you meet him, you'll like him. He'll like you too, that is, after he assures himself that you won't try to eat me up."

Hmmm.

She continued. "We'll go upcountry today. I wanted to take you to lunch at the Hali'imaile General Store, but they're closed for a party, so we'll eat at Kula Lodge. You'll like that, maybe better even. Then we'll zip back around to Wailea so you can see how the semirich live. We may even have time for a little nap on the beach before we hit happy hour at 5 Palms." She took her eyes off the road for a minute, scanned his face. "You *are* still allowed your one glass of wine each day?"

Damn woman, how did she know that? He nodded yes.

"Good. We'll have a grand day. I'm sure you've seen most of the sights already, but this should be pleasant for you. And at the end of the day, we'll know what to do next." Her eyes skipped from the road to him and then back. "By the way, nice shirt."

Damn woman.

Since it was clear there would be no serious talk for the moment, he settled his hat firmly on his head, held on, and prepared to enjoy the drive, still chuckling at the notion of a shape-shifting Mini and the unmitigated pleasure of laughter shared.

Chapter 21
Eliza Grace

A cutely aware of the man tucked in beside her, Eliza gripped the steering wheel with both hands, turned Gretchen away from the Maui Beach Hotel and headed upcountry. Her sides ached with the laughter. The man's imagination had gone right to sex and hers had no trouble following. Now she struggled to keep her face straight—another outburst might land them in the ditch—even as she wondered where she'd hidden her normal self.

She relished the wolfish gleam in his eyes when she mentioned Jaime and chided herself for wishful thinking as it faded. Harrison McLean did look pretty darn cute with his Wolf Pack hat and the carefully tended stubble on his cheeks. He had a lived-in face, not classically handsome but pleasant—"full of character," her grandmother would have said—a man who knew himself, or had, before his heart had betrayed him and his body had become a stranger.

But what a body, she thought wistfully as she glanced his way again. And that shirt—Tommy Bahama, mainlanders' snooty idea of what an island shirt should be. He'd mumbled something about a personal shopper, and she couldn't wait to hear that story.

He deserves an explanation. Anyway, what does he want with me?

Her mind ticking like a metronome, Eliza forced herself to concentrate on driving as she guided Gretchen through the lunch throngs in Paia, a one-stoplight town on Maui's north coast caught in a 1950s time warp. "Willie Nelson jams here sometimes," she told the man at her side, carefully avoiding eye contact in case he had something funny to say about Willie and jam, "and Paia Fish Market does a really good lunch."

He said he'd stopped at Anthony's Coffee Co. on his way to Hana. She nodded just as they whisked through town and the whistling wind made conversation difficult.

Raising her voice, she identified the flame trees lining the narrow road, directed his attention to glimpses of rough coastline and the waves crashing below, and then stopped a moment to appreciate the church constructed of native rock as they followed Baldwin Avenue toward the little town of Makawao.

Gretchen crept along a main street lined with shops and galleries and tourists, and the muggy air pressed upon them like a blanket too heavy for the season. Her body thrummed. Her skin tingled. Inside, unfamiliar locations clamored for attention.

She spoke to dispel this self she hardly recognized.

"Makawao celebrates its cowboy heritage with a rodeo every Fourth of July weekend. Maybe something else for you to do—that is, if you like men chasing cows. I always root for the cows."

He snorted. She paused. He didn't comment, but the thrumming and tingling had diminished so she continued, "And if you don't like cows, there's always the galleries. Lots of artists have located Upcountry; something about the view and the lazy afternoons inspires their craft."

She smiled. *For heaven's sake, I sound just like a tour guide.*

Absurd, but the man *was* a guest, and it was her job to make him comfortable. Beside her, Harrison did seem comfortable enough, having come to an agreement with Gretchen about how a maxi can be comfortable in a Mini and momentarily at ease with himself.

She wanted him to pepper her with questions. No, she didn't. She wanted to park under a tree and climb into his lap and see if he tasted as good in the daylight as he had last night. Yes, she so wanted that. Who knew her Eliza persona could be so much bolder than Grace's?

How strange.

She was glad when Gretchen hurried up the Haleakala Highway, and Makawao retreated into the rearview mirror, and the wind again whistled so loudly that the man surely couldn't hear her thoughts.

"Nice," Harrison said.

They'd pulled into the parking lot with its view of the Kula Lodge, valley and ocean in the distance, but when she glanced over, she wasn't sure where his eyes rested. She flushed, chose the impersonal. "Good view of the island. Food here is nice, and the ambiance—well, I'll let you judge for yourself." Her cheeks burned as she led him inside the quaint inn with its fireplace and wood beams and wraparound view.

The host settled them side by side at a table that overlooked the cabins and gardens to the ocean beyond. Harrison removed his hat and placed it on the chair beside him. "Don't let me forget this," he said. They ordered coffee and studied their menus, the companionship of shared laughter a distant memory.

Awkward.

Eliza's hands trembled as she raised the mug to her mouth, all thoughts of beards and bodies and kisses lost in regret. *What did I expect? He's being nice and this is more than awkward. What a mess. How can I fix it?*

She took a deep breath, wanted to bolt. He did deserve an explanation, but how to explain what she didn't quite understand herself?

Say something. Break the ice. Make a little polite conversation, for goodness' sake. Show some interest in the other person—that always worked with her patients. Then maybe she'd know what to do.

"Harrison," she said, "I know you've been here a few days. Tell me what all you've been up to."

No response for several beats. She could think of several song lyrics that would aptly describe the situation but didn't think he'd appreciate any of them. Really, though, this *was* just a tiny bit funny.

His pale blue eyes rested on her, considering, and humor fled, but when he spoke, his voice held only curiosity. "Eliza Grace, I'd be happy to describe my tourist activity just as soon as you let me in on the secret. In plain English, my girl, what the fuck is going on?"

CHAPTER 22
McLean

ELIZA FROWNED, AND HER VOICE HELD a defensive edge. "Well, Harrison, you showed up early and messed up my plan."

"You didn't answer my texts." If she'd had a plan, he was the King of England. "You didn't even know when, if, I was coming."

She reared back. "Well, yeah, I forgot my phone was off."

Voice sharp, no apology there. *Really, what the fuck?* He lifted his mug and gulped the tepid coffee, wishing for something very, very different as conflicting feelings scrabbled for his attention. He knew *his* emotions were all over the map, but really? He set the mug down a little harder than necessary. The table jumped.

Eliza sighed.

He looked up just in time to see her slender shoulders straighten. Gathering courage? Why? He hadn't been all that aggressive. What the hell, his students had survived worse.

Besides, she'd invited him.

Before he could say more, she continued. "I was going to pick you up and get you settled into the guest room and provide a space for you to get better."

A look flitted across her face that he couldn't interpret, but he was already responding to her words.

"Get better? I don't need a nurse."

In truth, when they'd met a month ago, he probably had, but now wasn't the time for that discussion. He gave her the look that had first-years cowering. "Do you rescue every stranger you run across?"

A lick of anger pushed her upright. "That's what my son says, and it's just not so."

Amused now, he leaned back in his chair, enjoying the flush that suffused her cheeks. Apparently, he had company on today's crazy roller coaster. "No? What then?"

She leaned toward him, face just inches from his own. Her breath held the memory of peppermint and her lips were bare and he wanted to taste them even as she spoke. "Well, Harrison Christian McLean, since you ask, I think I'm having a midlife crisis, and you've just become part of it."

Lightning flickered between them. Laughter was out of the question. Good sense told him to stand up and walk away, but when had good sense been his guide? He held himself still.

She crumpled into her chair, eyes filling. "I am sorry, Harrison, believe me that I didn't mean things to be this way." She swiped angrily at the tears. "And I darn well never cry."

His sprite of the previous evening had become a tearful waif, and his desire to possess her warred with his need to comfort. Deeming neither appropriate here in the Kula Lodge, he handed her a napkin. "Here. Wipe. Blow."

"Thanks." She sniffed and dabbed and pulled her legs up under her in the chair. "Sorry."

"No need." He leaned forward. "You promised me an explanation and I would like to hear it. But believe this, Eliza Grace, whatever the hell your name is, I wouldn't be here if I didn't want to be, and I am very glad for your impetuous invitation."

He smiled as he said the words and realized they were true.

CHAPTER 23
ELIZA GRACE

SHE WIPED AWAY TEARS AND BLEW her nose on the Kula Lodge napkin. She'd thought last night's success and the disclosures that had followed would dispel her bubbling emotions. Apparently not. And sexual tension had just leavened the mix.

I must be losing my mind.

Harrison's voice smiled, and when she looked up, kindness and amusement shone in his eyes. Better that than the anger she deserved for dragging him into this mess.

"It's complicated."

"I figured it was."

Now she laughed, and he joined her, and when she reached toward him, he accepted her hand, let it disappear into his paw, and kept it.

She blinked her eyelashes at him in an almost-pretend flirt. "I'd meant to charm you first and then tell you just the bits you needed to know—that is, if you even honored my 'impetuous invitation.'"

"Well, I'm here and I'm charmed."

"I didn't mean . . ." Again, heat rose up her neck and stained her cheeks. "Oh, heck, bungling this badly." No way could he understand how she needed and wanted and feared. She didn't know herself. So she tugged her hand and he released it, and she said, "Let's order and I'll try to explain, and then I'll get you back to your hotel."

He sipped coffee gone cold and said, "I've got a better idea."

She flinched. Danger lurked under his words. Surprised, she felt only regret as she waited for his "better idea," but the server who had wisely chosen to ignore their table now approached. "Yes, sir."

"Could we have fresh coffee, please, and then we'll be ready to order."

Fresh mugs of steaming coffee arrived. They ordered. She watched in fascination as Harrison doctored his coffee—six or seven packets of sugar, cream to the brim, vigorous stir. A sip, then a gulp. She wanted to remind him that so much sugar and saturated fat weren't good for him but chose silence instead.

"Ahh, good coffee." Harrison leaned back in his chair as though this were a normal day and he was having a normal meal with a normal person. He smiled. "My idea. Let's just forget this happened, that I demanded, that you cried."

She stiffened. "I didn't."

He grinned. "Whatever." His finger followed the path of her tears, and he didn't seem to notice when she shivered. *Complicated* was an understatement.

Their food arrived. She stared at her BLTA, sure she couldn't swallow a bite. He looked at his burger as though he didn't remember ordering it. Whatever had happened to the ease they'd enjoyed in the McCloud Hotel, the hours passed in unselfconscious conversation? Before Eliza could think of something witty to say, to apologize, or to jump up and hide in the ladies' room, he touched her hand.

She looked up and met his eyes, the kindness and amusement now highlighted with an evil gleam.

"Let's follow your original plan," he said. "We'll eat this pretty food and chat about everyday things, and you can even charm me, if you'd like. Then we'll drive to that beach and take a nap in the shade, following which we'll go to happy hour where I will have my one glass of wine and you will have something nonalcoholic as you are driving. Then we can exchange *complications.*"

CHAPTER 24
McLean

FULL OF A LUNCH HE'D HARDLY tasted, McLean watched Eliza as she drove. Small, competent hands, nails neat and polished with white tips just as he remembered, but the tidy hairdo had slipped its bonds and lustrous curls fluttered around her baseball cap. Color rode her cheeks, and tension radiated from her body. Tension and something he couldn't quite name.

They had eaten and chatted and argued about who would pay, and when they'd left he'd forgotten his hat, so they'd had to backtrack to retrieve it. Now, hat tightly in place, he shifted in Gretchen's front seat, glad the top was down. He knew what was riding him. He wanted this woman, complications and all, especially the complications. He'd never known anyone with two lives. He remembered Grace's gentle hand on his cheek as they stood on the stairs of the McCloud Hotel, the electricity that had flared as their eyes met last night, and wondered if sex with Eliza would be different from sex with Grace.

Kinky.

Humming a tune he didn't recognize, Eliza downshifted onto the shortcut to Mokulele Highway, and once again they were speeding past cane fields and nature preserves and the West Maui mountains with their cap of white clouds, toward the sparkling ocean in the distance. Neither spoke. For the moment, he was content to leave it so. At the light, Mokulele became Pi'ilani Highway. He read the signs, saying each name in his head, practicing the way he'd practiced throwing sutures so many years ago. His heart bumped just as Eliza fluttered her hand toward the right. "My apartment is over there, on South Kihei Road. I'll show you later."

He put aside memory. Decisions made, he could wait.

Before long she turned off the highway, and they wended through streets lined with grassy green slopes, tall trees, and palatial homes, always with a view of the sea, then right along a row of resorts whose names he didn't recognize. *The land of the semirich*, she'd called it. He wondered where the rich played.

Turning again, she maneuvered down a small drive into a graveled parking lot murmuring, "Hail Mary full of grace, help me find a parking space," and chortled as one appeared. She flashed a grin. "Works every time."

Doubting it would be as successful in the nation's capital, he grinned back.

Gretchen—God, he was doing it already—came to a halt between two blue rental sedans, and Eliza hopped out and began to unload. McLean extricated himself. "I'll carry the chairs," he said, and she nodded. "Anything else?"

"Thanks, I've got the rest." She glanced at his slacks. "You brought your suit?"

"In the bag." His backpack hung from his shoulder. He didn't tell her he had no intention of donning his proper Hawaiian beachwear in her presence.

"Good." She slung her bag over one shoulder, hefted a small cooler, and led the way to a grassy berm just above the sand. Beyond, the waves crashed and children squealed as they were tumbled ashore and then scrambled back into the water. "Let's stop here. Too hot on the beach right now."

Shade dappled the grass. A breeze rustled leaves and cooled air heavy with the scent of the white flowers that adorned the nearest tree. He dumped his load, helped her set up the chairs, and spread the towels.

She waved toward the resort. "You can change there. The hostess at the bar will give you the bathroom code."

He shook his head, sank into his chair. "Not much of a swimmer, probably won't need a suit today."

She let it pass and slipped out of her shirt to reveal a multicolored bikini top that molded the breasts he had imagined, small and firm and high. *I want*, he thought, savoring the spasm of desire long absent. His eyes swept the slender form and his breath caught as he imagined the rest.

I want.

Eliza kept her tan shorts on, a disappointment for sure, and seemed unaware of his scrutiny as she settled into her chair and opened the cooler. "How about some lemonade? Then we'll nap away the rest of our lunch calories and be ready for happy hour."

CHAPTER 25
ELIZA GRACE

AFTER THE LEMONADE, ELIZA ADJUSTED THE ubiquitous Tommy Bahama beach chairs into their reclining position. Harrison leaned back and pulled his hat down over his face, and faint snores soon ruffled the air. She wondered where he'd developed that talent, wished sleep came as easily to her.

Now that his gaze wasn't on her, she could take her time and look him over. Full head of sandy hair with a hint of curl, nicely trimmed beard of the same color, both visible around the edges of his baseball cap. At lunch, after they had agreed to have a normal conversation, she'd rocked with laughter as he'd told his story—Nene and Tutti getting him gussied up for his date—and she smiled now, remembering. Harrison McLean was definitely a nice man, even when his blue eyes iced over and he demanded explanations she wasn't ready to give.

Her eyes traveled over his considerable length. More sandy curls peeked out at the neck of the brightly flowered happy shirt. His barrel chest rose and fell with his resting breaths. Long legs encased in khaki tickled her imagination. Heavy or thin? Hairy?

Not hairy? Would she ever see them? Heat throbbed in her core just before her muscles contracted and the spasm swept her.

Jiminy Cricket. Aroused by legs I'll probably never see. Pathetic.

Resolutely she opened her *Rolling Stone* magazine and pretended to read until her eyelids drooped and she slept.

Languorous, Eliza drifted upward from a delicious dream, stretched, and sighed, and a blush rose as she felt the man's gaze on her. Her eyes popped open, and she scrambled to her feet. "Sorry. Must have fallen asleep."

His lazy hand encircled her ankle and tugged her back down to the chair. "No worries. You prescribed sleep to finish off our calories, remember."

Her skin burned under his hand. The heat traveled upward. She trembled. *Let go,* she prayed, *let go so I can think.*

Breathe. Count. Under her breath—*ten, nine, eight*—the way she used to when she wanted to smack a little hand doing something naughty. *Three, two, one.* With a final deep breath and a large measure of relief, she came back to herself.

"What?" Harrison released her ankle, and she realized she'd spoken aloud.

She shook her head. "Nothing." Bridging the small space between their chairs, she ruffled her hand over his cheek.

His eyes changed.

She tingled. *Oops, maybe not quite myself yet.* "Nice beard," she said. "Tutti mentioned you wanted to keep it because I liked it."

"Tutti should honor hairdresser confidentiality." One eyebrow quirked upward. "And how did she know it was you, anyway?"

"Island drums."

A pretty name for gossip, Eliza thought. Tutti to Nene to Rosie, who had had no difficulty identifying Eliza's big stranger. "Island drums," she repeated as heat rose up her neck and flamed her cheeks. Thank goodness Jaime was in court on Oahu.

With a glance at her watch, she jumped to her feet. Enough with the blushing and tingling and wanting something that was never going to happen. "No time for a swim. Let's fold things up and check out happy hour."

They stowed the chairs and the cooler and the towels, then crossed the lawn and stepped into 5 Palms. Conversation buzzed. To the left, over crowded tables, ocean and sky were visible. To the right was a long bar, stools fully occupied, with a bar back that mirrored the view of ocean and sky. A man who could have adorned any romance novel's cover called out, "Hey, Eliza, come on in," as he secured a bit of pineapple beside a miniature umbrella on the lip of a frosty glass.

"Hey, Paul, aloha." Eliza shouldered her way between two patrons and leaned over the bar's shiny surface for a smooch. "How's it going?"

He returned her kiss, shrugged, gestured at the crowded room. "Big night. Summer vacations. Almost holiday. Can't complain." A wide grin belied the casual comments.

"Oh, right, July fourth coming up." She tugged McLean forward. "Hey, Paul, this is Harrison. He's here from the mainland and we're slumming."

Before Paul could defend his five-star establishment, a woman erupted from behind the bar, wrapped Eliza in a hug, and then danced her in place. "Eliza, Eliza, you were so good last night. How can you be that good? And your song, the one you wrote, it made my eyes water."

Pure pleasure rose inside even as self-consciousness pinked her cheeks. "Enough, Kanani, enough. You're embarrassing me." Keeping an arm around the younger woman, she turned to McLean. "Kanani, this is my friend, Harrison. He's come from the mainland to hear me sing, even if he didn't know it."

"Aloha, Harrison, you will enjoy the island and the singing."

"Aloha, Kanani. I am already enjoying the singing and the island surprises."

Eliza saw the puzzled look on her friend's face. *Oh dear, another beat for the island drums.*

"Can you find a tiny spot for us, Kanani? I promised Harrison a glass of your most delicious merlot."

Without any questions—they would come later, Eliza knew, and probably from Kanani's Uncle Jaime, who took his position as head of the family very seriously indeed—Kanani escorted them to a cocktail table overlooking the formal dining room and the crashing waves beyond. "Always a table for you."

"Mahalo, my friend, this is perfect."

Eliza slid in across from McLean, ordered their drinks, and then excused herself to the ladies' room. She had barely punched in the door code when Kanani's breath was hot on her neck. She grabbed the younger woman's arm and dragged her into the restroom, which was, for a change, blessedly empty.

"Do *not* tell your uncle I brought the man here."

Kanani grinned, bubbling over with the drama. "But why, auntie? He seems very polite. He is handsome, too, but he *is* old."

Eliza spluttered out a laugh. "And so am I, little one, so am I. But, really, your uncle just believes he must meet the man first and make sure he is safe for me." She shrugged. "You know how uncles are."

Kanani's expression held both understanding and glee. Not every day did a secret this juicy come along. She swiped her fingers across her lips—zip. "Not a word. At least not until he tickles it out of me." She pushed Eliza toward the mirror. "Now pretty up and go find out for yourself how safe *you* want this man to be."

CHAPTER 26
McLean

Happy hour at 5 Palms was loudly happy, and Chris McLean was happily entertained. For years he'd been too busy, always had an agenda—to operate, to teach, to rescue, even to seduce—never time to sit and watch. Now he watched, dividing his attention between the antics of a courting couple more enthusiastic than experienced and the hall to the right down which Eliza and then her friend, Kanani, had disappeared. After what seemed a longer time than necessary, the two emerged together. Kanani flipped her long black hair over one shoulder, leaned in, and whispered something in Eliza's ear. Both women glanced in his direction. Then Kanani grinned and scooted behind the bar, and Eliza smoothed her own curls with both hands before she wended her way back to him.

Chris stood, ready to steady the table and drinks and nearby patrons if need be, but Eliza slid gracefully into the tight space. How could this be the woman who had tripped and tipped and jiggled and spilled and declared her name a misnomer? One more question for his growing list.

She raised her glass, touched its rim to his. "Cheers. The wine is good?"

"Excellent, thank you. As is our table and the view."

She glanced up to see his gaze not on the sea but on her, and her eyes darted away, but not before he saw confusion. *Good, her turn to be off balance.* Besides, he liked that he could raise that pink on her cheeks.

She sipped her virgin piña colada, coughed as though it had gone down too fast, and lifted her eyes to his. "Harrison, I promised an explanation. Please ask any questions that you might have." She chuckled. "But do remember, happy hour is over at seven."

He hadn't laughed so much in months. Following her moods, chasing a butterfly—same thing. "Mahalo. I think that's the right word. Anyway, thank you, and I'm sure the explanation will be fascinating."

She winced at his sarcasm, looking like one of his students when the day had gone wrong.

Easy, McLean, you want to know her, not browbeat her.

Her hand lay still on the table. He covered it with his own, curled his fingers around hers, and enjoyed the way her eyes flashed and then glazed over as he brought her fingers to his lips. When he released her hand, she hastily tucked it into her lap. Stifling a grin, he stood, nodded in the direction from which she'd come. "Restrooms that way?"

"Yes," she said, relief in the word. "Get the key code from Paul."

Chris kept his smile to himself as he headed toward the bar where Kanani watched with avid interest.

When he returned Eliza was staring out toward the setting sun. The not-quite-sure-of-herself look had returned, but she smiled when he resumed his seat. The level of the piña colada had dropped, and he was pretty sure she wished it wasn't virgin.

"Sorry," he said. "Didn't mean to get ahead of myself earlier. Perhaps an interrogation isn't such a good idea. How about we abandon happy hour and go in for dinner instead." He gestured toward the white-clad tables, gleaming silver, sparkling glasses in the room below. "We could move into a quieter, more comfortable place and over a nice meal spend time getting to know one another like normal people. Normal people on a first date," he added and enjoyed the shock in her eyes. "If we can call it that?"

He hadn't seduced a woman sober since he was about fifteen, and that, he remembered, had not gone well. Now he was not only sober, but old . . . old and broken. He reached for her hand, felt it tremble, thought his own might be trembling as well.

"But Harrison," she stuttered, "it's too expensive, I'm not dressed, I didn't mean . . ."

He trailed a kiss onto her palm. "Kanani says there is a table perfect for sunset."

She snatched her hand back. "You watch out for that Kanani; she's nothing but trouble." She stuck out her tongue and made a face as the woman in question moved toward their table, laughter dancing in her eyes. "But yes, in Maui, it *is* all about the sunset."

Around them, early diners enjoyed their meals, barely looking up as the host—Kanani had introduced him as Mr. Matsuki—led the way to a distant table and seated them side by side facing the setting sun. Their drinks magically reappeared as did wine lists and menus.

Eliza picked up the wine list. "Since we are having a meal, Harrison, I will have one glass of wine." She glanced sideways. "That is, if you have no objection."

He had none.

When her wine arrived, she raised her glass. "To you. Mahalo for such a wonderful treat."

His own glass was still half full as he returned her toast.

They discussed the menus, ordered, and murmured neutral words about the coolness of the air, the magnificent colors of the western sky.

Salads arrived.

McLean sipped his wine, observed the other guests, knew the woman at his side, with her sandy shorts and T-shirt and unruly curls, was by far the most beautiful woman in the room. He sighed.

"Sorry, Harrison, I just don't know quite where to start."

He realized she had taken his contented sigh for one of impatience. "Shh, it's all good." He speared a tiny shrimp, transferred it to her mouth. "Eat. While you chew, I'll regale you with the fascinating story of H. Christian McLean."

Her expression doubtful, she accepted the shrimp, chewed twice and swallowed, then reached for her glass and held it in both hands—a shield—no trust in her eyes as she prepared for whatever story he might concoct.

He sucked in a deep breath and put his fork down. Gently, he lifted the glass from her death grip, set it on the table, and took both her hands in his own. If he wanted her truth, then truth she should have from him.

Damn, this would be much easier with a bottle of wine under my belt.

She stared at their hands; hers trembled. "You have my full attention. Proceed."

"Okay," he said. "Just remember, you asked."

His hands were shaky now, too, and damp, but when he started to let her go, she held on. Support? God knew he needed it. His heart pounded. His chest hurt. He couldn't get a deep breath.

Get over yourself, man. This is anxiety, not another heart attack. And if she doesn't like what you have to say, you can enjoy the evening and go home—no harm, no foul.

Just do it.

He cleared his throat and began. "You heard a lot about me already—ex-wife, children, career. What you don't know is this—I drink too much, binges mostly, and that may never change; six years ago I fell in love with a much younger woman, the love of my life, I called her in my head. But she married someone else, and now I love her husband and their children also."

Eliza stared, eyes wide and mouth open.

His chest tightened, and he looked away. *Enough.* He freed his hands from her grasp, gasped for the breath that seemed stuck in his throat. *Finish it, man. Walk away.*

He dared another glance. Gray eyes full of understanding and sympathy and . . . what? Mischief? Daring?

Never one to dodge a dare, he straightened his spine. Besides, having promised truth, he was determined to get it all out. "I've neglected my own children and grandchildren; I have a habit of short-term relationships, and behind my back I've been called Heartbreak Harry. And two months ago I suffered a heart attack and had a triple bypass from which I almost didn't recover." One more deep breath before he mumbled, "Now I'm afraid I'll never be myself again."

Silence hovered over the last surprising admission.

He grabbed the stemmed glass, sipped the wine he wanted to gulp, and said, "There. Perhaps that will make your story a little easier to tell."

Out of the corner of his eye, McLean saw their server move toward their table. He paused, seemed to consider the situation, and turned away. Wise man.

Eliza shook her head as though emerging from a trance.

Not very subtle, McLean, but at least it's all out there. Now it's up to her. He ignored the thundering of his heart. When had he become such a fearful dick? How had this become so important?

The sea sparkled in the distance. Still hovering above the water, the setting sun reflected in Eliza's eyes. Noises melted into the background and there was only this one woman.

The corners of her mouth turned up, and she danced her fingers up his arm and slid her hand back into his. "Well, Harrison Christian McLean, I expected a good story, but . . . wow." She brought his hand to her mouth, kissed his fingers as he had kissed hers, then took one into her mouth and bit him.

He jerked, even as the hairs on his arms rose and his body tightened, and the little devil laughed. Before he could decide whether he was affronted or annoyed or amused—being honest hadn't been that easy—his laugh boomed once again to link with hers.

Still laughing, Eliza leaned in and claimed his mouth.

Ahhh.

The lingering kiss soothed him as words could never do. He tasted shrimp and raspberry and curiosity before she released them both and settled back into her chair with a sigh of her own.

"Oh my." She reached for her drink. "Hmmm. I will have many questions of course, but, like Scheherazade, you have earned your reward. And mahalo, Harrison, this does make *my* story sound a little less nuts."

CHAPTER 27
ELIZA

BY THE TIME HARRISON HAD COMPLETED his disclosure—
she'd expected him to say something like "just the facts,
ma'am" and recite his Social Security number—his fist was
scrubbing the center of his chest and his eyes were troubled. Not
much surprising. She hadn't ignored the signs—alcohol, women,
health issues, and feelings in long-term lockdown—but she *had*
wanted to laugh when he'd mentioned Heartbreak Harry.

Even if I'd already figured it out, I'm glad he told me, she
thought as the man grabbed his wine. And she'd seen the
despair in his eyes as they'd sat together that first morning in
McCloud. Whether he knew it or not, Harrison McLean was
a vulnerable man. He was also kind, and his laughter synched
with hers, and his touch sent electricity through her body.

What the heck, what's a few more complications? she thought
just before she bit him. After that, it was easy.

They finished their meal as Eliza recounted her story
much as she'd told Jaime and Rosie and the guys the night
before, again omitting Martin Grimes and her sons' continued

ignorance, and she was grateful when Harrison listened without question or comment. Even with his blunt history ringing in her ears, some secrets were not ready to be released.

As she spooned up her last bite of berries and crème fraîche, their server coughed behind her and she looked up. The other tables were empty, the diners long gone, and the sky was dark.

"Oh my, Harrison, we have developed a very bad habit."

He was still chuckling as he settled their bill, refusing her offer to share. "First date, remember. There must be a rule that says guys pay even in this day and age."

"Mahalo," She smiled up at him. "Thank you for an unusual evening. I'm sorry we missed the sunset."

"I'm not." His eyes gleamed and his teeth flashed white as they stepped into the dusky evening.

What now?

She scurried to the car, hopped in, and started the motor. Enough challenges for one day.

Eliza drove slowly into the night, letting the breeze play with her hair, cool her skin, kiss her neck. In the mirror, she saw his eyes and knew that Harrison wanted to do the same. She shivered. It had been a long time, maybe never, since she'd felt this desirable.

Deciding just to enjoy, she slid her hand under her hair, raised it up to improve his view as she guided Gretchen through the darkness.

"I wanted to know," McLean said after they'd driven several miles in silence, "how Nurse Grace could become the diva, Eliza K. I get it now, not sure I really understand, but that's okay. Thank you for telling me. I know it was hard."

"It *was* hard. For you, too. When secrets are held so tight, it's difficult to let them loose. Before last night, only Jaime knew mine, and he didn't really know them all."

She reached across to ruffle his beard. "But enough of serious talk for now, if that's okay with you. Let's listen to the night and appreciate the stars and the moon as I take you back to your Maui Beach Hotel. Tomorrow, if you would like, you will come to my apartment. I could pick you up, but it's probably best if you keep your rental car. If you like the second room, please stay with me and be my guest."

Shy again, she didn't look over to gauge the effect of her words. Silence lengthened between them.

"I've never had a guest before."

She heard his sigh, didn't know what it meant. This was no longer an impulsive invitation, she wanted him in her home. Not sure why . . . oh yes, she wanted him. She forced her voice to stay even. "But no pressure."

His response was slow in coming. "Eliza Grace, I'd love to see your apartment and be your guest, but you don't have to do this. Your plate is full right now. I would understand if—"

"No, Harrison McLean. I admit the invitation was crazy impulsive, but I felt it in my heart and I still do. It would honor my new home to have you there."

"Then I would be happy to be your first guest." Another sigh.

She could only hope it was one of happiness. He was, after all, a man of experience. If he wanted to say no, he could do it kindly. And he had said yes. She hummed and smiled and thought about tomorrow.

Twenty minutes later, under the portico of the Maui Beach Hotel, Eliza put Gretchen in park but didn't turn off the engine. She marveled that, in the few hours since she'd picked him up at this very spot, whole lives had been led.

Harrison climbed out, more nimble now from the practice, retrieved his pack from Gretchen's back seat, and walked around to the driver's door. She tipped her face up. He leaned in, brushed his lips over hers, echoed her earlier words. "Thank you for a most unusual evening."

He started toward the lobby.

She remembered, hoisted herself up to the seat back. "Harrison, wait."

He turned back.

"My address."

"Got it."

"How?"

He grinned. "I know how to Google, too."

While she was still digesting that, he returned to the car, wrapped his arm around her, and ravished her mouth, then stepped away and disappeared into the hotel.

Heart pounding, lungs heaving, lips dancing with joy, Eliza had only one coherent thought: *Island drums will be busy tonight.*

CHAPTER 28
MCLEAN

CHRIS WOKE EARLY ENOUGH TO WATCH the sun rise. A pale blue sky streaked with pinks and salmons and reds insufficient to lift the dark cloud inside. Flat, the heady feelings of the past two days no longer buoying him up, he slumped in the veranda chair and clutched his coffee mug.

Stupid, stupid, stupid, stupid. I'm fucking old, and weak, and not thinking straight—pumphead. He shuddered. Pumphead, a neurocognitive decline following open heart surgery, was most feared of all. *I should just chuck it all, go find some backwater where no one knows me, and drink 'til I die.* He slurped more coffee and conjured up still more black thoughts. When he picked up the pot of coffee he'd ordered from room service and found it empty, he had to clamp down hard to keep from hurling it into the morning.

"November in my soul." His voice loud, almost a shout, he repeated the words even as he cursed Ishmael and the all-too-apt quote stuck in his head. Breathing hard, heart thumping, Chris McLean sat unmoving until the angry surge subsided.

Fuck it, I've been muddling around in my psyche these past two months and here I am. Not my way; not my way at all. I make decisions and I act on them, and that's what I'm going to do.

In that frame of mind, Chris packed his clothes, freshly laundered thanks to a resort service slyly pointed out by Nene the morning before, and settled his bill. He would stay in Eliza's guest room tonight and then—he imagined two different futures, wasn't sure which he preferred—he'd decide what to do next.

He loaded his things into the trunk and waved goodbye to the hotel. With time to kill before meeting Grace, no, Eliza, he drove to the Maui Memorial Medical Center.

In the past when on the road, he'd always checked out the local medical facilities. With that intention, he'd looked up this hospital's address earlier in the week. Now he found a slot in the almost-full parking area and presented himself to the receptionist at the front desk. Time to bone up on island medicine. Never hurts to know your options.

Surprised to find the hospital administrator at work on a Sunday, McLean followed a volunteer to the office of Barbara Carter, MD.

A tall, rangy woman in her mid-fifties who reminded him of DeMello stepped from behind a desk and held out both hands. "Aloha, Dr. McLean, welcome. Glad you caught me in." She gestured toward the piles on her desk. "Paperwork, trying to get caught up, you know. I've read several of your articles over the years, and it's nice to finally meet you. Are you here with an agenda, or may I offer you a tour of our facility?"

With a smile, he released her hands. "No agenda, Dr. Carter. Just a curious visitor."

"That was me, thirty years ago, when I came to the clinic as a locum after my residency. And here I am, almost thirty years later, still helping the sun go down."

She shook her head at the curious workings of fate, took his elbow, and escorted him on a very thorough tour, which ended in the hospital cafeteria.

"Excellent coffee," McLean said as he stirred in his usual amounts of cream and sugar. "And an excellent tour. Thank you. Your facility is something to be proud of."

"Always welcome, and mahalo. Excellent coffee is one of Maui's perks. If I may ask, are you thinking of relocating to the islands?" It had been clear that the surgical options were limited. "Our cardiac cases go to Honolulu."

McLean denied thoughts of relocation, and the two physicians chatted about the changes in medical care and the myriad problems with insurance companies until they finished their coffee. With words of appreciation, he took his leave.

Back in the car, he scrolled through his text messages until he found Eliza's: If it suits you, come around lunchtime and I'll feed you.

Suits me fine.

His heart bumped just a little faster. Thirty minutes later, it was racing as he turned into the Waipuilani parking area and found an empty visitor's slot. He wondered if she was rethinking her invitation. God knows, he wouldn't fault her for reclaiming sensibility.

Taking nothing for granted, he left his belongings in the trunk and started toward the plain brown building. Suddenly Eliza was at his side, almost hopping up and down as she grabbed his hand and pulled him down for a cheek kiss.

"Sorry, sorry, but I'm so excited. I was worried about you coming and then I decided I wouldn't be nervous because this is so cool and you are my first ever guest in my new home and I fixed a wonderful lunch and"—she paused to catch her breath—"and I'm just so glad you're here."

Her flip-flops slapped on the bare concrete as she released his hand and danced up the stairs. Grinning, no longer in doubt about his welcome, Chris followed her onto a second floor landing, damp and dark, the carpet worn and utilitarian. The doors along the exterior hallway eyed him with a flat, brown glare.

Didn't seem like much to get excited about.

He almost bumped into her as Eliza stopped at a door wearing a brightly painted ALOHA sign. She glanced over her shoulder—making sure he was still there?—then, eyes shining, smile wide, she opened the door and waved him in.

"Aloha, welcome to my home. If we were in Mexico I'd say, *Mi casa es su casa,* but here aloha says it all."

Eliza stood still, framed by a wall of windows open to the sea and the waves and the sky. He understood he was expected to admire the view, which he was sure was just fine, but he was too busy admiring the woman. Today she wore a white tee, this one cheerful with scattered red flowers—hibiscus, maybe—that left her arms bare and red shorts that left tanned legs open to view. A real island girl.

Oh, yes, this is good.

When he stepped forward to take her in his arms, she stepped back, seemed to just notice his empty hands. "No suitcase?" Her eyebrows rose, forehead creased.

"In the car."

"Good. I thought you might have changed your mind. Not that I would blame you." A little sniff. "Anyway, you're here. And lunch is ready." She pointed away from the windows. "Your bathroom is there. Wash up and we'll eat and then get you settled in."

Adrift—his role in her life, guest or lover, still unclear, his role in his own life just as unclear—he followed instructions and washed up in the sand-colored room with towels the blue of the ocean.

When he re-entered the main room, she was pouring juice into a stemmed glass, her back to him, a pale stripe of kissable flesh visible above the waistband of her shorts, and a wave of something stronger than lust swept over him. She looked so perfect in her shorts, bare feet, and tan skin—a match for this home she was creating. He coughed to clear the sudden lump in his throat.

She heard him and turned, gestured him to a high-backed stool facing the windows and the sea. "Sit. Food's ready."

The granite counter was set with multicolored dishes an exact match to his own back home in Georgetown. For some reason, this similarity in a sea of differences pleased him.

"The juice is POG—passion, orange, and guava—and the fruit on your plate is papaya, if you don't recognize it. Shrimp salad in papaya is one of my favorite island meals."

Chris sat and looked at the food she'd prepared for them. Each plate held half a papaya filled to overflowing with lettuce and avocado and shrimp. Butter and rolls sat on the counter close by, as did a cream pitcher and a sugar bowl that looked like the ones on his mother's table.

Grace—his thinking hadn't fully transitioned to *Eliza*—poured coffee, perched on the stool at his side, and pushed the rolls in his direction. "Eat—it's all good."

She cut her shrimp into neat, tidy pieces and ate each with a bit of the salad greens and a spoonful of the colorful fruit.

He did as she did, and he watched her.

She looked up. "What?"

"You lick your lips after each bite." He didn't mention what that made him want to do.

"No, I don't, but I meant *what?* You've got something on your mind."

"Just remember you asked." He put his fork down, kept his eyes on hers. "In McCloud, you dropped and spilled and

knocked over everything around you. You even called your name
a misnomer. Now you're this graceful creature who takes my
breath away."

"Graceful creature? I don't think so." She flushed as she
considered his words. "But you're right, and I'm not sure how
it happened. I wasn't clumsy in the hospital, of course. Totally
competent and capable there, but it never followed me home.
Everywhere else, in my previous life, I mean, I seemed to leave
chaos in my wake."

He followed her gaze as she took in her neatly appointed
kitchen, the seascape of her living room with its sand-colored
walls, the ocean-blue cushions on white wicker furniture, the
photographs of flowers he couldn't identify that decorated
one wall.

"Here, I can even pour coffee and it stays in its cup." She
shrugged and demonstrated. "Now, drink your coffee while the
maid cleans up."

"The maid?"

She rose from her stool, giggling again, and began stacking
the dishes. "Me, silly, me and DeLinda the dishwasher."

Thoughtful, he drank his coffee as she loaded the dishwasher
and put away the remains of the food. Competent, graceful,
funny, full of life—perhaps with her music and the big guitar
guy who clearly thought she walked on water, she could no
longer deny her own worth.

Enough, McLean, psychiatrist you're not. He was left to consider whether her husband had valued her enough.

Cleanup accomplished, Eliza showed him the guest room.
While she jumped on the bed a couple of times to demonstrate
its comfort and durability, he wondered if he'd ever sleep there.
The door to the other bedroom remained closed.

CHAPTER 29
ELIZA

ELIZA BOUNCED ON THE GUEST BED with its traditional Hawaiian quilt and multitude of pillows, then made herself sit still while Harrison looked around. Her mood swings were making her dizzy.

Be serious, Lizzie, he's your guest, not your playmate. She grinned at the notion and adopted her no-nonsense voice. "Go down and get your things, Harrison, if this meets your approval. Then we'll put on our suits and go to the beach. There's time for swim and nap before the luau tonight."

What would he question first?

"Luau?"

Of course it would be that one. "At Jaime's. To welcome you to our island."

She didn't need to add *and check you out*. That knowledge was written across his face. She turned away so he wouldn't see yet another grin she couldn't hide. "Swim first, though. We'll go to Ulua Beach. Nice waves and good shade. You'll like it."

She was itching to get a look at the swimsuit he clearly didn't want to put on. *And the legs*, she thought on a rising bubble of excitement. *Yes, the legs.*

"No work for you?"

"I'm the boss. I've given myself a whole day off." She shooed him out the door. "Hurry up. Get your stuff. The ocean is waiting."

No worries today. He didn't need to know that underneath her newfound joy lurked darkness: paradise found could so easily become paradise lost. He didn't need to know how many nights she sat alone with guitar and scored paper and prayers that words would appear.

Today only fun.

Alone in her room, wishing that she had more on top and less on the bottom and that her tummy was just a little bit flatter, she pulled a sundress—her favorite, white with red hibiscus like her T-shirt—over her suit. Nothing would change just by wishing it so. She'd learned that lesson the hard way.

She'd packed water and lemonade and snacks into her battered cooler and was ready to load up before McLean emerged from the guest room wearing sandals, a white T-shirt, and a beach towel tied sarong-fashion at his waist.

She coughed to disguise her laugh. "Ready?"

He frowned. "As I'll ever be."

Gretchen crawled through a Sunday crowd to Ulua Beach and another fortunate parking spot. Past the restrooms and the outdoor showers, Eliza found a shady nook for their chairs. She tucked her sunglasses into her bag, gathered her hair into a messy tail, and pulled the dress over her head. Then she grabbed the towel still tied at his waist and pulled it free.

"Last one in's a rotten egg." Waving the towel like a flag, she ran for the beach.

When she surfaced, laughing, he was beside her.

Faster than he looks, she thought, just before he grabbed her ankle and took her under.

She popped up, coughing and spluttering from the unexpected dunking, and pushed wet curls out of her eyes. Safely out of reach, a grinning Harrison treaded water and waited.

Thinking, *battle I won't win*, Eliza grinned back and extended her hand. "Truce?"

"Truce."

Their fingers met.

Cymbals clanged. Tympani rolled. No plebeian fireworks for this encounter. She reminded herself to breathe while exquisite licks of fire danced inside. Hands linked, alone in the crowd, Eliza King and Harrison McLean bobbed in the salty sea.

Finally she released him and swam beyond the breakers, alone.

When she emerged, winded, from the warm surf, he was sitting on his towel watching her. Such a big man, right at home there on her beach—white shirt, blue and white swim trunks, the glitter of salt drying in his sandy beard—a native god, or a man comfortable in his own skin.

But he winced as he handed her a towel, and she remembered that he wasn't.

Mopping at her streaming hair, she sank down beside him. Under lowered lashes, she continued her scrutiny—traditional Hawaiian leaf print on the suit, skin pale, as though it had never seen the sun, feet broad and neat like his hands, calves thick and well-shaped and covered with a mat of sand-dusted curls. She wasn't sure whether he'd been hiding the suit or the legs, but in her opinion both were fine. More than fine.

She shivered.

He must have felt it, misinterpreted. "You're cold." He took her towel, wrapped it around her shoulders, and brought her onto his lap. She started to wiggle away. He shifted and drew her closer, and she fit there, as though the space had been created just for her.

Looking up, she caught a wicked smile on his lips. Maybe he hadn't misinterpreted after all. Caught, she let her head relax onto his cool, damp shirt. For the moment, there was nowhere else she wanted to be.

As she drifted off, his lips pressed a kiss into her hair.

CHAPTER 30
McLean

H IS HEART BUMPED WHEN HE FELT her shiver—it didn't take genius to recognize interest—and, to be fair, her legs interested him as well, so he wrapped her in a towel and gathered her into his lap. After one feeble struggle, she snuggled in and fell instantly asleep. She fit as though the space had been created just for her.

Amused, he shifted her into the shade and settled beside her. The morning's "November" had dissipated, and he drifted with the susurrus of the trees and the crashing of the waves and the sleeping woman at his side. He didn't know how long this interlude would last, wasn't sure he wanted it to, but while he was here he damn well would enjoy himself.

"Harrison."

Her voice brought him awake. She was still cuddled against his chest and her eyes held confusion. "How . . . ?"

Her turn to suffer. "Do you remember that movie *From Here to Eternity?*"

She flushed and squirmed to a seated position, her expression letting him know how clearly she remembered the beach scene. "Did we?"

The rumble of his laugh disturbed his tender chest. Small price. "No, but we wanted to, just before you fell asleep."

Her laugh joined his. "Just as well, all that sand in all those places." She produced an imaginary shudder. "And thanks for dragging me out of the sun."

Some women might have been embarrassed. Eliza was not. She stood, shook out her curls, and pulled the sundress back on, hiding his view of well-muscled legs and a nicely rounded bottom, then rooted around in the cooler and produced lemonade and chips.

"Here. This'll hold us until dinner."

Throat suddenly dry, he sat up, accepted the glass, and swigged the lemonade. "Tell me about dinner."

"Jaime's family always does a luau around the Fourth of July," she told him, her voice soft with some undefined emotion. "Tonight's the night. He's Hawaiian and has a wonderful wife and four great kids and an extended family that populates the island."

The extended family was not a surprise; the wife and kids were.

She went on. "Anyway, family and friends and so much food, and music and hula. And this is the real deal, not one of those for-tourist things. Sometimes, when his nephews aren't working, they even do a fire dance."

Her eyes gleamed—wicked. "Of course, he will also want to make sure that your intentions are honorable. In Hawaii, being the eldest male is a tremendous responsibility."

Not quite sure how serious she was, he kept it light. "Well, then, it's good I'm on my best behavior."

In an instant, she was straddling him, her breath lemonade-sweet on his cheek. "But for how long, Harrison? How long?" Her body shuddered. Her mouth closed over his.

Taken by surprise, McLean surrendered to her kiss, then flipped her so he was on one elbow, his other arm holding her tight against his body, and took his turn. His tongue slid between lips sweet and salty, and he deepened the kiss until his blood thundered and his loins ached. Her free hand clenched his shirt and drew him closer.

Then with a sigh, she pulled away, and he let her go.

Her eyes twinkled. "Perhaps we don't need that fire dance."

Laughing and carefully avoiding touch, the two packed up their gear and headed home.

SHOWERED AND SHAVED AND DRESSED IN khakis and his second flowered shirt, McLean stepped into the living room. The pink and purple shreds of sunset reflected on the water, but his eyes went to the woman once again framed by the scene. She stood still, her gaze on the horizon. Her dress, flowered and frothy and blue as the ocean beyond, left her shoulders and most of her legs bare. He wondered where her thoughts were.

Think about me.

He paused, considered. *Yep, think about me.* He strode across the room to stand behind her, bent to trace the line of her shoulder with his lips. Her actions on the beach had certainly given him permission. Hadn't they?

She trembled and turned, touched his cheek. "You shaved?"

He nodded, didn't mention whisker burn.

She slipped away, retrieved a glass from the counter.

"Would you like me to drive?" he asked.

"You said sometimes you drink too much?"

"Not tonight."

She smiled. "Then yes, sometimes I enjoy more than one drink at the luau."

He gestured around him, at the view through the windows, this little home with its perfect fittings, even the bedroom he hadn't yet seen. "This is all beautiful. And the music, magical. You've created something very special. What do your sons think of it all?"

Her expression changed. "They don't know."

"They don't know?" He frowned. In McCloud, when she'd mentioned her family, he'd gotten the impression that they were close, especially the younger son. "Why?"

Flinty gray eyes. Smile gone as though it had never been. "That, Harrison McLean, is my business." Voice that could cut glass. "My business, and none of yours."

He went still. His own smile died, and hope fled his heart as she turned away. The space between them loomed as wide as the Grand Canyon.

CHAPTER 31
ELIZA

HARRISON OPENED THE DOOR OF HIS plain blue rental sedan, closed it after Eliza slipped in, and drove the forty minutes to Jaime's Upcountry home. Only Eliza's voice giving directions broke the silence.

By the time they arrived, the street was full of cars. Rosie's pickup stood in the drive, Derek's jeep tucked in behind it. From the front, the home seemed modest, a ranch-style edifice nestled at the foot of Haleakala.

Harrison found a parking space, and Eliza hopped out of the car before he could come around to open her door. She had been unspeakably rude, and she wasn't even sure why. It should have been natural just to say, "don't want them to think I'm crazy," then laugh and move on. But she hadn't.

Before she could apologize, she had seen his body go still, seen his eyes go pale and flat, and the apology died unspoken. Now she experienced his icy correctness, had earned it even, and she didn't know how to make it better.

"Hey, sister." Arms outstretched in welcome, Jaime met them on the lawn. He wrapped Eliza in a hug and kissed her cheek, then he tucked her against his body and turned toward the man at her side. His tone was pleasant enough. "Aloha. You must be Eliza's friend from the mainland." He held out his free hand just as Rosie came to stand with them. "I'm Jaime Hokoana, and this is my wife, Rosie."

After the handshaking and the introductions were complete, the two couples followed the scent of roasting pig into a wide backyard that opened to a view of valley, the sea black in the distance, and conversation centered on house history.

"I was born here," Jaime said. "My mother still lives in my birth home, and Rosie and I raised our boys there, but when two surprise girls arrived, we needed more space so we just wrapped rooms around it."

"It grew like Topsy," Rosie added.

Jaime smiled. Rosie smiled. Harrison said all the right things, the perfect guest. Tension roiled, rupturing the starlit night. *My fault, my fault,* Eliza mourned. *How do I fix this?*

Rosie finished describing their home's evolution and waved her arm toward the crowd. "And we like it best when it's full of people."

Tonight it was full to overflowing.

When the Hokoanas moved away to welcome other latecomers, Eliza was sure no one but her had felt the chill.

True to his word, Harrison refused beer and wine and the innocent-looking fruity concoction called Hokoana Punch that Eliza knew from experience was anything but innocent. He sipped from a sweaty bottle of water and smiled as though there were nowhere else he'd rather be. She introduced him to Derek, his arm wrapping a leggy blond he called Mindy, then

Rick, alone at the moment, and then to Hokoanas she knew and others whose names she didn't. Here, that didn't seem to matter.

In her haze of self-reproach, she hardly noticed when Harrison drifted away until she saw him deep in conversation with Lelani Hokoana, Jaime's mother and clan matriarch, a woman of Hawaiian stature whose face retained the beauty of her youth. Mama H, as she was known in the family, held Harrison's hand in hers as he leaned in to hear her words.

Curious, Eliza watched, wondering about a conversation between a worldly surgeon and an island-bound octogenarian. *He's easy with people*, she thought, liking that even as she accepted a second glass of wine and promptly spilled it down the front of her dress.

Shocked, she only had time to think *dear heavens, Grace is back* before Harrison reached her side, just in time to catch the tiki light she knocked askew as she mopped at her dress.

She tried to laugh it off. No one else seemed to notice.

When it was time to eat, Harrison carried their plates. He was, after all, the only one present who knew Grace. They settled at a table near the edge of the lawn. In the distance below, lights flickered on in the homes dotting the hillside.

Fairy lights. *This night should have been magical and I've ruined it.*

Grief sat inside, an uninvited guest. She wanted to call her psychologist and demand an explanation. She wanted to weep.

"Harrison," she began, "I'm—"

He touched her lips with one finger. "Later. Time for that later." His voice gave no clue to his feelings, but his eyes were no longer glacier blue.

She hoped.

They talked about the food as he worked his way through one plateful and went back for more. *Act normal*, Eliza ordered herself as she pushed barbecue around her plate, managed a few bites of Rosie's famous potato salad and chatted with those close by. Party noise grew quiet as everyone concentrated on the meal.

Rosie stopped at their table. "All good here?" Her eyes searched Eliza's.

Darn, not as normal as I thought.

"All good, Rosie Posey," she lied. "The food's great. Harrison's on his third helping. He liked everything but the poi."

Chuckling, Harrison nodded at his almost empty plate. "Delicious, Mrs. Hokoana. Thank you."

"Rosie," she corrected automatically. "Mahalo for being our guest."

Eliza heard suspicion in Rosie's voice. *Uh-oh.* Before she could say anything, Rick's cymbal clattered—the call to entertainment—so she stood and slung an arm around her friend's shoulders. "Harrison," she said, "they have asked me to sing, so I'll just go along with Rosie and decide what song to torture tonight." She didn't wait for his comment, just touched his shoulder and walked away.

As soon as they were around the corner, Rosie whirled on her. "There is something the matter. Is it the man? Does he hurt you?"

Tears rose and she tried to hold them back. "Oh, Rosie, I was rude to him, terribly, terribly rude, and for no reason. Maybe I'm a little afraid, but of me, not him. And now he is angry and will probably go away." She swiped at the one teardrop brave enough to fall. "Don't worry. I'll sing and we'll go home and see what happens."

Rosie looked doubtful, and if Rosie was not convinced, her husband would be doubly doubtful.

Eliza struggled to reassure. "Truly. It's all good. Tell Jaime it's all good."

Rosie nodded and said nothing more. They stood arm in arm as Jaime strummed his ukulele and six little girls—his twin daughters, three nieces, and a friend—swished their grass skirts and waved their arms and postured their hands in a preschool version of the traditional Hawaiian dance.

When they were done and the applause had subsided and everyone had secured another drink, it was her turn. Eliza took a deep breath. *Time to pull on my big girl panties.* She swaggered to the makeshift stage, grabbed the karaoke mic and sang.

MORE SONGS, MORE DRUMS, MORE HULA, more laughing, and then she could escape.

Before they reached the car, Harrison's big hand encircled her arm and drew her to a halt. She turned toward him, saw hurt and understanding in his eyes.

"Oh, Harrison, I am—"

"What's going on?"

Jaime sounded so like Dudley Do-Right that Eliza expected his next words to be "unhand her, you villain." She laughed.

"Let her go." Like a sword, Jaime's words sliced the night air.

For a moment no one moved. Eliza choked on her laugh. *Not funny. My fault.*

Rosie trotted over, stood beside her husband, one hand on his arm. "Tried to stop him," she said. "Like trying to stop a truck."

Harrison released Eliza's arm and stepped back.

Eliza inserted herself between the men, pushed her hand against Jaime's massive chest, stared up into his eyes, and prayed he could see the truth. "My fault. My fault. I was rude and Harrison was upset, but he is not hurting me. He doesn't hurt people. I'm sorry to cause a fuss."

She held her breath. One beat, then two, before she felt the tension drain from Jaime's body. Another beat, and he set her aside and threw his arms around McLean. "Sorry, man, this little one is too trusting, even if she is almost old enough to be my mother."

Another beat, then Harrison returned the hug.

A round of back-thumping and apologies followed before he said, "I get it, man, it's good to take care of the people you love."

Eliza felt so proud she wanted to cry. Now if she could only make it right.

Used to Jaime's outbreaks, the crowd that had gathered entered into the back-thumping and fist-bumping and finally dispersed for another round of the punch, and Eliza and Harrison stood alone beside his car. He opened the passenger door as though nothing untoward had occurred.

"Harrison, I—"

Once again his fingertips on her lips stopped her words. "It's okay. Haven't had that much excitement since Sally Lou's father discovered my bare ass in her bedroom."

On her astonished gurgle of laughter, he tucked her into the car. "Buckle up," he said with a chuckle, "and I'll tell you the whole sad story. Then you can sing to me until we get home."

CHAPTER 32
McLean

ONCE BACK IN HER APARTMENT, ELIZA fluttered around the kitchen, opening and closing the refrigerator door, lifting glasses from the shelves. As though taking a cue from its wearer, the frothy blue dress that had swirled so provocatively now drooped, dispirited.

Nerves. Her heart was as fragile as the ones he repaired. He hadn't realized that before.

McLean used the bathroom, scrubbed his hands with Eliza's plumeria soap, and returned to stare out at the black sea. Light touch required, he knew, even as he wondered about his end goal. She'd overreacted for sure, a simple "I don't want to talk about it" would have sufficed. *It's not like I had her on the rack.*

But my reaction?

Christ on a cross, that iceberg impersonation was as over-the-top as Hokoana's fiery face-off. An image of snarling junkyard dogs popped into his head. Embarrassed, he acknowledged his own vulnerability. Every second entangled him more tightly with this complex woman. Every second reminded him of all that he'd lost, had yet to lose.

Forcing fear aside, he turned toward Eliza. "Why don't you pour me a glass of your most excellent red," he said, "and a glass of white for yourself. We'll take them outside where it's cool. Then you can say your piece and I'll say mine and we can laugh again." He dipped a kiss to her forehead, knew he wanted this.

She stepped back, relief in her eyes. "Good idea, but I'll carry the chairs and you can bring the wine. It's safer that way."

Minutes later, wine glasses in hand, he followed Eliza down the stairs and through a gate he didn't know existed to the deserted lawn below her window. As he watched her unfold the chairs they'd napped in the previous day and place them side by side facing the water, he thought again that he'd never known a woman so beautiful. Her earlier outburst seemed inconsequential, here where the moon and two stars looked down and their light sparkled off the ever-moving sea and twinkled in her eyes.

Seating arranged to her satisfaction, she scanned his face. What she saw there must have reassured her. Without comment, she sank into her chair. He handed her the wine glasses, lowered himself into the second chair, and took back his glass. It was in him to listen now, let her story unfold, so he stoked his patience and sipped his wine.

He didn't have to wait long.

"I was rude, and I apologize." Her voice low, almost a whisper, her gaze toward the sea. "You were not to know my touchy spots, but you definitely tromped on one. I haven't told my sons . . . ." Her head was bowed now, gaze downward, curls like a curtain obscuring his view. Embarrassed? Ashamed? Then she lifted her head, shook her hair back, and faced him. "I haven't told my sons because I can't bear their disapproval."

Nor anyone's, he thought, remembering the spilled wine and the toppling tiki light as his own disapproval rang in her ears. Criticism and clumsiness, a matched set.

He met her unflinching bring-it-on gaze and quenched a smile, thinking of Eliza planted between the big brown man and himself. Courage, too.

She turned her face to the sea. Deciding what to say, what to tell him, *why* even. He was still nothing to her but an impetuous invitation with an unexpected dose of fireworks.

Hmmm.

He remained quiet. It was her story to tell and he wanted to hear it, and he certainly wanted more fireworks.

Hmmm.

Side by side they watched as the waves broke far from the shore, their sound swallowed by the night, and a single night bird called for its mate. When she was silent too long, he prompted, "Tell me."

She sniffed, sipped her wine, and kept her eyes on the horizon. "You know some of it already. I have two sons. Jed's the older one, he'll be thirty-five on his next birthday. He and his wife, Caroline, have two daughters, Alison and Aurora. I adore them, but they live too far away for much contact. Catalina Island near Los Angeles," she said before he could ask. "He's a real estate attorney, doing very well, and she's a psychiatrist. They don't have much visiting time."

Her laugh carried a bitter tinge he thought she didn't hear as she added to his store of Eliza Grace information.

"They do think I need to live near them so they can take care of me since I'm so old. That is, Jed does; the verdict's out on Caroline."

"I didn't know you were old enough to have such ancient children." He laughed when she laughed, wanted to spank the son.

She preened a little. "Almost sixty. Jacob's my baby. He has something to do with the Washington, DC, music scene, dangles the promise of great seats at the Kennedy Center when he wants me to visit. And he always delivers. Lucky me."

She paused, sipped her wine.

McLean looked at the moon, riding high this clear night, and wondered how he'd gotten to this place, this time, this woman who had the power to hurt him. How had that happened? He wanted his old life back—didn't he? His eyes moved from the moon to Eliza's face as her story resumed.

"Jacob and his partner, Raul . . ." She glanced at Harrison as though expecting a comment; none forthcoming, she continued. "He and Raul have a lovely flat and they dedicate a little corner for me. I don't see them often enough."

Her voice held adoration as she described the life Jacob and the man he wanted to marry had created, the space it held for her.

Thumbs up for son number two. He recognized the man's name, Jacob Dart, bassoonist for the National Symphony Orchestra, holder of a measure of fame in the tight-knit DC music community. Now was not the time to mention this— there was still more to her story.

Her gaze returned to the horizon. "It's just that I don't want to worry them. I always worried Cal, my husband, you see. When I told Jed I'd bought this apartment I thought he'd have apoplexy . . . . Is there really such a thing?"

Her laugh had a hollow ring. Her eyes did a little dance, making sure they didn't quite meet his, and she didn't wait for an answer. "Anyway, he was all over getting the sale canceled, telling the Realtor to take the Reno house off the market, sue whoever talked me into this foolishness. You can maybe understand why I haven't mentioned songwriting, let alone public singing or name changing. He would for sure think I'd gone off the deep end."

Silence stretched long into the darkness before she spoke again. "Finally, I just told him it was a done deal and hung up." A puzzled expression flitted across her face. "I've never done that before. Huh."

"And the sun came up the next morning."

Her smile blossomed, the first real one of the evening. "Yeah, it did."

"What about Jacob?"

"Dozens of texts from him and from Raul. I haven't looked at them. They won't be fussy like Jed was, but sometimes love carries its own disapproval, doesn't it?"

A rhetorical question. She stared into her wine glass, her face clouded, sad. "I didn't want to spoil today, but then I did anyway, didn't I?"

With great care, as though he held her heart in his hand, McLean put aside his glass, not caring as it tipped and spilled. He turned to Eliza and took her hand. "We had a bit of excitement, I'll agree," he said, "and for a moment I was in danger of losing my life, but all in all I think it's been a splendid day."

Slowly she raised her eyes and stared at him for a long moment before she freed her hand and laid it gently against his cheek, and he felt his own heart turn over.

"You're right, it *has* been a splendid day."

CHAPTER 33
ELIZA

HAND IN HAND, THEY FINISHED HER wine and watched the moon traverse the sky, then folded up the chairs and climbed the dark stairs to her apartment.

We both know what's next, Eliza thought, amazed that the evening's debacle could be so easily resolved, *but we don't seem to be getting on with it very efficiently. We're experienced adults. Well, at least one of us is.*

Her heart thudded so loudly she thought he might hear. She'd never imagined she'd find love, or at least a lover—hadn't sought it, didn't want it. Too many entanglements and demands, she'd said. No way could she lose the self she'd just found—just created, she'd remind herself. And her secret fear: who would even want her?

She'd already come to the conclusion that Cal was as stingy a lover as he'd been a husband and father. Since he was her N of 1, she had to grant tonight's experience factor to Harrison, but she was no longer a girl and, as unlikely as this seemed, she knew what she wanted. She hadn't sought love, yet here it was in all its loud and messy glory, and she wanted to know this man's body with her own.

She refilled their glasses, then moved to stare out the window and ponder her options.

"Eliza Grace."

Attuned to nuance, she recognized the hesitation in his voice. She turned.

He stood just out of reach, arms at his sides. His glass sat untouched on the counter. He cleared his throat.

Well, well. Apparently experience doesn't always help. She placed her glass beside his. "Harrison Christian."

He said something that sounded like swearing but in words Eliza didn't know. Irish maybe?

"Christ, woman, you're not makin' it aisy on a man."

And then it *was* easy.

She closed the gap between them, put her hands on his arms and looked up. In his eyes, she saw herself: wanted, desired, beautiful. She raised her hand to his cheek.

He covered it with his big hand, then turned it and kissed her palm.

A flame shot through her. She gasped. Every muscle tightened.

His lips brushed hers, then trailed kisses downward, his mouth pausing, teasing over her pounding pulse. A spasm coursed her body, leaving her limp, liquid, boneless, and only his quick hands at her waist kept her from slipping to the floor. His mouth came back to hers even as he boosted her to the granite counter and held her body against his. Her arms twined around his neck.

Heat rose. Lightning flashed. A full-on storm raged as tongues tangled and mouths demanded. Just when she thought she would never breathe again, he released her. His breathing was ragged, too, and she thought she could hear the thunder of his heart.

He looked into her eyes. "I want this," he said. "Do you?"

Now he asks? She chuckled. "Filled with desire doesn't begin to cover it."

With a half laugh, half groan, he scooped her into his arms. "Which way?"

"My room."

In four long strides he reached her bedroom door and shoved it open. Moonlight disclosed the realm of a very messy princess, all peach and white with curtains fluttering in the breeze and balls of crumpled paper carpeting the smooth tile floor and decorating the unmade bed. He dropped her into the tangle of sheets, releasing her scent, and sank down beside her.

Poor planning, she thought as the detritus of a night's good work crumpled under them. *Oh well, too late now.* Panting, she rose to her knees, and her trembling fingers found the buttons on his shirt.

His hand stopped hers.

Oh? The sternotomy? On the beach, the surgical scar had remained hidden under his T-shirt and she could only guess what it meant to him, but he sure as heck needed to get over it. She wanted her hands on his skin.

"Harrison, really," she said in a voice her sons would have recognized, "it's a little late for modesty."

He growled but released her hand, and she took that as a good sign. Hardly recognizing this bold new self, Eliza made a ceremony of the unbuttoning, kissing each one, taking her time. Then the buttons were undone.

She pushed the fabric aside, and a sob rose in her throat. The incision glared red and raised and lumpy in places where keloid had formed—angry. And it broke the perfection of the broad chest.

He didn't move, and she knew the stillness cost him.

Again she took her time, trailing a lifeline of kisses over the not fully healed wound, feeling him tremble. Her fingers fluttered through the stubble of sandy hair, over the scar, then on to his nipples, his shoulders, his belly. No words were spoken. When she looked up, she saw his furrowed brow, his pursed mouth. He didn't meet her gaze.

She leaned back and, in one fluid movement, pulled her dress over her head, then scooted forward until her own nipples were hard against his chest.

Hesitation. Then she felt his murmured "ahhh" in her hair as his arms came around her, and the scar held no more importance.

"Back to business?"

His chest rumbled, and she knew it for a laugh before his mouth took hers again and she was lost.

"More," she whispered. "More."

His lips burned kisses over neck, shoulders, breasts, until his mouth found her nipple. He moaned as he slipped it into his mouth. She arched to him even as another spasm took her. Never since her children had anyone touched her this way. He suckled. Never had such pain and pleasure tortured her.

Still on her knees, she pulled herself closer. "Please." A stab of fear. Lost.

He let her go.

Bereft, she crumpled. "Harrison." It was a plea.

His hand skimmed her side.

Ahhh. She stretched catlike for more. Who was this new woman in her skin?

He slid her no-nonsense panties down and off her pliant body, and she lay naked on her own wrinkled sheets. She wanted him, needed him, and, as his hands explored her body, laughed with the joy of it.

His eyes questioned.

She issued an unfamiliar sound, then giggled and answered. "I thought this only happened in romance novels."

He chuckled as his fingers found her center. Her laughter faded to a whimper. "Harrison, please. Now."

Still chuckling, he let his fingers play a little longer before he whispered, "In a minute, dear heart. Just a minute."

The bed moved as he stood and unzipped his slacks. She opened her eyes to watch, gasped. *Is there room?*

Yesterday's conversation remembered, she almost laughed again before the bed dipped with his weight and he lay beside her, long and hard and hairy against her body, and thought ceased. His hand raced up her inner thigh. Ripples of desire became a flood as his fingers resumed their play and in one exquisite motion took her to the peak.

Time stopped.

I will remember this moment always—the sweetness of plumeria flowing in on the night breeze, the curtains rustling, and, before she could catch her breath, his weight gently covering her shuddering body. She arched to take him in. She did know how to do this.

"I don't want to hurt you."

She wanted him now, snapped, "I accommodate, like Gretchen. I don't break."

Chuckling, he slid into her warmth, and he froze.

What?

Then she knew. She could almost see the ads, "Ask your doctor if your heart is strong enough for sex," and she knew this was his first time, that he was afraid. For a second, she didn't know what to do, and then she did.

"Roll over."

A long beat, then another before he complied.

She rolled with him. He had softened, but their bodies were still joined. Heart to heart, she felt his thunder as she rocked her hips, easy at first, then harder as her own fear dissipated and heat rose. Tight, she refused to let him slip away.

When she heard his breath catch, almost a sob, and his arms came around her once again, she straightened. Her head fell back, and her own breath released as she took him deeper.

"Now or never, dear man," she whispered, and she rode him until his fear broke and his rhythm matched her own, and they were lost together.

CHAPTER 34
McLEAN

Sweaty and limp, Eliza collapsed onto his chest. When coherent thought returned, McLean pulled a sheet over their cooling bodies and let himself revel in the scent of her—raspberry, plumeria, woman—maybe for the only time. What woman wants an unpredictable man?

She slid to his side, snuggled into his shoulder, and he felt her satisfied "hmmm."

It had always been his way to meet problems head on, but he hadn't expected the memory—crushing pain in his chest, his arm, his jaw; the fear bigger than any he'd experienced when aftershocks rocked or fires crackled around him. Christ, he'd known men who died in the throes of coitus. Paralyzed, he'd hung on the edge.

Eliza Grace had refused to let him retreat.

Grateful and embarrassed, he dropped a kiss into her hair. *Better get this over with*, he thought, *here in the dark where it will be easier for the both of us.*

"Sorry," he said, forcing the word over the sudden lump in his throat. "I didn't know that would happen."

Eliza ran a finger up the scar. "No worries. But for a minute that Viagra ad was scrolling in my head."

He could almost smile when she chuckled. "I didn't know you hadn't . . . I mean since . . ."

"Not since the MI. I should have told you. Next time will be better." *If there is a next time*, he thought as he waited for her words.

"Good Lord, Harrison, if next time's any better I'll be the one to expire." Snickering, she caressed his cheek, then snuggled deeper into his arms.

They were both smiling as they fell together into sleep.

HE WOKE TO THE PINK OF sunrise-tinted clouds visible through a strange bedroom window. Alone. Her scent surrounded him, aroused him. It had been a long time since he'd woken in a lover's bed. Usually alcohol and hot sex were enough, and he'd go home to his own bed. And there was always a cot in some physicians' lounge or a sleeping bag in a grimy Red Cross tent. He stretched.

What next?

Unbidden, memories of the night returned, and his fist pressed his chest even as a grin creased his face. He'd been afraid and yet . . .

Brimming with satisfaction—he'd made love with a beautiful woman and survived—he crawled out of bed and reached for the pants lying on the floor where he'd dropped them in his haste. He picked up one of the crumpled papers that littered the floor and smoothed it flat. Staff paper, scribbled black music notes that resembled sperm, scattered words, many heavily crossed out. Last night, songwriting had been on her list of things kept secret—perhaps this was work in progress. He folded the paper and slid it into his pocket.

He unearthed his shirt from under the quilt and started to put it on, then shook his head and tossed it down. Barefoot and bare-chested, he headed for the bathroom. Ten minutes later, he followed the aroma of coffee and the sound of music.

Eyes closed, Eliza sat cross-legged on the divan, fingers strumming the guitar in her lap. Light streamed into the living room, and through the window behind her he saw the monkey pod tree and the moving sea. His heart quickened. *New*, he thought, wondering what that meant. *I feel new.*

She looked up, no hint of shyness or regret in her smile. Crumpled papers littered the floor around her. A silky orange wrap covered her body but left her legs bare, and the morning sun highlighted the red in her hair.

"Good morning," she said. "I didn't mean to wake you. Inspiration is hard to ignore." She waved at the rejections around her. "But sometimes illusive. Coffee's in the kitchen, vanilla-macadamia nut blend. You'll like it."

New, alive, hopeful.

Lust rose. He'd thought he needed coffee, knew he needed this woman more. In a few steps he was at her side, dropped to a knee, and took her mouth.

For a moment she didn't move, then with a sigh she put the guitar aside and leaned into his kiss, her mouth soft under his.

Ahhh.

As she opened to him, he took the kiss deeper, tasting the vanilla of her coffee, the peppermint of her toothpaste, the sweetness that was her own. He could lose himself here. But when he felt her fingers on his zipper, he gave up her mouth, leaned back, and caught her hands. Desire aside, he wasn't sure morning sex was a good idea.

"Coffee first. No offense meant."

"None taken." She laughed and handed him her empty mug. "Me too, black."

The kitchen sparkled, all granite and stainless steel. Cream and sugar and an empty mug stood by a Cuisinart coffee maker that looked brand new. He fixed his coffee and hers and returned to sit in the chair facing her. "What are you doing?"

She looked around at the scattered pages. "Killing trees, mostly."

"Really, tell me."

"I write songs, lyrics anyway. Then I work with Jaime and the guys on the music. Sometimes people even want to hear them. Usually I have an idea of how it should sound, hence the guitar and the staff paper." She waved toward the stack beside her. "Sometimes I do better than others."

He sipped the very good coffee and waited, but she just ran her fingers over the guitar strings, apparently done with a completely unfinished topic.

What next?

Before the silence became awkward, she set aside her mug and moved uninvited into his lap. "I woke this morning with some new words and themes to play with, thanks to you."

She trailed a finger down his chest, pressed her lips against his collarbone, laughed as he firmed beneath her.

He caught her hand. "Not just a one-night stand then?"

Pursed lips, voice prim, eyes twinkling. "I don't do one-night stands, sir."

"Indeed." Her words were cocky, but her gray eyes clouded as they slid away from his. He was pretty sure she didn't do any kind of stand, but took her words as permission to proceed. "So let's keep your record intact." He slid a hand under her wrap and found only woman. "Will you let me see you? I was too busy to get a good look last night."

"Naked?"

He nodded.

"Here?"

Another nod.

He felt a deep sigh build in her. Then she released it with a little "huh" and unwound herself from his lap. Muttering what sounded like "in for a penny, in for a pound," she let the wrapper slide from her shoulders and puddle on the floor at her feet. Head high, eyes on his face, she stood naked before him.

His breath caught in his throat. Beautiful, small, vulnerable.

Her hands fluttered with the instinctive need to cover herself, then relaxed at her sides. She was smooth and tanned, with a thin white band around the high, firm breasts, another calling attention to hips generous enough to take him in. Her legs seemed long for such a small person, well-muscled and tapering to slender ankles and dainty feet. Not a girl, certainly, but what a delectable woman, a woman whose body was as lovely as her heart.

Words failed. Not for the first time, he envied his father's way with poetry. No matter, today he couldn't speak anyway over the lump that had formed in his throat.

She knelt beside him. "Are you okay?"

He nodded.

She hopped up. "Well, as long as you're okay, it's your turn now."

He'd sometimes wondered what flabbergasted felt like. Now he knew—eyes go wide, mouth drops open, stupid invades the brain. "Me? Naked?"

She nodded.

"Now? Here?"

He'd spent a fair amount of time naked with women—the things they did were easier done unclad—but no one had ever asked just to see his naked body.

"Oh, yes, Harrison, here and now and naked. I was too busy to get a good look at you last night." Mocking him, she grinned, then whirled away, teasing and striking poses, mimicking sexy.

She was not a girl, but she had a girl's spirit.

Mocked or not, he wanted her in his arms, under him, taking him in, but he had an old man's body, skin a little slack and marked by years in the sun, a layer of fat instead of a six-pack, everything drooping a little more than it had when he was forty. And the scar that heralded his brokenness.

In the daylight, his instinct was to cover himself, to back away. The life he knew had been structured to fit, didn't allow surprise—now everything was a surprise.

A joke from the universe? Maybe. Keeping his eyes on her face, McLean stood and stepped out of his pants.

The grin disappeared and her mouth formed an O. Her eyes sparkled as they raked him up and down. *Little devil, she's enjoying this.*

Then she stepped in front of him, put her hands on his forearms, and looked up into his eyes. "Harrison McLean, you are a big man, and so much better than my imagination."

CHAPTER 35
ELIZA

STANDING NAKED IN HER OWN LIVING room, pleased with the moment and with her own audacity, Eliza devoured the man's body with her eyes and released the breath she didn't realize she'd been holding.

"Harrison McLean, you are so much better than my imagination."

True. Her experience consisted of perfunctory kisses, pats on the butt, and unsatisfactory grapplings under the covers, often still partially clad and never with the light on. Not that she hadn't seen men naked—she'd been a nurse for years—but this was different.

Tall and broad, carrying some extra weight that on him looked good, he was the epitome of a strong man, a man in charge, a man who would always get things done. She'd seen despair in his eyes, and confusion, and now discomfort, and she knew he doubted himself. She also knew that doubt would fade as his life returned to normal, his scar a thin memory.

How long will such a man want me? More to the point, do I want such a man in my new life?

She almost laughed. What a question. In the past twenty-four hours she'd known joy and anger, laughter and pleasure, and a climax she hadn't known possible. It was too late, he was already in. She shivered. *What next?*

Putting dark thoughts aside, she caressed his stubbly cheek. "Do me a favor, please. Two, really."

"What?"

"Don't shave, and make love with me out here."

Surprise displaced discomfort on his broad face. "Here?" He looked at the tile under his feet. "Floors are hard."

She nodded. *He'll think I'm nuts, but what's one more nutty thing on my recent list of crazy.* "I've never had sex anywhere but in a bedroom."

The wicked man grinned. "Well, there's an oversight," he said, his expression changing as though he were considering the problem.

Before she could guess what he was thinking, he said, "Let's remedy the situation," and captured her hand. The kiss he delivered to her palm was shock enough to steady any heart, or to disrupt one. "Hold that thought," he ordered and disappeared into the guest room.

Heart beating wildly, Eliza had barely registered his words or his intent before he returned with a beach towel and spread it over the tiles. With a rumble from deep inside, he swooped her up and brought both of them to the floor. "Don't say I didn't warn you."

Laughing, she lay cradled in his arms. How could she laugh and want in the same moment? And here was another crazy request about to be granted as though it were normal.

His skin was warm against her nakedness. So much skin. He held still as her hand slid up his arm, over his shoulder, down his flank to belly and chest, but he sucked in a breath as her fingers caressed his nipple. It firmed. He trembled. She laughed again—sheer joy, such power at her fingertips.

Who knew?

Thrilled at her own daring, Eliza took the nipple in her mouth as this man had taken hers. Suckled. Flames leaped in her core. As though her body knew something she didn't, her hips undulated, and his desire rose beside her. *Amazing*.

With a moan, he pulled her closer. When she raised her head, he claimed her mouth.

All heat now as his mouth and his hands demanded. When she could bear the tension no longer, she slung one leg over him and fit her body to his.

Ahhh.

Harrison slid inside her as though that space had always been his, and she drew him deep. Of its own volition, her body moved with his slow, rhythmic thrusts and pleasure that already seemed complete erupted. Then she was only feeling, shiny and new, vibrating with the need for release and the wish that this moment would last forever.

His pace increased. Her world became his hands and his mouth and the earthquake building inside. Just when she thought there could be no more, he whispered, "Now, dear heart," pushed her to the edge, and fell with her.

"You were right," she said when the aftershocks had subsided, and she could speak, "the floor is hard." Pinned beneath him, she appreciated both his weight and the comforts of a good mattress.

"In a minute, just give me a minute and I'll move."

She giggled, amazed again. *Here I am, Eliza Grace, not too old after all.* She wanted to leap up and punch her fist into the air; she wanted to tell the world how marvelous she felt—instead she licked his skin, tasted salt and man, and licked her lips with the pure pleasure of it all. In a back corner of her brain where guilt and conscience and good sense resided, a little voice snickered, *Play now, pay later.* With a sigh, she flicked it away.

He rolled to his side, one arm keeping her close. "Sorry, didn't mean to squish you."

"No worries." She scooted up to kiss his mouth. "My pleasure to be squished. Now I'm hungry."

CHAPTER 36
MCLEAN

"I'M HUNGRY," SHE SAID AFTER THEY had all but devoured each other on the hard tile floor of her apartment.

"Me too," he said, still fighting to catch his breath. *If I died right now, I'd die happy.*

Stupid, he thought later, after they had laughingly separated to shower and dress. He wasn't dying. And life would only shrink away as much as he let it. God, today there was no shrinkage at all.

A half hour later, dressed and ready for the day, they settled into his sedan. He turned the key. "Where to?"

"Your choice." She sounded as happy as he felt.

"The Gazebo."

"Long drive." She frowned pro forma, and he remembered her telling him that people from Kihei were reluctant to go "to the other side."

"Worth it." He grinned and turned toward Lahaina and Napili Bay.

The pinks of sunrise had given way to a cloudless sunny sky and a blue sea as beautiful as any Rembrandt or Van Gogh. As they drove along the coast in the early morning traffic, conversation flowed easily, punctuated by moments of silence, equally easy.

Chris had spent a lot of time with women; they were the nurses, students, colleagues, and rescue workers of his life. He liked women, especially smart women who were good at their jobs and good in bed. This morning, he couldn't remember a single moment when he'd so enjoyed a woman's simple presence.

He wanted to touch her.

The wind had whipped up whitecaps and the sun held dominion over the sky by the time they joined the long queue of couples and families sheltering under Gazebo-provided umbrellas.

Finally the hostess—not Lisa today but a woman who reminded him of the comedienne Jane Curtin—beckoned them. McLean returned their umbrella to its holder, Eliza straightened the round-brimmed straw hat that struggled to contain her curls, and they followed her into the crowded open-air restaurant.

"This had better be good," Eliza whispered after they'd squeezed into a space overlooking the water. "I've never stood in line this long for anything."

He just smiled and looked at the menu. She'd spent most of the hour cheerfully chatting with everyone around them.

They shared a Mexican omelet and the macadamia nut pancakes that he'd found so delicious a few days earlier. Not much remained when Eliza pushed her plate away. "Full, very full. Golly, that was good, but you have to eat this last bite." She gestured toward the pile of crumbs that remained. "I've filled out every last wrinkle I own." She poofed out her cheeks. "And I feel like a puffer fish."

He laughed and complied, washing the crumbs down with the last of his coffee. While she went to the ladies' room, he paid their bill and then wandered to the sea wall near the pole where the whale-sighting bell hung ready. Waves crashed on the rocks below and wind now pushed heavy clouds across the deep blue sky. His belly was full and his mind, for a change, was quiet.

He started when her hand slipped into his.

"Time for a walk."

He resisted. "Too full. Besides, we already had our morning exercise."

She giggled. "Never too full. And *that* doesn't really count." Pulling her hand free, she made a face at him and strode off toward the car. When he caught up, she stood on tiptoe to kiss him. She won.

THE KAPALUA COASTAL TRAIL BEGAN AT the beach where Chris had encountered turtle and sunburn. He parked along the street, and Eliza, looking quite pleased with herself, set the pace. Waving palms, pounding surf, and the heat of the sun soothed him further. His heart beat an efficient and steady seventy-six per minute, and his breathing was unlabored. Only his legs grew tired from the ups and downs of the trail. She paused frequently to admire the view, rest stops he suspected were for his benefit, but, since each stop was punctuated by a kiss, he didn't protest. At one viewpoint, where the waves crashed against the volcanic cliffs and sent up a salty spray that cooled them both, he took out his phone and snapped her picture.

She laughed and demanded selfies of the both of them. "My goodness," she said as she made him pose, "you look just like a little boy playing hooky."

Exactly. That's just how I feel. From then on, he kept his phone handy and snapped pictures at any opportunity.

After they walked and laughed and got good and sweaty, they returned to the car and drove the few miles back to

Lahaina, where they wandered along the crowded sidewalks, ducking into gift shops and exclaiming over the goods and the prices. In the ABC Store, Chris found a refrigerator magnet with a saying he thought she'd like, purchased it while she tried on flowered baseball caps (which she refused to let him buy), and tucked it into his pocket for later.

Sitting under the famous banyan tree in the town center, they slurped shave ice and watched people until Eliza glanced at her watch. "Oh, dear," she exclaimed and scrambled to her feet, almost knocking him off the bench. "Sorry, sorry."

Chris righted himself and stood beside her, not sure what the fuss was about.

She pointed at her watch. "Look, we've done it again."

He checked his own watch. 3:12. He caught her hand. "Still confused."

She tossed her plastic cup into the trash and pulled him toward the car. "Sorry. I don't know where the time goes when we're together, but I'm due at practice at four."

"Practice?"

"Rehearsal with the guys—twice a week always, more often just before a gig. And tonight's special; we're scoring a new song."

As Chris negotiated the curves back toward Kihei, Eliza snuggled into the corner of the passenger seat, leaned back, and closed her eyes. He thought about long-ago rides with the girlfriend of the moment tucked under his arm, close enough to change gears and still keep her in his adolescent grip. Annoyed at the console that separated modern front seats, he contented himself with thoughts of Eliza's apartment and the delights awaiting. The silence provided adequate canvas for the erotic fantasy he was creating when her cell phone vibrated.

"Huh, what?" She pushed her sunglasses up into her curls and rummaged in her bag, a brightly colored twin to the one she'd carried when he'd first met her. She located the phone, uttered a triumphant "gotcha," and peered at its tiny screen. A troubled look crossed her face.

"Problem?"

"Nope, no worries." Her curls bounced in a vigorous *no* as she punched a button and tossed the phone back into the bag.

Too emphatically?

"Just a little nuisance off island." She glanced away. "No biggie. Serves me right for leaving the darn thing on."

He knew from personal experience how easily she could turn her phone off and leave it off, but this was a little white lie, for sure, or maybe a big one. However, as she'd so dramatically demonstrated the previous night, her problems were not his concern. She'd tell him when she was ready, or not, and he would have to be fine with that.

He asked no more questions, couldn't help worrying as her brow furrowed and she feigned sleep until they pulled into the Waipuilani parking lot.

"Jaime and I have work to do before the guys get there," she told him as they hurried up the stairs to her apartment. The worrisome call was not mentioned. On the landing, she dug around in her bag, found keys, and opened the door.

The staggering view of trees and ocean once again welcomed them.

She paused just inside and sighed. "I don't think I'll ever get tired of walking into this room."

He stood behind her, suddenly awkward, not quite sure what he was supposed to do.

"Sorry, not being a good host, but I really do have to go." She fumbled again in the bottomless bag and pulled out another set of keys. "Here." She handed him a "Welcome to Hawai'i" key ring. "Yours. House key and gate key, which is also the pool key. If you don't have anything else to do, you could hang out at the pool. There's leftovers in the fridge if you get hungry. I'll be home in time for sunset." She threw him a grin as she darted into her room. "Don't start without me."

He wanted to go with her, keep watching her, but understood he'd be as welcome at her rehearsal as she'd be in his operating room with its klieg lights and chaotic efficiency, so he acquiesced and waited instead as she changed from yellow, flowered sundress to no-nonsense shorts and dark blue T-shirt. Ready, she slung the bag over her shoulder, grabbed her guitar by its neck, and hurried out the door.

In a minute she was back. "Forgot something." Rising up on tiptoe, she planted a kiss on his surprised mouth. "Bye now."

The rickety screen slammed behind her as Chris ran his tongue over lips still tingling, thinking, *Can't remember the last time I got a goodbye kiss*, and felt a smile blossom.

Alone, he wandered around the apartment. Beside the small television he hadn't noticed stood a framed photo—a younger Eliza between two handsome youths, Jed and Jacob, obviously, though neither looked like ogres. *She'll feel better after she calls them*, he thought with a sigh, some small part of him wishing he could call his own kids. Deep breath. *Too late.*

He looked in the refrigerator, decided he wasn't hungry, went into the guest room and looked at the bed, decided he wasn't tired, unearthed the *Journal of Cardiothoracic Medicine* from his backpack and carried it to the living room before he decided he wasn't interested in that either, and tossed it on the coffee table, unopened. So far, neither journals nor the professional papers he should be reading had seen Hawaiian daylight. Right now, he felt no need to remedy that.

What do I want to do?

A novel question. He couldn't remember a time since childhood when he hadn't had things that needed to be done. Not sure whether this was good or bad, he donned his blue suit with the white Hawaiian leaf print and looked down: legs that hadn't seen the sun since summers when he was a lad; legs always clad in khakis or scrubs or the occasional fine wool suit, which he wore when he was impressing a hospital administrator or soliciting funds for the Red Cross or begging blood for the blood bank; feet always in sturdy boots or shoes draped in blue booties now looking back at him from the rubber sandals she called flip-flops.

Ugly buggers. He grinned. *I did say I wanted a change.*

He gave more thought to the original question, decided he wanted to lie with Eliza, but, this option being temporarily unavailable, he wanted to sit in the sunshine and reread one of his favorite books. Whatever else he wanted, he'd figure out later.

In renewed good humor, he stuffed a towel, a bottle of water, and his battered copy of *The Prophet* into a blue Walmart bag he'd discovered in the closet. After discerning which key was which and carefully locking the door, he headed downstairs. Halfway down, he remembered sunscreen and went back to fetch it.

When he finally opened the gate and stepped into the pool enclosure, he found sparkling water and empty lounge chairs lined up to face the sun and a tree heavy with white flowers that exuded Eliza's scent. Plumeria. With no one to witness, Chris removed his shirt, slathered on sunscreen, and let the sun warm his damaged chest while he thought about the woman who was taking root in his heart.

"Hey, sleepyhead, rise and shine."

Eliza's voice yanked him from an erotic dream, and he shot a glance down. *Nope, no incriminating evidence.*

"You looked like you were enjoying that dream." She laughed as he looked down again. "No worries, just save some for me."

The laugh sounded a little forced, and there was no welcoming kiss.

"Come on, we need to hurry so we don't miss the sunset."

He was surprised—a glance at his watch showed 6:51—to find he'd napped for almost two hours. His mother would have said, "Oh, my, where has the day gone?"

Thoughts of his mother produced a warm feeling as he got to his feet and pulled his T-shirt back on. Colleen McLean had been an Irish woman burdened by three great lunks who adored her. She'd only completed sixth grade herself and was fiercely proud of her college-educated sons. *Especially me*, he thought, *with my gift of healing*. Wonder what she'd be thinking now.

"Harrison, come on. We don't have all day."

One look at her sulky expression warned him to keep his mouth shut and follow instructions. She carried a thermos and two plastic glasses. Beach chairs waited just outside the pool gate. Obviously, there was a sunset-watching ritual not to be interrupted. Shaking off his reverie and the irritation he felt at still needing naps, Chris settled his hat on what he hoped wasn't a sunburned pate and picked up the chairs.

The lawn on the beach side of Eliza's apartment teemed with people, the number surprising. Last night, the area had seemed so private he'd thought of it as hers. Now they were sharing it: couples standing arm in arm or silhouetted as they sat on the dune's edge, three boys tossing a football and trying to attract the attention of two long-legged girls strolling and giggling nearby, dogs getting acquainted as their owners found seats on the grass. Apparently in Maui, the sun needed daily admiration to set properly.

Over it all, tall palms swayed, paying tribute. He hadn't been around these trees much, enjoyed watching them move as though they, too, could hula. But Eliza's back was straight and her voice was petulant so, without comment, he followed her commands and set up their chairs. He was, after all, no stranger to moody nurses.

When things were arranged to her satisfaction, Eliza sank into her chair with an exaggerated huff and poured from the thermos. Red wine, not the lemonade he'd expected. She handed him his glass and took a big drink from her own.

"If you want water," she said, not looking at him, "you can get your own."

Hmmm. Apparently divas got moody, too. "This is fine, thanks. Hard day?"

He waited.

The set of her jaw provided his answer. She stared straight ahead, but eventually she nodded yes.

The sun was much closer to the horizon when she spoke. "One of those times when things are not as they should be. Jaime was crabby, and Derek kept cracking stupid jokes, and I kept hitting a flat that should have been a sharp, but we soldiered on and finally got one or two things to go right. At times like this, I wonder if Jed might be right. But then . . . ," she sighed, "I'm here."

Glancing toward him, she worked up a smile and clinked their glasses. "Aloha. Now *we* are here."

"Aloha." He raised the plastic glass to lips stiff with a less-than-genuine smile.

Merlot, a good one. *Ahhh.* A real smile emerged as the wine pleased his palate. Moody diva or not, this woman paid attention to a person's likes—cream and sugar this morning, now a good vintage of his favorite red. He wondered: Were Jaime

Hokoana's grumps because Chris McLean was still in town? Were her sulks about the phone call she hadn't taken? Was she having second thoughts about him?

He didn't ask.

Eliza drained her glass and set it aside, then kicked off her sandals, stretched her legs out in front of her, and let her head fall back. Loose, her hair fell around her shoulders and ruffled in the wind.

He imagined plunging his fingers into that mass of curls, drank his wine instead, and waited for her to unwind. If her bad mood had to do with him, he'd find out soon enough.

The sun had almost completed its daily journey before she straightened, laughed, and poured herself another glass of wine. "Sorry. Some days are like that. Then I sit here and get my daily reminder—the sun comes up in the morning and goes down at night and everything that happens in between is just passing through."

The day's stress seemed to have passed through, leaving her body relaxed and her voice serene. McLean felt a pang. *Am I just passing through?*

She scooted her chair closer to his and linked their fingers, and they watched the sun travel its final inches. When it touched down, the crowd applauded. As though she knew his earlier thoughts, Eliza said, "I don't know what we will be to each other. I'm going to enjoy each moment while I can."

She looked at him as though asking if he could do the same.

With her sunglasses still on, he couldn't read her eyes, but her hand was steady in his. He had already come to the same conclusion. "Good idea," he said and raised his glass. "Here's to many days in paradise."

What could possibly be wrong with another few days of island bliss?

CHAPTER 37
ELIZA

ORCING HERSELF NOT TO POUT, ELIZA touched her glass to his. *What did I expect, a profession of undying love? I don't think so. A week ago I didn't even know I wanted him.*

She amended that to a month and looked at this man she wanted very much.

"I know a world awaits you. How long can you stay?"

In the dusk, his expression grew pensive, and she wished she could know his thoughts. She imagined he'd done this many times, met and lusted and then moved on. She wondered about the woman he said he'd loved—DeMello, he'd called her. That seemed different somehow. She ran frustrated fingers through her hair and wondered if he could ever love her, then plucked that thought out like a seed that couldn't be allowed to take root. Lust was safer. Love implied shackles she no longer wanted. But he had called her "dear heart."

His answer was too long in coming. "Harrison?"

"Sorry, just calculating. My return-to-work evaluation is scheduled for August sixth. No one has been nagging at me yet but they'll start soon. I've left quite a bit of unfinished business, hard to predict a heart attack. So, to answer your question, I can stay until the end of July, if it suits you."

Her heart thumped. A lifetime of good sex in a month. She could handle that, and if she was sad when he left, well, she would handle that, too. It was all more than she'd ever expected. "I'd love to have you for July."

His eyebrows gathered.

She giggled—she *had* meant it both ways—and raised her now-empty glass. "Aloha. Aloha means hello and goodbye and cheers and everything in between. So aloha, Harrison McLean. Here's to many more days in Paradise."

He leaned toward her and his mouth found hers. His hands framed her face as he took the kiss deeper. She trembled. He released her and stood. "Let's go up, before we become part of the evening's entertainment."

As though their conversation had loosened something within him, they were barely in the door when he engulfed her. No gentle explorations now—hard, frantic even, as his mouth demanded and his hands tore at her clothes.

Caught in his firestorm, Eliza held on for the ride. When she finally caught her breath, they were lying on her bed, both naked and drenched in sweat.

"Did I hurt you?"

"Goodness no." What else to say? Her own demands seemed insatiable, the passion he aroused revealing both her own needs and her fear that she might be consumed by the fire. As her breathing evened out and her voice approached normal, she danced her fingers down his side, tickling, needing to lighten the moment. "No, dear man," she added, "it was a reasonably pleasant encounter."

He quivered and pulled her close with such a contented rumble she thought she'd imagined the earlier desperation.

They lay wrapped in each other's arms until her stomach growled, and she realized it had been a long time since her macadamia nut pancakes. She poked him. "I'm starved. I'm going to shower and then fix us something to eat, since apparently there are no calories in sex."

With a laugh, he let her go.

She stood under the spray, enjoying the cool water and plumeria-scented soap on her overheated body. The glass door opened, and he stepped in behind her.

"Do you mind?"

Hunger vanished. *Oh my God, of course I don't mind.* Blessing the oversized shower Rosie had talked her into, she moved forward to allow him space. His body hard against her back sent shivers in all directions, and she started to turn.

Gentle hands held her shoulders. "Wait."

He rescued the bar of soap from nerveless fingers and proceeded to lather her—shoulders and back, buttocks and legs—each stroke of his soapy hands sending off erotic sparks until she was a quivering mess leaning against the tile for support. He turned her to face him, pushed wet hair off her face for a quick kiss, and then went to work on her front—arms, breasts, belly—and then lingered at the V of her legs.

She heard a whimper, realized it as her own, and wanted. *Oh yes, I want.*

An embarrassed giggle escaped when he chuckled and she realized she'd said the words out loud.

She shuddered as his hand cupped her. "Please, before I melt down the drain." Another shudder, earthquake velocity. "Please. I've never had sex in the shower."

"Another oversight," he said with an exaggerated sigh as he boosted her up against the shower wall, then let her slide onto him.

"Oh my," she whispered into his shoulder, "I'm glad you know how to do this."

She felt his chest rumble again and looked up into a grinning face. Her own flaming now, she muttered, "I'd have us both drowned before I figured it out."

His laugh reverberated in the enclosed space and his arms tightened.

Guess I've got it right, she thought as she twined her arms around his neck, wrapped her legs around his body, and opened herself to him.

For a moment they stood, suspended, and then he drove into her and took her beyond thought.

SOME TIME LATER, THEY DRIED EACH other off. She wrapped a towel around her wet hair and pulled on the orange wrap.

"Now I'm really hungry," she said and started out the bathroom door, stopped when his hand curled around her arm. "No . . . no . . . don't even touch me or we'll just be desiccated bones when they find us."

His laugh again filled the small space as he tugged her to him. "Just one more kiss, I promise."

She was shaky inside when he let her go. *Kitchen*, she thought. *Food*.

The counter was set, and shrimp scampi was bubbling. She lifted it from the microwave just as Harrison, wearing shorts and a white tee, settled onto a kitchen stool. She pushed a glass of ice water toward him, stirred the shrimp, and pulled a chilled bottle from the fridge.

"Wine?" She had decided she was not the arbiter of his drinking.

He shook his head. "Water's good. And that smells delicious. What are we eating?"

"Rice, salad, shrimp. I'm not much of a cook, but I can do this without poisoning anyone. Besides, I made it a few days ago when my brain still worked."

Chuckling, he emptied his glass, went to the sink for more, and on the way caught her up in a hug that left her breathless. *Always touching, kissing, holding—like he can't get enough of me. Never happened before, but I could get used to it. Really used to it.* She sighed and put that thought away, too.

They were mopping up the last of the meal when she yawned and then yawned again. No wonder—she'd been up since before dawn and had lived more in this one day than she had in most years.

"Past your bedtime, I'm thinking."

He wasn't yawning, but then he'd had his nap, not the soul-searching confrontation with Jaime before they settled down to work on her newest song, and not the nagging worry about Martin's latest contact.

That's not fair, she reminded herself. *Harrison is still recuperating. Major surgery, life-altering events, unknown future. He should be more tired that I am.* She shook her head, denying fatigue. Truth told, she didn't want to sleep through a minute of this July gift she'd been given, but suddenly she couldn't keep her eyes open.

He frowned. "Come on, sleepyhead, I'll tuck you in. Remember, the sun *will* come up tomorrow." He scooped her up as though she were weightless, carried her to her room, and dumped her on the rumpled sheets.

Eyelids drooping, she clung to his hand. "You'll sleep with me?"

"I will." The ceiling fan lazily moved the air, and the room was cool. He pulled the sheet up to her chin, sat beside her. "But I'll do kitchen duty first."

She tried to protest but her mouth wouldn't form words, and she dropped like a rock into sleep.

CHAPTER 38
McLean

I COULD GET USED TO THIS, McLean thought, *really used to this.*

He waited a minute before he slid his hand from her slackened grasp. When she didn't even wiggle, he stood and quietly left her to sleep. In the kitchen, he packaged the leftovers and wiped the counter, couldn't remember the last time he'd done dishes.

Connie cooks and cleans and I just write the check.

Connie Marvel, his longtime housekeeper, was even now taking care of his home in Georgetown. Plunging his hands into soapy water, Chris decided he rather liked the chores.

When he was done, he hung up the dishtowel and walked around the counter. Visible through windows open to the night breeze, the moon cast its reflection on still water. Birds asleep, silence complete. So much stillness, too much time to think.

What am I going to do?

And then there was the woman. He liked her goodbye kisses, he liked every minute spent in her company, he even liked doing chores in her kitchen at the end of the day—but playing house with Eliza King did not answer the question. It just raised more.

As he'd told her, his return-to-work evaluation was sched-uled—he'd received notice yesterday, an order nicely phrased as a request—August sixth, a minute or a lifetime away. He knew it was necessary that others observe and assess, determine whether his brain and body still functioned competently, safely. It had to be about the patient, after all. He'd evaluated other poor souls, now it would be his turn.

A chill ran up his back. *Necessary, yes, but I don't have to like it, or look forward to it.* The idea of someone looking over his shoulder gave him the willies.

Not long ago he'd been convinced that part of his life was over, nothing left to look forward to, but his hands had come alive in Anita Juarez's operating room, and now he wanted more than anything to be a surgeon again.

He glanced toward the darkened bedroom. Well, maybe more than *almost* anything. He didn't know what he wanted with this woman, but he did want. He stepped to her door.

She lay where he had left her. Beguilingly ordinary: one delicate foot with cheerful orange toenails peeking out from under the sheet, sooty lashes trembling with REM sleep, an occasional riffle as her breath escaped her lips. His body tight-ened as he looked.

She wasn't beautiful, he recognized, though he'd already deemed her so. Her forehead was high and lightly wrinkled, her eyes round and large for her small face, her teeth slightly askew, the front one chipped on one corner.

He stepped back, thought about the bed in the guest room, large enough for him to sleep in comfort. Last night had been an anomaly. He didn't *sleep* with women, he always slept alone. But she had clung to his hand, said, "You'll sleep with me?" and he'd said yes.

He moved to the side of her bed. *She's not beautiful,* he thought again, *but even sound asleep she moves me.* Good enough—no, better than good. The guest bed would have to remain empty. With time, his breathing steadied and his heart rate returned to normal and the ache in his balls lessened. Then he gently disentangled the orange wrapper from her sleeping form and laid it on the end of the bed, but he kept his shorts on as he slid under the sheet beside her.

"Shorts, Harrison? Really?"

Her teasing voice brought him instantly awake. Morning light filled the room, all of the bedclothes had migrated to the floor, and the damn shorts were on full display. Before embarrassment could register, he saw understanding and then wicked glee flash across her face.

"Really?"

Maintaining a serious countenance with difficulty, he nodded. "You were sleeping so soundly, I didn't want to wake you."

Standing at the bedside, two steaming mugs in her hands, she said, "Well, I'm awake now." She placed the mugs on the nightstand. "Shall we—"

He pulled her onto his chest and stopped her words with his mouth.

On Maui, the island of romance, Tuesday the twenty-sixth of June was unusually blustery. Neither Chris nor Eliza noticed.

The following morning, McLean woke to coffee and music and birdsong. He stretched lazily, wondering what this new day in paradise had in store. *Whatever*, he thought. Not much could top yesterday.

Now, rather than interrupt her work, he showered but didn't shave, donned clean clothes, and changed the sheets. Just as he pulled the quilt into place, her phone rang.

Eliza said hello.

He stepped into the living room to see the color drain from her face, the phone slip from her fingers, her knees buckle. He reached her side only in time to keep her head from striking the tile.

His fingers were searching for a pulse when her eyes fluttered open.

"Huh?" She struggled to sit up.

"You're a nurse, you know better. Stay down. You fainted." Heart pounding like a jackhammer, he finally found her pulse, fast but steady.

"I don't faint," she said, but she obeyed, head now cradled in his lap. "I never faint."

"You just did," he snapped, annoyance concealing his fear. He wanted an ambulance, EMTs, a proper hospital—recognized his overreaction. It was a simple faint.

Her heart rate slowed. Her cheeks lost their pallor. His recalcitrant heart refused to cooperate. *A simple faint*, he reassured himself as he stroked her hair and strove for composure. When his breathing steadied, he started to lift her to the divan, but she batted his hands away and got to her feet, then stood still.

"Dizzy?"

"Just fuzzy." She pushed him away again. "Don't need a doctor. Do need coffee."

She wasn't wobbling, so he went for the coffee.

When he returned, she was seated on the divan, eyes troubled.

"Thanks." With both hands, she accepted the steaming mug he proffered and moved a little to make room for him beside her.

He sat, steadied the shaking mug, and helped her raise it to her mouth.

She sipped. "Thanks again," she said. "Sorry I snarled. I obviously haven't mastered proper faint protocol. I always wondered why my patients acted the way they did." She managed a shaky laugh.

He recognized the feint for what it was. She didn't want him to ask about the phone call.

Not your business, man, he told himself, but he felt her body tremble, a leaf in the wind, and knew he lied. "Just before you went down," he said, "I heard you answer the phone. Bad news?"

She dropped her eyes to the hands clutching the mug. "No, no big deal."

"Big enough deal to drop you like a rock, you who doesn't faint." He put two fingers beneath her chin and lifted so her eyes met his. "I know it's none of my business, Eliza Grace, but please tell me what's going on."

He held her chin, wouldn't let her look away, wondered again what he was doing here.

Deflated, Eliza sighed. "All right. There's this man in Reno who's decided he needs to take care of me. I usually don't take his calls, but this morning I was working and just forgot to look at caller ID."

The same jerk who called before, he thought, even as he cautioned himself to keep it light, even as he wanted to reach through the phone and throttle the pervert who'd dropped her to the floor. "He doesn't know you very well if he thinks you need caretaking."

As she laughed, heartier now, and shifted her eyes, Chris knew there was more to the story.

CHAPTER 39
ELIZA

IT WAS THE SHOCK, ELIZA TOLD herself, the shock of hearing his voice and listening to his words. She'd been deep into the lyrics she was writing, humming a possible tune, away in the place she called her sparkle spot when the phone chimed. Without thinking, she'd stood, clicked on, and said, "Hello."

"I know you're in Hawaii, Grace." Martin Grimes's usually well-modulated and professional voice was now high-pitched and whiney.

Surprise, then fear, as something dark slithered into paradise. She couldn't move.

"I love you, Grace," Martin went on more conversationally, "and you love me. Why don't you just tell me where you are, and I'll come get you. You don't have to continue this hide-and-seek game to make me prove my love. You know I love you, but you're being naughty." It wasn't her imagination that his voice took on a more ominous tone. "And you know what happens to naughty girls. You know I'll find you. Nothing can keep us apart."

If he'd said more, she didn't remember. Her world had gone black.

Now, as Harrison steadied her shaking hands and helped raise her mug to her mouth, she was grateful she wasn't alone. Her big man was here, right next to her on the divan in her own living room. He'd just made her laugh, and he didn't think she needed a caretaker.

"Jed would disagree," she said after the coffee had soothed. "I should have taken his advice about the restraining order, but I couldn't get it fast enough and I just wanted to be here and—"

Harrison raised one hand. "Wait, wait, wait. I need to catch up. Your lawyer son advised you to get a restraining order against this person who made you faint?"

She nodded, eyes on the cooling coffee.

"And you didn't do it. Why?"

"Don't interrogate me. You are not my keeper."

"Sorry."

She peeked up at his face. He didn't look sorry. He looked angry.

Her cheeks grew warm. "Me too. Sorry, I mean. That was rude of me. I know it's confusing and, darn it, Jed *was* right, and I was wrong. This person's name is Martin Grimes. He's an accountant in Reno, a CPA. I consulted him about some tax issues after Cal, my husband, died. He looked sad and lonely, and I felt sorry for him."

Harrison winced. "Like me."

Again, he made her laugh. "I don't think so. You bring out something else in me."

She accepted his kiss, linked her fingers behind his neck, and pulled him closer. In his arms, the fear she'd felt just before the world had disappeared became smaller, negligible, a dot on the horizon. She relaxed against him and closed her eyes.

But still a dot. *Sit up and deal.*

She straightened. "Shall I finish?"

"In a minute." Harrison dropped a kiss into her hair and let her go. "I'll make more coffee."

It was easier talking to his back.

While he made coffee and rummaged in the fridge, she filled in the details. When she repeated Martin's latest words, Harrison's hands fisted and his whole body tensed.

Oh, dear.

Before she could say, "What's wrong?" he shook himself like a big bear and resumed breakfast preparation. By the time he turned so she could see his face, everything seemed normal, and she wondered if she'd been imagining things.

"Come and eat," he said. "We'll both feel better with something in our stomachs."

He'd shoved aside the jigsaw puzzle they'd been working on the day before, one of their many blustery-day activities, and set two places at the counter. She joined him there.

Hot coffee, orange papaya one scoop at a time right out of its skin, crispy toast, and raspberry jam she didn't remember buying—she'd been sure she couldn't eat a bite and was surprised when her plate was empty. She pushed it away. "You were right, I do feel better."

"Good. Your color's back to normal."

He refilled their mugs from the fresh pot of coffee, then sat next to her at the counter and placed two fingers on her wrist. "And your heart's doing its job. So can we make sure I've got this straight?"

She nodded, apprehension flooding her. *Now he'll tell me how stupid I am. He'll say Jed was right. He'll make sure I know I really can't take care of myself.*

Even if it were true, she could hardly bear to hear from Harrison's lips what she'd heard so often from Cal's. She clutched her coffee mug and the hot liquid sloshed over her fingers. Skin burning, she braced for his words.

Obviously unaware of her plight, Harrison paused as though organizing his thoughts and then summarized: "You consulted this guy professionally and felt sorry for him so you had coffee with him."

"Twice." She didn't want to admit that at first she'd enjoyed the attention.

Harrison waved it away. "Once, twice, no difference. Based on that, he decided you were soulmates and won't take no for an answer. Now he's looking for you, no, *hunting* you. The only reason Jed knows is the guy contacted him to locate you. You needed some additional information to get the restraining order, so it's pending, and you came here, and now he's found you. And if I hadn't caught you in a faint, you'd still be dealing with this on your own. Is that about right?"

Eyes still down, she nodded again. The bald recitation made it sound even stupider.

He turned her swivel stool so she was facing him. "Dear God, woman, if I were in your shoes I'd be quivering in a corner or demanding twenty-four-seven police protection. The guy's a nut case, a stalker. You are the bravest, most self-sufficient person—"

Eliza lifted her eyes to his face, hardly believing what she was hearing. Not criticism but praise. Faint with relief, even though she was still judging herself to be dumb as a post, she touched his lips to stop the extravagant words.

"Thank you, thank you. I thought I'd brought it on myself. I'm a nurse. I really should have recognized that he wasn't quite right, but I didn't until it was too late."

He scooted her onto his lap, stopped her words with a kiss. "Not your fault, his. It's *his* behavior that's way out of line."

"I thought I could handle it." She kissed him back, then returned to her own stool. "That wasn't too smart, and I agree with Jed on that point, but it's always been my job to handle things, to make them right." She paused, sensing a contradiction—*my job to handle things, never doing it right*—but before she could consider further the thought slipped away.

Harrison cleared his throat.

She took a deep breath, felt some of the weight leave her shoulders, and said, "But maybe now it's time to get some allies?"

CHAPTER 40
McLean

McLean agreed. Eliza *did* need allies. As far as he was concerned, she should call out the fucking Mounted Police, or at least Hawaii 5-0. A sliver of fear pricked him; Martin Grimes held danger, and if what he'd heard so far was any indication, the danger was escalating. McLean was well aware that once a person had set this course, he would be very hard to deter.

Damn the man. Chris's hands clenched. He wanted to track the bastard down and beat him to a pulp. *That'd make me feel better, much better.* He reeled himself in tight. He hadn't known he held such a capacity for violence. But Eliza needed support, not a Rocky Balboa or a heavy-handed pseudo-savior telling her what to do.

Again, he kept it light.

"Pick me, pick me, pick me," he said, mimicking the DeMello-Johnson children in their constant competition.

Eliza giggled, and the haunted look she'd been wearing retreated. "I think you've got more than enough roles already.

Right now, if you don't mind, will you help me figure out a plan? I do need to deal with this. Head in the sand is not working."

Chris put on a third pot of coffee and for the next hour they discussed her options. She stopped protesting his interrogation techniques as his questions and her answers to them drew a textbook-clear and frightening picture—deteriorating personality, accelerating threat.

"I couldn't see it, Harrison," she admitted in a voice not quite steady. "At first there were just a few emails, a text or two, and once in a while I thought I saw his car cruising my neighborhood. I just figured he was being silly and kind of needy, you know—high-schoolish. I felt bad for him until that day he came to my house." Color left her cheeks as she described the prickly feeling that had suffused her as Martin Grimes stood beside her on the driveway and she knew she couldn't let him inside.

Chris stood and pulled her close.

"I should have realized," she said into his shirt, "with all the texts and emails."

"How many?"

She raised her eyes to his. The haunted look was back.

"Ten to one hundred each day." She grimaced. "That's why my phone was turned off when you were trying to contact me. The dings were making me crazy. Mostly, I didn't read 'em, just deleted them until the legal lady told me I needed proof that he really was bothering me."

Obviously thinking about the few she *had* read, she shivered. "Some of them were pretty weird."

"Show me."

He sensed her resistance, then felt it slide away. She retrieved her phone from the floor where it still lay. "Here." She turned it on and placed it in his outstretched hand. "Be my guest," she murmured and went to stare out the window.

He let her go. He didn't want to read any of them, but if he was to help he needed to know. He scrolled. Most of the messages were short, of the "please don't ignore me" and "I love you" variety. The more recent ones were longer, more detailed, less concise, crazier even. In them he called her "my lovely" and "my darling," but also "you little tease" and "my bad girl."

Chris reached the last one, the one that must have frightened her as they were driving:

Grace, I grow weary of your game. WE MUST MEET. My heart beats for you i tremble at the thought of your Touch your existence makes my life complete. I CANNOT WAIT MUCH LONGER!!! I will NOT!!!

Worse than he'd thought. Thank God the man lived in Nevada. When he was sure he had control of his features, Chris laid the phone on the counter and went to her. She said nothing. When she turned, he gathered her back against his chest and just held on.

She rested against him for a minute, then yawned and pulled away. "Enough. I'm too tired to think anymore, and I know what I have to do."

Today before rehearsal, Eliza would tell Jaime the whole story, seek his counsel as both lawyer and friend. Tomorrow she would send along the additional information required for the restraining order in Reno, specifically the emails and texts that had bombarded her. And she would tell about this morning's call and the menace it contained.

Still yawning, she gathered their breakfast dishes, set them in the sink, started rinsing the plates. "I am exhausted. I usually sleep midday when I work really late or really early—I think it's time for my nap."

He stopped her busy hands, didn't remind her that fear and fainting make a body tired, too. "I'll tuck you in and then clean up. But one more question—your kids?"

This time she didn't snap at him, just took a deep breath and said, "I hate for them to worry about me." Her tongue fussed at the chipped tooth.

He scowled and kept quiet.

"I know, I know. I need to tell them all of it. Jed knows a little. Jacob probably knows whatever Jed thinks he knows. I'll call them both tomorrow. By then I'll have discussed it with Jaime and sent on the information to Reno so I'll have something positive to report."

She grinned at him, the first in a while. "And they'll want to know about you. They've probably googled Harrison Christian McLean, MD, by now and know more about your life than you do. Maybe not, though, I don't think I told Jed your whole name. But he is a nosy one."

His heart skipped a beat. He'd never been checked out by anyone's children before. Then the absurdity of it struck him, and he chuckled.

"What?"

"Nothing really. Just odd—in the old days it was parents checking out their kids' dates, now it's topsy turvy. Hope I pass muster."

She pulled him down for a kiss. "No matter. Parents or kids, they still don't get a vote. Now come snuggle me to sleep."

With pleasure, he did.

WHEN SHE WAS SOUND ASLEEP, HE slipped out of bed and cleaned up the kitchen, then took his phone out to the lawn beneath the monkey pod tree and called Owen Johnson, DeMello's husband and his own very good friend.

"Chris," Owen answered his phone. "Where the hell are you? Quinn's been dithering around worrying about your health and your rehab and some woman. What's up?"

McLean laughed. "I'm fine. I'm in Maui with a very nice woman, and I need to pick your accountant's brain."

"Slim pickings, I'm pretty much into five-year-old logic these days, but go for it."

No questions. Just matter-of-fact acceptance. McLean felt his own worry diminish. He told his friend what he knew.

"Well, I don't know this Martin Grimes," Owen said when Chris finished, "but he sounds like he's certifiable. I can certainly check on him. The community isn't large so someone will know something. And there's a licensing board, too. Quinn has a friend, a judge in family court, so maybe she can get some information from that quarter. It's okay to tell her?"

"God, yes, we need all the help we can get."

Without commenting on the *we* that had slipped out unbidden, Owen promised to call when he had something to report. "And you'll probably hear from Quinn sooner." With that warning, the line went dead.

McLean settled himself on the grass under the tree to watch the birds and wait. Four minutes later, DeMello's ring tone alerted him.

"McLean, can't you stay out of trouble for one minute?"

He laughed. "And hello to you, too. I'm not in trouble, but Eliza is, and I want to help if I can."

There was a long silence. "Tell me about her."

"This is awkward, DeMello."

"Awkward smawkward. Tell me."

So he did, and she listened without comment as he tried to explain the Grace he'd met and the Eliza she was and where he fit in the picture.

"So you're in love with this Eliza Grace person?"

"No . . . maybe . . . damn it, yes."

"Good." Then in a TV announcer voice she said, "And have you asked your doctor if your heart is strong enough for sex?"

He cracked up. When their laughter finally turned to chuckles, he said, "It may have come up."

"I'm jealous." There was silence for a moment. "But seriously, McLean, she'd better be good enough for you. I'll be checking. And I'll talk with my judge friend. Her son's in a play group with Will. She may have some ideas of how to take care of your lady."

Before he could say thank you, she'd kissed the air and was gone.

Under the spreading branches of the monkey pod tree, while he watched the waves break and the clouds move through the sky and the mynahs stalk across the grass, he thought about the woman sleeping upstairs. Brave and foolhardy, courageous and timid, funny and sulky in fits and starts. And above all, lusty and generous. Lust or love—where does one stop and the other begin? Can a man have both?

This is more than just a roll in the hay . . . and I'm not sure I want it.

Unbidden, other issues presented themselves, making a mockery of his simple love-or-lust dichotomy: his health, precarious; his work in DC, questionable; Red Cross rescue, questionable, too; and Quinn DeMello, the woman he would have married, the one he'd thought to be his last love. Then it all faded to gray, and his mind filled with Eliza Grace—the sleeping dynamo upstairs who had him tied up in knots of love and lust, tenderness and, now, worry.

He couldn't pound Martin Grimes into dog food or sit by Eliza's door with a shotgun, but he needed to do something. What?

His mother's voice popped into his head. For some reason, she seemed close these days. "Nothing's so bad that good food won't make it better," she'd say when he was sad or mad or discouraged, or when he'd been sent home from school for hitting one of the bullies who deviled his smaller brothers, and she'd fix his favorite food.

He'd believed her, and he'd felt better. But now . . . cooking? Him who'd never cooked a meal in his life? He needed allies, too. With a half smile at the thought, he called Vivian, Owen's sister, who ran the bed and breakfast in Unionville and was almost a better cook than his mother.

No questions, no teasing, just an instant menu: "Fish is easy. Get salmon—not Atlantic farmed, Alaska wild. I'll email you the recipe. And tabouleh, it's easy. I'll send that recipe, too. And some fresh bread—there must be a local bakery. You'll be fine."

He wasn't so sure.

Quietly, he let himself back into the apartment. Finding Eliza still asleep, he left a note, made sure Vivian's recipes were in his email, and went grocery shopping.

ELIZA WAS JUST STIRRING WHEN HE slipped naked under the sheets. "Hello, sleepyhead, welcome back to the world."

She yawned and stretched and straddled him. "I thought only men wanted sex when they woke up. I was wrong."

Lust or love, right now it didn't matter. He was ready. And when she took him in, he shuddered and was glad.

CHAPTER 41
ELIZA

"Izzy, come on in." Jaime greeted her with a giant hug and pulled her into his office. Located upcountry in a two-story building not far from his home in Makawao, the unpretentious concrete exterior of Jaime Hokoana, Esq., could be anyone's, but the interior—wow.

Even today, tightly wrapped in her own woes, Eliza appreciated the dark furniture, the massive original oil on the wall, the view of island and ocean visible through wraparound windows, and knew the office, the view, the man himself would be equally comfortable in New York City or Paris or the movies.

Thank God he's here.

Jaime indicated a chair near his desk. "Sit."

Wishing she could enjoy the chair's comforts, Eliza perched on its edge, knees primly together, and smoothed the fabric of her denim skirt. If Jaime noted her nerves, he didn't comment as he settled into her chair's larger twin, clearly constructed for a man of substance.

"Okay, what's so important that it couldn't wait an hour until practice?"

She told him.

Halfway through her recitation, Jaime was on his feet.

He peeled off his bespoke suit coat and tossed it aside like a secondhand rag as he paced, gesticulated, and threw rapid-fire questions, which she struggled to answer. If Harrison's response to her story had seemed cool and contained, Jaime's reaction was volcanic. She had expected nothing less from a best friend, especially this friend who also did pro bono work for the local women's shelter and had deep feelings about men who hurt women.

Now he railed at Martin Grimes, cursed her for not telling him sooner, profaned the legal system for its tortoise-like speed, and finally sank back into the chair, sweating and breathing hard.

"Done?"

He nodded.

"Good."

Good that he is done, and good that I have told him.

Widening her eyes to keep grateful tears from falling, Eliza rose and retrieved two bottles of water from the small refrigerator hidden among the law books. She opened them and handed him one. "Here, hydrate. Just watching you makes me tired." She laid her palm on his smooth cheek. "And thanks for being angry for me."

Jaime let out a huff, then emptied the bottle in one gulp. "Sorry. I just get so mad . . . well, you know." He pulled a handkerchief from his pocket and wiped his sweaty face as Eliza curled back into her chair. "So now that I've got that out of my system, what can I do to help?"

She told him. Jaime made some additions of his own.

She refused the Glock he kept in his safe, and she refused the bodyguard services of his second cousin, Kimo. She promised she would tell her sons the whole story. With a few phone calls, he got her set up with a lawyer "who knows how to handle those shits."

When Eliza stood to leave, Jaime wrapped her in his arms and rocked them back and forth. "You be watchful, little sister, and you tell me if anything seems off. We are family, we take care of each other." He planted a kiss on the top of her head. "Now, let's go make some music."

WHEN SHE GOT HOME, HARRISON STOOD at the bottom of the stairs. In wrinkled khaki shorts, flowered shirt, and flip-flips, he looked like he belonged.

"Sorry I'm late."

"No worries, but the sun won't wait much longer." He blocked her passage. "Let's go straight out, chairs are waiting."

She really wanted to wash her face and put on something a little less smelly. Her skin and her clothes were sweat-salty after the afternoon's hot and productive practice. "Sweat equity," Jaime called it when the others complained. Right now she longed to wash it all off with her flowery soap and put on a pretty dress and arouse that certain light in Harrison's eyes.

"You're fine," he said, covering her protests with his mouth and urging her away from the stairway.

Usually amiable, tonight Harrison seemed downright surgeon-like, and she wondered what was going on as she followed him through the gate, glad that she didn't need to pee.

Their chairs were arranged in the shade with a perfect view of crowd and sunset. The sea lapped softly against the sand,

and the air hung sweet and heavy, with a breeze so gentle the kiteboarders had already packed up their equipment in disgust.

Slipping off her sandals, Eliza sank into her chair and dug her toes into the cool grass. *Hard to believe I fainted just this morning,* she thought, as her fear and the memory of Martin's words drained like water straight into the ground. She looked around. Right now it didn't matter that she was still sweaty, that her teeth needed brushing, that the man beside her was acting very strange. The sun, the sea, the man: *home.*

Harrison rummaged in a cooler she didn't remember owning and decanted a sweating wine bottle and frosty round-bottomed glasses that she was certain were also new.

"White tonight, I think," he said, ignoring her questioning look. "Chardonnay." He filled the glasses, placed one in her hand, and raised his own in salute. "Aloha."

"Aloha." She clinked the rim of her glass to his and a lovely sound issued forth. Not just new, but fine. She sipped. And the icy wine tasted better than any she'd ever tasted. *Ahh, this is nice.*

Slowly, slowly the sun descended, now partially hidden by a rogue cloud, now bright again as the cloud full of sundrenched oranges and reds and pinks poofed away. Eliza pulled up her skirt and stretched her legs to catch the cooling breeze.

The last few minutes before sunset always seemed longer than other minutes. The murmur of the watchers and the yips and yaps of the dogs grew muffled until it seemed the whole world held its breath. That sandbags-on-her-shoulders sensation slid away then, too, and she savored the wine's crisp flavor on her tongue.

Drifting in this unexpected well-being, she started to tell Harrison about her talk with Jaime, but her stomach clenched and she decided it could wait. Slipping her hand into Harrison's large one, she let that tension also slip away.

He linked their fingers. "Ahh, this is nice. Can't believe I just discovered Maui sunsets."

And me, she wanted him to add and was glad he didn't. It was a new thing to want and not want in equal measure. The sun seemed to hesitate, then slid out of sight.

No matter what, I'll have July.

Before sunset's reds and purples had faded into darkness, Harrison was on his feet. "Drink up, woman. Show's over. Time's a-wasting."

She'd barely emptied her glass before he'd plucked it from her hand and packed it away, and his kiss, when he pulled her to her feet, was definitely perfunctory.

"What's the rush?"

He just grinned and hustled her through the gate and up the stairs.

When she opened the apartment door, a new scent assailed her. Food? Something cooking? Definitely something cooking in her kitchen.

She turned to Harrison. "What's going on?"

A sheepish grin on a big man was definitely novel. "Just thought I'd try something new, being on vacation and all, as I am. Not sure how it'll turn out, but I figured you'd be brave enough to try anything once."

Taking in the diffident look, the almost shoe-scuffing stance, and his failure to meet her eyes, she was baffled, and then she knew. *He wants to do something nice for me.*

Tears sprang to her eyes.

He saw. "Don't cry. You don't have to eat it."

She laughed, peered into the oven, sniffed. "No worries. It smells delicious. And it's about time my stove got used for something besides boiling water." Her eyes twinkled and she nodded her head toward her bedroom. "But do we have time for . . ."

The stove timer dinged. His face comically sad, Harrison said, "Ah, no, dear one, dinner calls."

She pouted, then squeaked as his hand slipped under her skirt. "But perhaps enough time for a quickie."

The quickie didn't live up to its name.

He had removed the food from the oven, so their hot meal was a cold one when they finally returned to the kitchen. Humming happily, Harrison plated the salmon with its lemon mint sauce, added a generous scoop of a dish she didn't recognize. "Tabouleh," he said. "Hope you like it."

When he'd filled their glasses and sat beside her, Eliza looked at the food on her plate. She knew that even if it tasted like sawdust, it would be the nicest present anyone had ever given her, but she didn't need to fib. Each bite was wonderful.

"This is delicious. I know you meant to serve it warm and it's my fault that it's cold, but I don't think it could be any better."

Flashing the grin she'd come to treasure, he raised his glass. "Mahalo. But if I remember correctly, we were equally involved in the delay."

She clinked glasses. "Indeed."

Eliza savored a few more bites, then looked over at the man who'd gone quiet beside her, his expression inscrutable. Her appetite fled as her treacherous imagination filled in the blanks. *Worries? Secrets? Loaded questions with no good answers?* Whatever it was, she could tell he didn't want to say. She reached for her wine.

The turbulent silence lengthened until she couldn't stand it. She clinked her spoon against her glass. "Hello. Hello. Earth to Harrison."

Another beat. "Sorry, just relishing the moment."

A lie, but for now she let it rest. "Cooking?"

"I can't, I mean not really." He laughed then, and she could almost feel his return to the room, to his body, to her.

Back from wherever his troubled thoughts had taken him, Harrison refilled their glasses and launched into storytelling.

An observant man by nature, he wove in color and texture and the one-off details that turned the ordinary into the hilarious: Vivian's social media recipes and directions, his subsequent search for salmon—Alaska fresh, not Atlantic farmed—in Kihei, his mother's voice prescribing food as the remedy for all ills. Who knew that any story told with an Irish lilt would be spellbinding?

His own shopping and cooking adventures segued into tales of his cobbled-together rehab at the Wildflower Inn Bed and Breakfast and the twins who owned it. Her sides ached from laughing as he recounted some nonsense about a guest whose foot had been humped by a horny toad.

But under the laughter, her uncertainty roiled: *This is about her, the one he loves. Don't ask, don't torture yourself. It's just for July—you don't need to know.*

Eliza sipped at her third glass of wine. "The twins, they're related to the woman you mentioned? The one you're in love with?" She couldn't meet his eyes. She wanted to plug her ears and pretend she'd never spoken.

He went quiet.

Awkward, painful. "Sorry, I shouldn't have asked."

"I want you to know."

He turned her stool so she faced him. His expression was one she hadn't seen before. His delivering-bad-news-to-patients look, she thought, and steadied herself, but his voice held only confusion as he continued. "I was just figuring out how to say it so it makes sense. Most days it doesn't even make sense to me."

Curious now, more than fearful, Eliza listened.

"Her name is Quinn DeMello. She worked rescue with me at the Pentagon after 9/11." He told about the quirky, flute-playing woman who had caught his eye and gradually become an obsession; how she'd come to him after she'd broken up with her boyfriend and they'd spent a drunken weekend together; how he'd invited her to his home to work on a Red Cross project; and how he'd nursed her through the morning sickness of an unexpected pregnancy.

"By the time she left me to marry the boyfriend, I thought my heart would be broken forever."

Sometime in the recitation, Eliza had taken his hand, and he clutched hers now like a lifeline. This was not a story told so much as facts recited, brief and bald. The Irish lilt had disappeared. She felt his pain.

"So she married the other guy, Owen Johnson is his name, and had the baby. Triplets, it turned out. And for some reason, I've been part of their family ever since. At first I visited to celebrate the kids' birthday. The boy, Will, is my godson, you see. Now I go more often because they *are* family, all of them and the sisters, too. I love them, I love her, but I'm not in love with her anymore. Crazy, huh? I don't know how it happened, but it's good."

He squeezed her hand, let it go. "More answer than you wanted?" He turned his face away.

She sighed. There was certainly more to this story, but what he'd told her made sense. She understood how people got together in times of stress, especially death, kind of an affirmation of life, wondered if that was what she was doing. And this man who'd given his life to helping others wasn't very introspective. No surprise that it didn't make sense to him, especially now that she had inserted herself into his life. There really wasn't anything to say.

She laid her palm on his cheek and turned him back to face her. His eyes held tears.

"Thank you, Harrison, for telling me. It was a hard thing to do, I think, especially since you, we . . ." She waggled her hand toward the bedroom. "You know. Anyway, mahalo."

Now it's up to me. This can be awkward or not.

She made her decision, leaned forward for a kiss. "So with all this storytelling and cooking and soul-baring, do you have anything left for a dip in the pool?"

CHAPTER 42
McLean

Grateful for Eliza's matter-of-fact invitation, McLean stowed the leftovers and changed into his suit, no longer giving bare legs or flip-flops a second thought. Eliza flashed him a smile as she emerged from her room in a neon green bikini briefer than the one she'd worn on the beach. A statement? A defense? He decided for now it didn't matter as she slipped her hand into his and they stepped into the night.

He'd enjoyed the pool during the day, hadn't thought much about it otherwise. Now, visible as they descended the stairs, underwater lights showcased the blue water and emphasized the surrounding darkness. *Magical.*

Eliza unlocked the gate and they went through, mindful of the association's mandates for evening quiet. The space was theirs alone.

Her face serene, Eliza stepped out of her sandals and slid like a mermaid into water still warm from the sun. He kicked off his flip-flops and settled onto the steps, watching as her efficient strokes carried her up and down the pool's length—smooth, sensual, hypnotic. *Magical.*

He desperately wanted to know what she was thinking.

She hadn't said much in the minutes since he'd delivered his thumbnail Harrison Christian McLean history. His brain had telegraphed—*TMI, TMI*—but the message had gone unheeded in his need to tell her. Fact is, once he started, he just couldn't seem to stop. He wondered now why he hadn't said the babies were not his. A sexual relationship was obvious. And he hadn't mentioned the cardiac surgery that had saved DeMello's life.

Have I chased her away? He rubbed at his chest. *God knows I left her with questions that she hadn't asked. And doubts? Was that what I wanted? For her to send me away?* He ached with anticipated loss. Immersed in uncertainty, Chris jerked as Eliza surfaced beside him, hair dripping, eyes laughing.

"Come on in. The water's fine. And," she said conspiratorially, "we are alone."

In the dim light, her eyes teased just before she surged up and whispered in his ear, "I've never had sex in a swimming pool."

A mock laugh masked his relief.

"Oh dear, sigh, another oversight needing correction." Hands already busy, he plunged in and floated with her toward the deep end.

MORNING. HE WOKE EASILY, RISING INTO consciousness without the jolt that usually marked his days' beginnings. Cool air, whirring fan, snippets of music from the other room, an almost unrecognized sense of well-being—and the center of his chest no longer throbbed. *I could lie here forever,* he thought, savoring the rumpled sheets and the scent of plumeria and the memory of her body, soft and warm, beside him, wanting it all to last forever, knowing it could not.

Last night, after much stifled laughter and swallowed pool water, they had managed to couple. Later, wrapped in a towel and cradled in his arms as they lay on a lounge chair, she whispered, "Harrison, I hope you will understand when I tell you this. Pool sex is okay, but it just isn't my favorite." She had popped into a sitting position so she could look him in the eye. "Maybe we can try some other venues?"

Entranced by this inventive and adventurous being who had taken over his days and filled his nights, Chris had laughed and promised to see what they could do. In their lust and laughter, it had been easy to forget his worries.

Now he forced aside thoughts of the future, stretched, and got up. No word about his disclosures. Not a single question asked. Good or bad—he didn't know.

For now, shower, coffee, another day in paradise. "One day at a time." He whispered the motto of the organization he'd eschewed. By the time he needed a decision, he'd know what to do. At least he hoped he would.

Eliza stood at the bathroom door when he emerged, still damp from the shower, towel secured around his middle. She handed him a steamy mug. "Thought you'd be ready for coffee."

He bent to savor her mouth, accepted the coffee. "Thanks. How's it going out there?"

"Pretty good, I think." She followed him into the guest room and sat, cross-legged, in the center of the bed. "I've got some interesting inspiration." She waggled her eyebrows and grinned.

Shorts on, he settled down beside her. "Happy to oblige."

Her expression changed. "I talked to Jaime yesterday."

Oh God, I didn't ask. A pang of guilt—he had monopolized the evening. He caught her hand, brought it to his lips. "My bad, dear heart. Selfish and one-track mind, I could only worry about whether you'd like what I cooked. I should have asked."

Her lips curved upward and she seemed to accept his apology, no trace of yesterday's pale, frightened woman in sight. "No worries. I think you are not used to thinking about things without a calendar to remind you. Besides, I needed a break, and your wonderful food and *other things* were so delightful, I just decided to put it all aside for the evening. But I did tell him."

Remembering his own introduction to Jaime Hokoana, Chris grimaced. "And how did that go?"

Her smile tried to take over her entire face. "Needless to say, he was upset. Enraged really. You should see him when he's mad."

His face must have shown his thoughts.

"Oh, right, you have seen him mad."

He endured several minutes of wheezing laughter before she hiccupped, dried her tears, and raised up to give him a smoochy kiss.

"Sorry," she said, settling back on the bed. "You want the rest?"

Feeling like comic relief, he nodded.

"Okay. He was mad at Martin, upset that I'd been dealing with it alone, angry at the slow-motion legal system. But when he got all that out of his system, he offered me a gun, a Glock, I think he called it, and he offered me second-cousin Kimo as a bodyguard, and he got me an appointment with a lawyer who deals in this kind of thing. I see her this morning at ten."

At his unintelligible snort, she looked up. "Goodness, Harrison, you should see your face."

"A Glock?"

"Yep. A gun and a bodyguard. Guess that's what friends are for. I refused, though. Not sure how second-cousin Kimo would fit into our correction of oversights."

In a sudden move, she launched herself forward, pushing him onto his back, and the last drops of her coffee dribbled unnoticed onto the flowered spread. Huffing, he struggled to capture busy hands seeking his ticklish spots. They rolled on the bed like litter mates, tickling and nipping and forgetting the gun and the guard and the very real threat.

Giving up on her hands, he pinned her with his body. "Gotcha."

"No fair." But she plastered herself to him and began the slow, sweet undulation that was hers alone.

All's fair, he thought as he heard the sweet hum of her arousal and his body responded. *All's fair*. She made him laugh. She made him lust. And when her mouth found him, she made him tremble.

CHAPTER 43
ELIZA

ELIZA HAD DECLINED HARRISON'S OFFER OF moral support, determined to act the independent woman she wanted to be. Now her heart pounded and her steps slowed as she approached the lawyer's office, and she wished Harrison was beside her, holding her hand. Right now, she felt about twelve.

Before she could knock, the door swung open. "Eliza, aloha. Come in. I'm Anika Reyes."

Eliza gaped—Mr. Rogers in drag.

A woman of her own age, fifty-nine not twelve, Anika Reyes wore a man's brown sweater too large for her slender frame. It only partially disguised a flowery, not-quite-pressed dress with a frayed hem. A single red chopstick secured the woman's salt and pepper hair in a messy topknot that bounced precariously with each step. With difficulty, Eliza suppressed the urge to laugh and fell in behind her new attorney.

The twinkle in her eyes was the only clue that Anika Reyes recognized Eliza's struggle as she ushered her new client into an office that was the antithesis of Jaime Hokoana's: soft cushions and overstuffed chairs; a children's corner overflowing with stuffed whales and dolphins and fish of many colors; a tiny sliver of ocean just visible from the window behind a desk piled high with books and files; a framed photo of the lawyer in the same brown sweater bracketed by a smiling President Clinton and an equally smiling first lady. The room and the woman a perfect match.

By the time Ms. Reyes ("Call me Anika, if you don't mind. Ms. Reyes is my much older sister.") had settled her into a chair and placed a cup of fragrant jasmine tea in her hands, Eliza felt as though she'd been transported into the safety of Grammie King's lap.

Ms. Reyes, Anika, listened to her story. "Your phone, please," she requested when Eliza's account of events dwindled into silence. Expression opaque, eyes stony, the attorney maneuvered through the texts and emails with nimble fingers, then looked up. "Is this all?"

"I deleted the first ones . . . there were so many." Chagrined, Eliza hastened to explain. "I know I should have kept them. At first I was kind of . . . flattered. Then I thought he was just . . . sad, silly . . . . I didn't . . . should have . . ."

"Shush, shhhh." The attorney held up two fingers to dam the torrent. "You weren't to know. That's how it starts. Not *your* fault, his."

Harrison's words, Jaime's too.

Anika handed Eliza a handful of tissues.

Eliza blew her nose and dabbed her eyes.

In a matter-of-face voice, Anika asked more questions, made notes, and explained the precious few legal options. Impatient to put fear behind her, Eliza hardly listened as the woman cited studies about the psychology of stalkers and the difficulties such situations presented.

They went together to file the second restraining order.

Martin Grimes would be served in a few days. He would understand and leave her alone. Done and done: *safe.*

ELATED, ELIZA HURRIED HOME, EAGER TO share the morning's adventure, the good news: Martin Grimes wouldn't be bothering her anymore. Harrison's car was not in its usual spot. *Drat.* Where was the man when she wanted him? Inside the apartment, no man, no cryptic note defining his whereabouts. Nothing. Huh?

Alone, feeling like last week's birthday balloon, she set about cleaning house. She vacuumed, dusted, wiped down the shower, even scrubbed both toilets. Hot and sweaty, she poured passion tea into a glass full of ice cubes, collapsed into the papasan chair, and ruefully considered her actions—procrastination. She needed to call her sons. And where the heck was Harrison?

Thinking about her own foolishness, she grimaced. Harrison McLean was not hers to command. She hadn't even wanted a man. *When did I get so needy? So greedy?*

With an exaggerated sigh, she picked up the phone.

Jed snorted when she told him about Anika Reyes, took down the woman's name, and promised to check her out. Otherwise his response was much the same as it had been the previous week, with the addition of a few terse comments about the benefits of following his advice and a repeated invitation to move closer. She thanked him and declined.

Jacob was in tears before she finished her story. "Of course, I knew what was happening, Mom. Jed gave me several earfuls. Scary, scary bad. I left messages, but you didn't call me back. Now I'm hearing your voice, and I can tell you're dealing with things. I was so worried, and I wanted to come help, but Raul keeps reminding me that you can handle anything." He hiccupped a sob. "I know it, but still."

She reassured him as best she could, glad that one of her sons thought she could do something right. Then Raul took the phone.

"Mamacita, I told this worrywart you could handle anything. And see, I was right. But about this man, this Harrison person, I did Google him, and I think you should keep him."

She burst into laughter. A moment later, Jacob giggled and Raul hooted, and the call devolved into a babble of who should visit whom and when, especially now that her location was as desirable as theirs. She was smiling and her heart felt lighter when they said goodbye.

For a long time after the call ended, Eliza remained as she was, curled up in her favorite chair, phone clutched to her chest. Outside, the sun floated high in the sky, and gigantic waves dived toward the shore. She had told her boys everything, and the earth still turned on its axis. Who knew?

Harrison's steps on the stairs roused her. Still smiling, she jumped up and met him at the door. "Guess what, guess what, guess what," she said before he could utter a word. "I just talked to the boys, and you are now officially a keeper."

After they'd properly celebrated his new official status, she lay beside her man and answered his questions. Yes, she'd liked the attorney and they had filed a restraining order. No, Jed hadn't sent out people from the funny farm to take her into protective custody. Yes, Jacob and Raul had really Googled H. Christian McLean and found him to be quite satisfactory.

"What did they say about your new name?"

Uh-oh. She made a face. "Didn't quite get around to that."

Before he could comment, she rolled over and started to get up. "And where were you this morning?"

He grinned and pulled her back against his sweaty chest. "Okay, you get to change the subject. I'll have my answer later. And where was I?" He kissed her hair. "I was out arranging an after-snorkeling repast."

Life just kept getting better and better. They gathered up their things and went to Baby Beach for his initiation into the fine art of snorkeling.

DAYS LATER, AFTER A SECOND EXPEDITION to a deeper venue, Harrison dropped to the sand beside her with a sigh that held no worries.

Chilled from their hour in the sea, Eliza linked her fingers with his, relaxed into the heat of the sand, and sighed her own deep sigh. There had been one text, a terse, "Grace, you have made a terrible mistake," and then no more, and it was easy to let Martin Grimes slither away. No more worries for her either; she would enjoy the days she'd been given.

Side by side, they let the island work its magic.

"Did you like it today," she asked, "the snorkeling, the fish?"

"I did, especially the turtle that was almost as big as I am. But that eel . . . it *was* a bit unnerving when it glared at me and I had nowhere to run."

She giggled. "I don't think they like the taste of people, but I know what you mean."

He was quiet then, and she thought he'd dozed off. He didn't nap much anymore, and it was easy to forget that he was still . . . still what? Not fully recovered? She rolled over and propped herself on her forearms. Just looking at him—the big body brown from the sun, the scar on his chest almost hidden now by the mat of sandy curls—took her breath away. Sturdy, strong, safe, and oh, so sexy. Leonard Cohen's words said it all, and whether Harrison knew it yet or not, his broken places had let the light in.

Tears gathered behind her eyes. She wasn't sure how it had happened, but Harrison McLean had become as essential as the air she breathed, almost as essential as the island where they lay.

"What?"

She started. "Huh?"

"You were staring."

She blinked hard. "Just thinking what a hunk you are."

His chest rumbled, his chuckle deep.

Tears put away for later, she ran a playful finger down his side and then sat up to face him. "Not to change the subject, but . . . remember I told you about Makawao's Fourth of July celebration?"

"Uh-huh." He raised one lazy eyelid. "Cowboys and cows and you root for the cows. Of course I remember."

Oh, yes, their first day together. Her cheeks were immediately warmer than the sun. "Well, tomorrow's the parade. I think we should go."

THE PANIOLO PARADE WAS ALL THAT it should be: Hawaiian cowboys, known as *paniolos*, on their gussied-up horses, miles of old cars, and marching bands and music and people, all happy to celebrate America. They munched street food, sat on the curb and sucked on shave ice, and then went to the rodeo where even Harrison rooted for the cows.

At the end of day, they helped the sun set from Eliza's favorite spot, the lawn outside her apartment. Darkness settled, and fireworks sparkled in the distance. From somewhere behind them came the sound of music. She recognized "Lady in Red"—not a song she sang but one she admired.

Her heart fluttered when Harrison stood and held out his hand. "May I have this dance?"

No ballroom, no dance floor, no fancy dress nor dancing shoes. What might have seemed corny was not, and when she took his hand and he moved them smoothly over the grass, she was a woman in the arms of the man she loved.

AND SO, WITH LOVE IN HER heart and uncertainty in her future, Eliza settled into a routine: she worked late into the night or early in the morning and then slept while Harrison instituted the long walks he had been prescribed and had neglected; she rehearsed with the band three days a week, and on those days, he cooked their dinner; they swam at a different beach every afternoon; they made love at every opportunity.

Eliza put thoughts of the other woman out of her mind. "It's like being jealous of a ghost," she told Rosie one day before practice. "Nothing to be gained, so I'm not going to dwell on it."

When Rosie asked, "What happens next?" Eliza shrugged. "Not dwelling on that either."

Neither statement was quite true, and, without her permission, July inched toward August.

Some mornings when she woke early with wisps of new music in her head, Harrison was already up and on the phone, and she knew the time difference made his East Coast connections difficult. Both fear and passion colored his voice when he talked about his work. Certain of his dedication and his talent, her heart ached. She knew just as certainly that he could not walk away from it.

Their lovemaking was fierce one day, gentle enough to bring tears another, and true to his word, Harrison continued to correct oversights. She could now claim to have had sex in the back seat of a car, on several beaches, in a national park, and in the crater of a volcano, but she liked it best when they lay together in her bed and she could forget that August was fast approaching.

Then Jaime called. "Willy K cancelled. Fourth Friday is ours again if we want it."

Of course, they wanted it.

As though it were written in the stars, she knew this, too—in one week, while Harrison was still by her side—Eliza K and the Hawaiian Cowboys would give him "In His Arms."

Chapter 44
McLean

Before Eliza pocketed her phone and leaned toward him, quivering with excitement, McLean heard it in her voice—something momentous. He turned toward the sunset, sudden pain a serrated knife in his chest. *This is it. This is how it ends.*

Twenty-nine days in paradise. He'd rediscovered his child-self with Eliza. They'd laughed and explored and played in the salty sea.

Most surprising: No black dog, no craving.

They'd spent two days enjoying Makawao's Fourth of July rodeo—three hundred fifty cowboys riding bulls, roping cows, swaggering in the way of cowboys everywhere—where Eliza, as promised, rooted for the cows. Then they sat on the curb as old cars and homemade floats and horses and bands and a woman in a long pink dress riding sidesaddle passed by in the Paniolo Parade. That evening, when he held her lightly in his arms and danced her across the grass, his mouth formed, "I love you," but the words did not emerge. He loved her then, but tomorrow?

Those twenty-nine days had passed so slowly it had seemed that they might go on forever. While she worked, he cooked and walked and read and found satisfaction in those activities, but he could not ignore the siren call of his OR. Occasionally, as Eliza swam her laps and he stretched like a lion in the shade, he would notice his fingers, of their own volition, practicing the complicated motions of his craft. At those times, he would count the little brown birds that scoured the sand around him until the longing passed.

One day, with a whir of feathers and wings, the small brown birds scattered and a bird with a bright red crown dropped into their midst. The Hawaiian cardinal—for surely this was the haughty bird Eliza had described—strutted and preened while the smaller birds hovered like supplicants. *That would be me. Top dog, king of the roost, ruler of all he surveys. But how can I be different? Less? Dear God, who would I be?*

Then, at the sight of Eliza rising from the sea like a water sprite, his heart sang, and the unflattering portrait disappeared.

Eliza Grace. He slept every night with her curled into his body, and he woke every morning to her scent and her music. In his waking fantasy, he was healthy and competent, and Eliza Grace was with him in Georgetown.

Twenty-nine days in paradise. He'd come to believe it didn't have to end.

He blinked away the dream. *Pay attention, fool.*

"Oh my goodness, Harrison," Eliza was saying, "you'll never believe this." Her hand splayed open against her chest as though she needed to hold herself together. "That was Jaime. They want us to play Fourth Friday. In Kihei. Again. This Friday. No one ever performs twice in one year. Willy K was supposed to play and something came up, and Jaime thinks there might be an agent on island."

Running her words together, bouncing up and down, sloshing her wine. His heart hurt.

Sunset on the lawn. He'd poured them each a glass of the Chardonnay she liked, ready to invite her to his home, into his real life. She was lover and companion. He could no longer imagine his life alone.

"This might be it, our big chance." She tugged him to his feet and crooned "big chance, big chance" as she danced him around in the thin shade of the palm tree he'd come to regard as theirs.

He scooped her up and swung her around like a child, his body demonstrating an enthusiasm his heart lacked. "That's fantastic, incredible, wonderful. Next stop, CW Music Awards." He knew how to pretend, and he did so now.

He would not ask her to choose.

LATER THAT NIGHT, AFTER ALL THE details had been discussed and plans for the rest of the week formulated, McLean stood in the doorway of the bedroom they shared and watched her. Asleep, she sprawled over more than her half of the bed—her small self gorgeous, sexy, vulnerable. Tenderness crept over him, as though she were a child whose heart beat in his hand; then crashing loneliness almost dropped him to his knees.

God, I'll miss her.

He thought about the devastating weeks and months after DeMello had left him. *Good that I'm not really in love*, he consoled himself, half knowing it for a lie, but he couldn't survive another heartbreak.

Surrendering to her gravitational pull, he climbed into bed, and in her sleep Eliza turned to him. His arms went around her and tears filled his eyes. Five days until Fourth Friday, then four more before he went home.

Nine days. He would make them the best nine days of their lives.

Time passed unnoticed as the band ramped up its rehearsal time, and McLean applied his newly discovered cooking skills to preparing food for musicians who might otherwise forget to eat. Days earlier, he'd discovered Pacific Fish Market, located near the airport, where pompano and ahi and scores of fish he'd never heard of rested in gigantic, ice-filled white coolers that filled the store. Having also discovered YouTube, he could now cook just about anything.

Last night it had been a chowder; tonight, for a change, an Irish stew. To celebrate the unprecedented Fourth Friday performance, he planned a seafood extravaganza. He hadn't eaten this much fish since the church had dispensed with the no-meat-on-Friday rule. Rosie had even promised poi, though he himself didn't see that as a treat.

Whenever he struggled into Jaime's garage, laden with hot pots and pulling a cooler, the band would take a break, devour whatever he brought, and then let him remain for the rest of their practice. A couple times when he entered unannounced, they stopped in the middle of something they had been working on and didn't pick it up again, and he wondered what that was about. Then they'd go back to work, and he'd forget to ask.

While he was there, he listened.

Jaime's voice was deep and full, and the duets he and Eliza sang were achingly beautiful. Drum and bass solos rocked the oversized garage. Eliza strutted and sang, and he could see her confidence grow. They were good, and he knew she was better than good.

On Thursday, he was packing up the remnants of the night's meal when Jaime touched his arm. "Walk with me," he said. "We need to talk."

McLean glanced around. Eliza and Derek had their heads together. Rick was adjusting his drums. No one noticed as Jaime motioned toward the front of the house.

The men walked around the corner. "What's up?"

"Eliza says you are leaving soon?"

McLean nodded. "August one. My sick leave's up."

"She's in love with you, you know."

"She said that?"

Jaime scowled as though McLean were deranged. "No, but I know her."

In an instant, the night seemed darker. After several beats of silence, McLean nodded. "Maybe she thinks she is. I'm the first person she's been with since—"

"Her husband." Jaime's voice held contempt. "I know. That man was a jerk who didn't appreciate his wife. If you don't know that, you're stupid in spite of your fancy degrees and your fat Google page. She may be afraid. I'm sure you were unexpected. But I know love when I see it."

"She's making a new life for herself, and she's damn good at it." McLean was not going to mention his own equivocal emotions. "It's not right to ask her to choose."

"Choose?" The big man looked confused. "I don't get you, man."

"My life is in Washington, DC. I was going to ask her to come with me until this new opportunity arose. Her life is here. I can't ask her to leave it all. Besides, we don't know one another well enough to make decisions like that." Spoken aloud, the reasons did sound lame.

Jaime rolled his eyes with an impatient huff. "Don't make up her mind for her. Don't disrespect her like that. If her heart is broken, so be it, but not her spirit. If there is a choice to be made, it is her right to make it for herself."

He looked like he wanted to say more. Then he held out his hand. "Remember, man, she's family."

McLean shook his hand then watched Jaime walk back to the group, pick up his guitar, and strum the notes that called the others back to practice.

I handled that badly, he thought as he loaded up the car. *Jaime's right. Saturday we'll talk.*

Chapter 45
Eliza

It was long after midnight when Eliza climbed into bed, exhausted and exhilarated. Too wired to sleep after their final rehearsal, she'd been working on a Celine Dion song. Her voice wasn't Celine's, but maybe she could do "Tell Him" and the guys would let her know if it didn't work. She chuckled softly. You bet they'd let her know.

Maybe she'd even follow Celine's advice and tell Harrison that the sun and moon really did rise in his eyes. Shoot, maybe she'd just say, "Harrison, I love you," and see what he made of that tidbit.

A sad little cloud rose. He couldn't stay, of course, and of course she really didn't want him to, but . . . maybe it would bring him back, once in a while.

Saturday. Her heart skipped a beat. *I'll tell him Saturday.*

She snuggled into Harrison's sleeping body and smiled to herself as he grew hard even before his snoring stopped and his lips sought her mouth. Knowing each kiss, each touch, each crescendo they shared was a little miracle, Eliza sighed and rocked her body against his, gently at first, then with increasing demand until his exploring mouth found her nipple, and the first orgasm ripped her.

Then the demand was his as he thrust deep inside, faster, harder, until nothing existed but the man who rode her. He took her up, held her at the peak. Just when she thought she couldn't stand it any longer, he pushed her even higher, and they fell together, *I love you* her only thought.

She woke Friday morning, stretched, smiled. *Ahhh, luxury—no practice, no worries, just a long, lazy day to savor and Fourth Friday tonight.* Outside her window, the *k-kio, k-kio* of the birds echoed her joy.

Humming "in his arms, resting in his arms," she climbed out of bed. On the other side of the door a delicious man waited— she tingled in anticipation—and tonight he would hear the song she had written for him.

As she left the bathroom, she heard Harrison speaking. Someone in the house? She scrambled into her clothes. Telephone? Indistinct words, but the urgency in his voice spurred her toward the kitchen.

Half on, half off the bar stool, phone clenched in his hand. "I need the earliest you have. No, that won't work." Taut, commanding, a surgeon's voice. "Look harder."

She approached. Harrison slipped an arm around her, drew her close, and mouthed "in a minute" while he waited.

A woman's voice came on the line. Eliza couldn't decipher the words, but when Harrison's arm tightened, she glanced up and saw his frown.

"If that's the best you can come up with," he said, "it'll have to do. Book it, please." He did not sound pleased.

Eliza's heart staggered. *Book it? Not good.* Struggling with a rising panic, she kissed his bare shoulder, then left the safety of his embrace and went to pour coffee. Clearly, they would need it.

He was staring at the silent phone when she returned and put the mug in his hand. "Here. You look like you could use this."

Harrison set the mug on the counter and enclosed her in his arms. "This is bad, dear heart," he mumbled. "Not how I planned, not what I . . ." More words, unintelligible, lost as he buried his face in her hair.

She pulled back. "Dear man, I know something's wrong, but I can't understand what you're saying."

"Sorry." He straightened his shoulders, a man used to delivering bad news. "Eliza Grace, I have to go home today."

Her stomach dropped, her world darkened, and she sank onto the stool beside him. Hands shaky, she pushed his coffee mug toward him and picked up her own, and she managed to keep her voice steady. "Tell me," she said.

He told her about the newborn, brother to a girl whose heart he had repaired three years earlier. "Big hole, congenital defect. Someone else could fix it. Elaine Meyers, my colleague and the most talented surgeon I ever trained, has tiny hands and may end up doing the job."

He looked at his own big hands, his expression so uncertain that her heart crumbled.

"I'm not even sure I can do it, you know, but they trust me and want me there anyway, so I need to go. Every minute makes it harder for the little guy." His eyes were ice, unreadable, as they met hers. "I'm almost packed. My plane leaves at one."

One o'clock. Seven now. Not enough hours to last a lifetime.

Not sure she could speak, Eliza straightened her own shoulders and took his hand. "Then let's make the most of the time we have," she whispered and led him back to bed.

They loved furiously, then gently, and when she climaxed her throat was full of tears.

He shifted his weight and pulled her tight against him. "Don't cry, dear heart. I have to go. I know this isn't what we planned, but—"

"Don't say it, don't you say it, Harrison McLean. I know we had July. It's just not enough. I thought it would be. I don't want it to be true, but it is. I didn't ask for this, and now I have to find a place to put it so it doesn't hurt so darn much."

"Come with me. We could be together in DC."

Filled with surprise and gratitude, she snuggled closer, drenching herself with his scent and his strength and his sweat for the last time. Her voice felt thick with tears. "Oh, you tempt me. But you know that can't happen. My life is here. Yours is there." One shuddering breath, then another. "Just know this is one of the best things that's ever happened to me, and I will thank you for this time every day of my life. Now kiss me and go shower or you'll be late for your ride."

CHAPTER 46
McLean

H IS PHONE VIBRATING IN THE DARK had awakened him from an erotic dream and plunged him deep into reality. Dr. Elaine Meyers herself had made the call. Compassion in her voice, she told him about the child and about the parents' request. She of all people could understand his dilemma. Decision time: a *no* would effectively end his career; a *yes* would take him away from Eliza, from Maui, before he was ready. Even as he parsed his options, he knew he would go. They needed him, impaired or no, and that was enough.

His invitation to Eliza was not the Saturday conversation he had intended. "Come with me," he'd said.

"You know that can't happen," she'd replied, and it was done. Their lovemaking had been exquisite, agonizing, too brief.

Now H. Christian McLean, MD, stood in line, boarding pass in hand. The warm and humid Maui air caressed his skin like the soft, sad hand of a rejected lover as he waited to board the plane that would take him to the mainland and, ultimately, to Washington Dulles and his old life.

Was that what he wanted? What the fuck did he want?

He knew he was stronger, healthier. How could he not be with a rehab that had included walking on sandy beaches, snorkeling with turtles and eels, and making love with the most wonderful woman he'd ever known? His belt was cinched in so far he needed another new one. His mind was clear. His hands were steady.

He'd been talking with his colleagues, with the hospital administrator, with the GW faculty coordinator for days, trying to figure things out. They wanted him back, apparently unconcerned about the evaluation scheduled for August sixth. Elaine would scrub in with him a few times and that would be that.

He'd created the pediatric surgery protocols almost single-handedly, yet he wondered himself if he were still competent. In Mexico City, Nita Juarez had encouraged him; in their bed, Eliza had challenged him—did he have the courage to face failure? What did he want? What could he do? He'd thought he would know when the time came. Turned out he was wrong.

And he'd just received a text message from Owen Johnson: Grimes is clean, no priors, no history, just gossip about his first wife leaving Reno in a hurry. Relief—at least he didn't have to worry for Eliza's safety.

He refused to think about Eliza as he'd last seen her, waving and whispering *au hui ho*—until we meet again—as tears coursed down her cheeks, just before he turned left out of the Waipuilani parking lot and she was lost to sight.

He knew he was better. But his heart held a pain worse than any he'd ever known, and he knew this one was irreparable. There had been no other possible ending.

Trailing a carry-on stuffed with flowered shirts and leafy swim trunks and a month's worth of hopes and dreams, Harrison Christian McLean handed over his boarding pass and strode down the ramp to the waiting plane.

Chapter 47
Eliza

"*Au hui ho. Au hui ho.*" Eliza whispered the words, knowing in her heart they would never meet again.

She waved long after his car vanished onto South Kihei Street. Then, like an old, old woman, she shuffled home. No birdsong, no breeze ruffling the palms, and if anyone witnessed her despair, she didn't notice. Tears flowed unchecked as she dragged herself up the stairs and crawled back into bed.

Sobbing. Kicking. Pounding pillows. Harrison's scent—soap and man and sex—lingered, and she wallowed in it until, exhausted, she dropped into sleep. She woke at one. By sheer force of will, she blocked the image of his plane rising into the sky.

Get up. Make the bed. Life goes on. She held her breath as she wrestled sheets that still held his essence into the washing machine and turned the water on hot.

It was good and now it is over. You knew this would happen. There had been no other possible ending.

Then she turned and saw the magnet: "Go confidently in

the direction of your dreams!" it said. Thoreau's words. "Live the life you've imagined."

She ripped it from the fridge door. With all the strength she could muster, she threw it onto the floor and stamped on it with both feet. How dare he go away and just leave this . . . this *thing*.

The black letters under her feet mocked her, so she snatched up the white square and buried it in the garbage beneath the coffee grounds, but she could still envision Harrison's big hand placing the words of hope where she might see them.

I want him, not this fucking magnet.

She sank to the floor, unable to stem another flood of tears. *I want him, I want him, I want him.* Rocking, crying as a pile of wet paper towels grew beside her, but finally the sobs turned into hiccups and the tears dried up, and she blew her nose until she could breathe again.

"I want him and I can't have him and that's all there is to that." She spoke aloud, as though hearing the words might make them true. "In a few days, when my heart pieces itself back together, I'll appreciate the time we had. For now, there's a performance tonight, and maybe an agent, and isn't that what this is all about?"

Shaking her head—*no, no, no*—Eliza retrieved Harrison's gift. With fingers as gentle as if they were touching the man himself, she smoothed away wet coffee grounds and round black papaya seeds, and, when it was again pristine, she tucked the little thing deep in her saving drawer. *Someday this will remind me of him and I'll smile. Just not today.*

Holding that thought, she put on her bathing suit, drove to her favorite beach, and threw herself into the water.

She emerged beyond the crashing surf and swam until her arms ached and her body shook. On the way in, she misjudged a wave and got tumbled twice before she could regain her balance and inch onto the beach.

Crap, crap, crap. My heart's broke and my butt's full of sand.

She repeated the words, searching for a laugh. Finding none, she stood under the cold spray of the beach shower and rinsed off as best she could, then climbed into Gretchen and went home to get ready.

At six-thirty, clad in a swirling white skirt and a bright red blouse, she walked the mile to the Azeka Shopping Center and Fourth Friday. In a few terse words, she brought the guys up to date, told them she was fine, and started tuning h.er guitar.

She didn't miss the look—three men trying to decide what to do with her.

Rick patted her back.

Derek dropped a shy kiss in the vicinity of her cheek.

Jaime grabbed her arm and pulled her aside. "I know you're not 'fine,' and I know you'll be okay, but are we still doing the song?"

A smile hovered—the first genuine smile of this very sad day—and she nodded. "You bet. He'll never know what he missed."

When it was their turn, she was on. Once again, the white folding chairs were full. In front of the flatbed trailer that was the stage, all manner of people danced and clapped and sang along. If she teared up a little with "Angel of the Morning," no one seemed to mind, and they laughed with her when the band played several renditions of "Love's Been a Little Bit Hard on Me." Even the audience could tell something was going on.

Then it was time. Rick muted his drums. Derek's bass took on a softness. Jaime stepped forward and, in Eliza's mind, the noise of the crowd faded. "Ladies and gentlemen," he said, "we give you something new."

She stood at the microphone, head down, arms at her sides.

Jaime strummed the intro, the men hummed the refrain,

then Jaime's guitar and Rick's drums went quiet, and, as Derek's bass set the rhythm, Eliza raised her head and smiled. In a voice low and slow she began:

> There are days when I am weary
> And I can't get out of bed.
> And I doubt that I will ever
> Have the strength to rise again.

She looked out on her audience, rapt and silent, and knew they'd all had days like that. They swayed as she went on:

> Without words of blame or comfort
> He offers me his hand
> And I go into his big arms
> Until I am strong again.

With her, Jaime's baritone and Derek's sweet tenor sang the first refrain: "Resting in the arms, resting in the arms, resting in the arms of a big man."

Alone, Eliza continued:

> There are days when I am fearful
> And I cannot find my way
> And I cower in the darkness
> Afraid to face the day.

> Without false praise or censure
> he offers me his hand
> And I go into his big arms
> Until I am brave again.

Humming, singing, the audience joined in: "Safe in the arms, safe in the arms, safe in the arms of a big man."

Energized by the crowd, the words, and her own voice, and almost overcome with the love she felt, Eliza sang as though Harrison could hear.

Two more verses, then the last. Derek played, then Rick—touching the skins so gently that tears filled her eyes—then Jaime strummed. Eliza stepped to the front of the stage, raised her arms to the sky, and let her voice soar:

There are days when I am joyful
And I know just how to fly
So I raise my voice in praise and song
And I can touch the sky.

Without words to keep me earthbound
He offers me his hand
And releases me from his big arms
Knowing I'll come home again.

She stood still as the music died and tears streamed down her cheeks. Silence reigned. When she bowed her head, the audience roared and rose en masse. *Hana hou! Hana hou!* Encore, do it again.

Arm in arm, Eliza, Jaime, Rick, and Derek repeated the chorus a cappella: "Resting in the arms, safe in the arms, rocking in the arms," and then, as though singing to the heavens, "home in the arms of a big man."

When the last words faded, even as the applause continued, Jaime hugged her, the guys took a bow, and it was done.

FLAT DAYS FOLLOWED, DAYS WITHOUT SUNRISE or sunset, days whose beginnings and endings coalesced into a litany of misery. Time marked only by the changing voices of the birds.

Eliza ached for him. She missed the rumble that was his laugh. She missed the hands that wrapped hers so firmly. She missed his comments on anything and everything. Most of all she missed loving him.

Someday I'll be whole again, she thought, *but for now, I'll just spare the world my misery*, and she took to her bed. She slept as long as she could, curtains pulled closed to shut out the light, and she cried when she reached for him in her sleep and found only emptiness. She turned off her phone.

She knew Jaime and Rosie would worry, but she couldn't bear to talk about him, and she couldn't bear to talk about anything else. When sleep refused her, she wrote, and then she tore up the songs that echoed her sadness. She kept only one:

My heart is breaking
What words can I say?
My arms clasp tight,
Gently
Keeping my pieces from flying into space
until the glue of time sets
and I emerge, reconfigured.

One week, she bargained. *I'll give myself a week, then I'll be better.*

On the Thursday following Harrison's departure, a *bang-bang-bang* on her front door jerked Eliza from sleep. She pulled a pillow over her head, but the noise continued, louder, more insistent. Afraid the door would splinter, she dragged herself out of bed and went to open it.

Jaime Hokoana stood there, fist raised to strike again.

"Jaime, what?"

He burst in as though afraid she'd slam the door in his face. "Lizzy, what the hell's wrong with you? You don't answer your phone. Your voice mail is full. Nobody's seen you in a week, and we thought you might be dead." His gaze swept her disheveled state. "Jesus, Liz, you look like shit."

"Sorry, sorry." Her eyes filled with tears.

A big man faced with a woman's tears, he warded off her words. "No worries. No worries. You're just a mess, and I can fix that." He picked her up, carried her into her bathroom, and deposited her in the shower. "Wash your hair, get clean, then get out here. There's amazing stuff happening."

She was still spluttering excuses and apologies when he turned the water on.

By the time she joined him in the kitchen, clean and smelling of plumeria, Jaime had the coffee going and a papaya cut and ready for her, and she felt almost whole again. "Jaime, I am truly sorry. I didn't mean to worry anyone. I gave myself a week to wallow so I turned off the phone." She shut up, confused. Her best friend was fiddling with something in his hand and not paying any attention.

Suddenly her voice rang out from what appeared to be a phone: "resting in the arms of—"

Her mouth dropped open. "That's me? Us? What?"

He held the device so she could see.

There she was, in her white skirt and red blouse, hair all wild and curly, singing away like her life depended on it. The Azeka Shopping Center sign was just visible to her right, and the guys behind her. Then small-screen Jaime stepped to her side, and they sang the refrain.

"That's us!"

"YouTube. Somebody videoed us Friday night and posted it and it's gone viral." He sounded like a little kid who'd finally gotten his Christmas pony. "We've had so many hits I can't read the number, and at least four agents want to talk to us. Even that jerk who said he wasn't on island."

Jaime hit play again, and their music filled the apartment. "It's a miracle, little sister, and it's your song that's made it happen."

Eliza stared at the short clip, mostly the four of them singing the first refrain, and felt as though she'd stepped into an alternate universe.

Jaime kept talking. "Four clips in all. The best is when you sang the last verse alone—you know, arms up like you could touch the sky."

She remembered, watched in amazement as he played that one.

"You should turn on your phone. You probably have messages from everyone you've ever known, and a whole bunch you've never heard of." He laughed at her as she dug in her bag, found her phone, and brought it to life.

"You're right." She watched the messages populate the screen: Jed, Jacob, Raul, her sister Florence in Vermont who only talked to her on her birthday, the boys again and then again, names she didn't recognize and didn't know how they'd found her phone number, her neighbor Jackie from down the street in Reno. Then her breath caught—Martin Grimes, a single word in the subject line: "soon."

Jaime heard the gasp. "What?"

She showed him the message: "Soon my love we'll be together forever."

"Batshit crazy." Scowling, Jaime tapped numbers into his phone, spoke to someone. "Just alerted the sheriff. His office will contact Reno, just in case. You keep your door locked." He flashed a grin. "Sure you won't reconsider the Glock and second-cousin Kimo? Too fucking bad that man of yours isn't here."

It was too bad. She'd felt safe with him here, unfair and unreasonable as that might be. Now she was on her own, by her own choice. Eliza drank her coffee, looked at messages until her heart rate returned to normal. She'd seen the worry in Jaime's eyes, but it would be all right. Martin was just a lonely man who was obsessed with the idea of love. She could relate to that.

They finished the breakfast Jaime had made.

"No gun and no bodyguard," she told him, "but I'll keep my door locked. If we have a meeting with an agent at noon, I've got to make myself presentable. But first, I've got to call my boys. Go now, I'll see you at noon."

She shooed him out the door, locked the screen door as promised. Then, armed with fresh coffee and apprehension, she called her sons.

All my secrets revealed.

It went better than expected if she didn't count the number of apologies and explanations required. Jed, predictably, wanted to know why she hadn't told him and then berated her until she interrupted. "Jed, enough. This is just why I didn't tell you."

He subsided with a grudging, "Dad would be proud," before he hung up.

His words elicited a sad smile. *I don't think so, my son. More like, "Grace Dart, whatever were you thinking to make such a spectacle of yourself?"*

She shook her head. *No. That was then, and this is now.* Easier to believe when she heard the words of praise from her younger son. Jacob and Raul double-teamed her, talking non-stop, so loud that she held her phone away from her ear and laughed as their excitement filled her world.

"Gosh, Mamacita," Raul said after they had calmed to a normal volume, "I didn't even know you could carry a tune, let alone write one."

Jacob cut him off. "Oh, I knew she could sing. My question is, what happens next?"

Eliza had no answer. She promised to let them know when she knew and basked some more in their praise. Then they were gone, she was alone, and Harrison hadn't called.

The pain of unshed tears clawed the back of her throat. She tried to focus on something else, anything else, but the pain took over, moving into her jaw and her face as the tears followed their inescapable path, pooling in her eyes as she stood paralyzed, until one tipped over the edge and fell.

CHAPTER 48
MCLEAN

CHRIS MCLEAN SAT AT HIS DESK. His white coat hung on the back of his closed office door, and the business of the university hospital rustled just outside. He reached for a half-empty bottle of Tums, shook out a few, and tossed them into his mouth. As though he'd never been away, the hospital life had closed seamlessly around him. He'd been home exactly a week.

The surgery on Baby Aguilar, Ramon, had been successful, and the infant would grow up strong and healthy with his sister, Maria, and his older brothers, Juan and Michael.

Job well done, Chris thought as he stared at the papers littering his desk. *Well done by Dr. Myers.* His protégé had surpassed her mentor, more skillful now than he'd been at his peak. Hard to be glad and sad at the same time, but that's the way it was. He'd heard all about "time to pass the torch" but had never considered that it might someday apply to him.

He reached for his phone, fingers itching to punch in the 808 number as familiar as his own. He'd called her after the surgery, not even sure why—to change her mind? Change his?—but her phone was turned off, and he didn't leave a message. What was the use? Each day, the same, then suddenly her voice mail was full. Now, receiver to his ear, dial tone inviting, he paused. Her life continued without him, and isn't that what he wanted?

But he hadn't known how much he would miss her, laughing, loving, holding her hand as they helped the sun set. With a sigh, he hung up the phone, pushed it away. No more calls. What was the point? Nothing had changed. What would he say? And hearing her voice would break his heart. Better to let her get on with her life while he struggled for some way to continue his own.

Rap-rap. Rap-rap.

Before he could speak, the door swung open to disclose a skeletal frame and a smiling face. Roused from morbid thinking, Chris stood to welcome his own mentor. "Jackson, come in. I thought you were out of the country."

Jackson Coombs, MD, FACS, had taught him how to hold a tiny heart, how to listen to its story, where to make the cut or place the stitch that would make it whole.

"Home just a day or two, Chris." The older man pushed the door closed behind him and lowered his stooped body into a chair opposite McLean. The creases of his summer linen slacks broke sharply over boney knees. "I heard you were back. Sorry I missed all your drama."

They laughed together, heart doctors and heart attacks an ironic mix.

Dr. Coombs accepted coffee from a pot on McLean's desk, settled back into the chair as though he might stay the night. The men exchanged pleasantries, then a little gossip that trailed into a not-quite-comfortable silence, and Chris realized this was more than a social call.

This man had taught him everything, encouraged him to teach and learn, and reveled when his prize student surpassed the teacher. Eighty-four years old now and still brilliant, Coombs wrote and taught an occasional seminar and traveled the world with Belle, his wife of fifty-five years. Eleven years earlier, for reasons not stated, he'd given up his surgical practice. Until this moment, Chris had never questioned. Now he braced himself for what his mentor would say.

Coombs's voice rasped away the silence. "Chris, you never asked why I stopped scrubbing in. No one did, and I wondered why. Guess oldies are always held in a little too much awe. But that's not my point. Boy, I quit the day I opened a chest and worried that I might fall in dead and contaminate that tiny body."

McLean sat up straighter, closed the mouth that had dropped open.

"Surprised you a bit, boy? Shocked even? Thought it couldn't happen? Me too, until that day when Lady Death looked me in the face and I knew those little ones deserved better. Lucky for me, you were better. I just needed to stay out of your way."

Before McLean could react, Coombs stood and was at the door. He leaned on his cane and waited until Chris reached his side, then took the younger man's hand and smiled up into his face. His faded blue eyes held humor and compassion and a hint of sympathy. "Just thought you should know is all. Now I'm off to take my bride to dinner."

McLean stood in the doorway and stared after the old man until he limped around the corner and was lost to view. Then he returned to his desk, slumped into his chair, and closed his eyes. Surgery had been his first love, one to which he'd given his all. And rescue work, almost as important. His life decisions were his own, but they had all felt organic, requiring only hard work and determination, not this gut-wrenching process. *What to do? How to know?*

In minutes, paperwork unattended, lights off, Chris locked his office door and left the hospital.

August was not the District's finest month. Stifling heat hung in the air, cooling only if rain pelted down to make things even muggier, and the familiar, tree-lined sidewalks provided no answers as McLean made his way from GWU to his Foggy Bottom townhouse. Detouring to sit at Abe Lincoln's feet was vetoed—he wasn't sure he could bear the answers old Abe might provide.

Feet dragging, McLean climbed the stairs and opened his heavy front door. Emptiness echoed. Once inside, he clicked on CBS for the ten o'clock news and relief from the haunting silence. In his bedroom, no scent of plumeria, no birdsong, only a king-sized bed mocking with its emptiness. A piece of crumpled staff paper rescued from a trouser pocket lay on his nightstand, Eliza's squiggles and music notes faded and the paper worn from his touch. The Tommy Bahama shirts hung in the back of the closet with his hopes and dreams.

What to do? What the hell!

Feigning ambivalence, he strolled into the kitchen. Arms braced on the refrigerator door, he stared at the photo collage mounted there: Eliza smiling as the ocean spray broke behind her; Eliza rising like Venus from the waves; Eliza walking away from him, deep footprints following her in the sand; Eliza smiling, laughing, talking, singing. Eliza. He drank her in, then closed his eyes, replaying in memory every moment of their time together. Front and center was his favorite, an image held only in his heart: beloved face, smoky eyes, lips curved into a smile of secrets and love as they rose together to the peak.

With a sigh almost a sob, he turned away, and, from the depths of the liquor cabinet, he unearthed the Maker's Mark. Allowing no time to consider his action, he poured three fingers of the amber liquid into a squat crystal glass, and, clothed in defeat, wandered back into the living room—once comfortable, a warm and accepting space where a man could sit and enjoy his spirits and his thoughts. Now sterile, rejecting—a surgical suite with no patient, a home with no heart, just right for this husk of a man. Chris McLean settled into the leather chair that had endured his weight for more than twenty years, sipped his liquid comfort, and mourned his loss.

The television droned in the background.

He was in the kitchen refilling his glass a third time when he heard her voice. His heart stuttered.

Eliza sang, "knowing I'll come home again."

He rushed to the living room. On the television screen, a radiant Eliza, white skirt swirling, rioting curls framing her face, raised her arms to the sky. Her voice soared as the clip replayed. Then she was gone, and the news anchor was raving about this newest YouTube sensation.

Heart pounding, thoughts ajumble, Chris stumbled into his chair and sat while the program moved on to other breaking news. He'd known, really known, from the first time she'd placed her neat hand over his. He'd spent all this time denying what was not to be denied. He loved her. He could be the best of himself when he was with her.

So why the fuck am I sitting here like a bump on a log?

He shook his head and the room came back into focus. All the obstacles were only pebbles in a shoe, not the mountains he had made them. When the late-night host was well into his monologue, Chris stood, emptied his glass and then the bottle down the drain, and picked up his phone.

CHAPTER 49
ELIZA

IN HER ORANGE WRAP, HAIR STILL damp from a morning swim, Eliza sat on her divan, strumming and thinking. Too much, too fast.

Three agents wanted to sign them. Willie's people, the ones who'd bought her first song, were sniffing around. The guys were, in Jaime's words, "in hog heaven."

Her own mood traveled from elation to despair and back so quickly she could hardly locate her sensible self. Jacob and Raul checked up on her every day, and she could even manage a laugh as they outlined the ways they could help spend her newfound millions. Mondays and Wednesdays were harder, but she showered and washed her hair and lugged herself to practice, pretending that everything was back to normal. She cried into her pillow each night.

Nothing from Harrison, and she'd be darned if she'd call him. He had left her after all. Besides, what would be the point? Nothing had changed.

The Prophet, left behind in his packing haste, had a permanent place beside her pillow. Each night she held it and read about children, and marriage, and giving, and if tears obscured Kahlil Gibran's words about love, she would stroke the leather worn smooth by Harrison's hands and pretend. She missed him with an ache that was physical, had not realized how much she valued his permission to touch until it had been revoked.

Good days and bad days. On the bad ones, when she had no strength to get out of bed, when her papaya tasted like dirt in her mouth, she would lock both her doors and huddle in the dark. On the good ones, when light streamed into her bedroom and the air seemed full of promise, she strummed her guitar, hummed new tunes, and escaped to the beach. Work kept her grounded. The ocean supported her grief.

Some days were bad, more and more passably good, a few outstanding. So far, today promised to be one of the good ones.

Permission to touch. Good idea for a new song? Hmmm. Maybe.

Harrison had granted it when her Grace-self had dropped that first chaste kiss on his sad and lonely cheek. And she'd invited his touch just as simply. Who knew? They certainly had not, or at least she hadn't. Now even her skin yearned.

If that's not enough pathos for a good love song, I don't know what is.

She'd just jotted a promising verse when the doorbell rang. *Huh?* No one rang the bell. They knocked or helloed or just walked right in.

"Come on in," she called out before she remembered the screen door was locked and looked up.

Martin Grimes stood at the door.

"Martin?" Her voice caught, and she reached for her phone. Not there. Charging. In the bedroom. *Oh God.* She wrapped her arms around the guitar as though it could provide protection. "Martin, what are you doing here?"

"Hello, Grace. You sent your message, you knew I'd come." Soft. Calm. Soothing.

Fear's ice tickled her back.

"Batshit crazy," Jaime had called him. Now she knew he was right.

With an effort, Eliza steadied her voice and chose her words with care. "I'm working, Martin. I'm sorry you've come so far, but I can't visit right now."

"Enough, Grace. No more games. We both know we are meant to be together. I saw the Azeka sign, God's message, your message, telling me you were ready. There will be no more delay. I've come to take you home." With each word his voice grew shriller.

Do something, fool, before he walks right through the screen.

Shaking inside, Eliza slid off the divan, and the cold tile under her bare feet steadied her. She waited until her legs felt solid enough to support her and started toward the door. "I'm sorry, Martin, I didn't realize you felt so strongly. Wait a minute. I'll let you in, and we can talk."

She'd almost reached the door when his eyes changed. Just as he wrenched the screen from its hinges, she slammed the inner door, threw the bolt, and raced for her phone.

"Lizzie! Lizzie!" Jaime's shout rose over the sirens' scream, and she was sobbing in his arms before the police stomped up the stairs to her broken door. A perfunctory knock and a deep voice announced, "Maui Police, Officers Lim and Bailey."

Face buried in his chest, Eliza felt Jaime motion them inside.

"Kimo will be hanging with you for a bit," Jaime whispered into her ear as her sobs subsided into hiccups. Still tight in his arms, Eliza nodded, no arguments left.

He set her out of his safe embrace. "Go get dressed and then you can tell us what happened."

At his words, she realized she wore only the orange wrapper. Her cheeks flamed and she ran for her room.

In the shower, she scrubbed at the dirty feeling that clung like sand from a tumbling wave. He hadn't touched her, but he'd invaded her space.

Violated. She felt violated.

She'd heard other women use that word. As she lathered up for the third time, she understood and ordered herself to stop. All the soap in the world wouldn't wash him away, and it wouldn't help him either. She rinsed, turned off the scalding water, and got dressed.

Jaime had brewed a pot of coffee, and the three men had mugs in their hands when Eliza, armored in jeans and a faded Nevada Wolf Pack sweatshirt, returned to the living room. The officers stood and introduced themselves again, asked how she was.

"I'm fine," she said, knowing she was not.

"He's gone," Jaime said, answering the question she hadn't asked. He handed her a mug of steaming coffee. "Here."

Glad to have something for her shaking hands to do, Eliza accepted the mug, slopped coffee down her front as she turned to the officers who still stood at her counter, waiting as though they had all the time in the world. In their sharply creased, dark blue uniforms and gleaming Maui County Police badges, they exuded safety, but she didn't feel it.

"I'm sorry. I know you have questions." She willed her voice not to quiver, her tears not to fall. "Sorry you had to wait so long." She walked past them, curled into the papasan chair, and tucked her bare feet under her. "Sit, please. Ask away. I'll tell you what I can."

The men again identified themselves. Officer Bailey pulled a notebook from his breast pocket and sat, and, for a minute, she thought the sofa might give way. The other man, Officer Lim, tall and slender, took a knee beside her. At eye level, she could meet his gaze, and she was grateful that he wasn't hovering above her barking questions she couldn't answer, her only previous experience being late-night police drama reruns. Lim's eyes smiled. *He knows what I'm thinking*, she thought. *I like him.*

His voice gentle, Lim asked his questions, and silent Bailey jotted down her answers. Finally Lim stood. "I think that's all, Ms. King. Thank you. Someone will be keeping an eye on things here until that man is apprehended. We will keep you informed." He shook her hand, shook Jaime's. At the door, he turned back. "I really enjoyed your Fourth Friday concert. That angel song is my wife's favorite, and she made me dance to it." Lim inclined his head toward Eliza. "Thank you." Then they were gone.

She stared after them until a man in boxers and bedhead peeked around the wreckage of her screen door. "You all right?"

"Am now."

"Good." Curiosity apparently satisfied, the man disappeared.

"You have strange neighbors, little sister," Jaime commented as he refilled her coffee mug.

A little smile. "No argument from me." Jaime didn't smile back.

Her insides still felt like Jell-o as she stood and walked to Jaime's side. One hand on his arm, she said, "Thank you, my best friend, for the most awesome rescue a woman could desire. And you ordered up really nice policemen to interrogate me. All in all, that wasn't so bad, but now it's time to get on with things."

At that, he laughed and wrapped her in his arms.

Finally, she extricated herself from the hug and got on with things. Kitchen tidied, she settled in with her phone, now charged and ready in her pocket, and made arrangements for the installation of a safety screen. Mission accomplished, she poured the last of the coffee, slopping only a few drops, then stared out her window at the ocean and willed Eliza back as Jaime worked his cell phone and waited for second-cousin Kimo to arrive.

She jumped as a house-sized man strode past her shattered screen and thumped Jaime on the back. When he turned toward her, she shrank away, unaware that she held the mug like a weapon until he plucked it from her hand. Face of a cherub, physique of a sumo wrestler, voice soft as a whisper, the giant said, "Hello, Eliza K, I am second-cousin Kimo, and while I am here, you won't be needing this."

Eliza believed him. Weak with relief and furious at her need, she forced a smile.

As though sensing her feelings, Kimo smiled back. "You take good care of yourself, little sister, but I would be honored to assist, just for a little while. Besides, I make better coffee than my cousin."

For the first time that awful morning, Eliza laughed. She pointed him toward the guest room that had never been used. "You're on, second-cousin Kimo. Settle in and we'll see if you fit in Gretchen."

By evening, Kimo had established himself as chauffeur extraordinaire, and Martin Grimes had been apprehended.

"They found him at the airport and took him in," Jaime told her from night court, "but since the only real charges against him were violation of the restraining order and breaking an old screen door, they let him go on his own recognizance and his promise to leave the island. An officer is waiting with him at the airport. His flight leaves at midnight."

"Thank God." Eliza heaved a sigh, only partly theatrical. "But do I have to give up Kimo?"

Jaime chuckled, and she felt his worry dissipate. "Not yet, little sister. He has to stay a bit longer. His girlfriend kicked him out for flirting with a beautiful haole, and it always takes at least two days to talk his way back into her good graces."

Relieved, Eliza paced her apartment and thought about second-cousin Kimo channel-surfing on her couch, about Jaime in his lawyer suit holding forth before some judge, even about Harrison, who'd poured her coffee and cooked her meals.

Huh. Big men. She paced some more. *I'm surrounded by big men and they all want to take care of me.* Finally she poured herself a glass of water, perched on a stool, and stared into the darkness.

She thought for a long time and felt fear in her throat like a permanent lodger, then hopped off the stool and grabbed her bag. *Not today. Some days a girl has to take care of herself.*

"Headed out, Kimo." She crossed to the door, her voice shakier than she liked.

He looked up. "Out, little sister?"

"Yep, to the airport to straighten out that sad little man." She grinned at his look of surprise. "You wanna ride shotgun?"

Chapter 50
McLean

Pale summer light filtered through a crack in the heavy drapery when Chris McLean woke. His dream—a white sandy beach at sunset, a couple hand in hand, his own self just ready to whisper, "I love you"—vanished like smoke into the shrill of his alarm.

Now, no birdsong. No crashing ocean. No warm hand in his. No chance to say the words in his heart. One fist pressed tight against the anguish in his chest, he grabbed his phone and punched in the eight-zero-eight number. Before his feet were on the floor, the mechanized voice he'd come to despise informed him once again that Eliza King's mailbox was full.

Dratted woman, did she never check her messages?

Cursing Eliza's mailbox and her known propensity to keep her phone turned off, then cursing phones and the universe in general, McLean drank his black coffee and fiddled with his own new iPhone until he located the YouTube video and Eliza's voice filled his sun-drenched kitchen. He ate his cereal and read the morning paper wrapped in her voice. Then he dug sturdy shoes out from the depths of his closet and stepped out into Georgetown's late summer heat. He didn't yet have a plan, but he needed to be ready.

That morning and the mornings that followed, he walked, and he thought, and he ached for Eliza.

What do I want?

The familiar tree-lined streets still returned no answer.

I want my old life back.

Again no comment from the trees, but he knew what they'd say. His old life was just that—old, gone, done, *fini*. In fact, there was no old life to retrieve, just this new one where his heart had failed, his mind and spirit questioned, and his body yearned.

I miss her.

It was true—he missed pulling her small form against him even before he was fully awake, falling asleep with her curled beside him, loving her with his body and his heart—love and lust. But more: her hand in his as they helped the sun set; her head cocked to one side like a little bird as she listened to him blather on; her fierce concentration as she worked; her kisses soothing his damaged chest. Ahh yes, he missed her.

And he missed the easy camaraderie with Jaime and the guys, too. He missed fixing dinners, walking on the beach, driving upcountry with Gretchen's top down and the wind threatening his hat. Big surprise, he wasn't at all missing the stress of rescue work or the adrenalin flow of his OR.

What do I want?

He wanted to talk things over with Jackson Coombs, now that the old dickens had once again appointed himself role model, but Dr. Coombs had taken his bride off on an Alaska cruise and wasn't available for consultation. DeMello would listen, but somehow it seemed a little off to discuss Eliza with his former lover, no matter that she'd see the humor in it.

So he walked and he thought. He hadn't resumed his surgical practice, so at work he consulted and rounded, even taught
a seminar class. Going through the motions, he knew, his heart
no longer engaged, but no one complained. And he consulted
his financial advisor, his banker, and his personal physician. On
Friday, one week after Coombs's surprise visit and six days of
Eliza's voice filling his every waking hour, McLean called Gen,
the ex-wife who had become his friend.

"Genevieve McLean, Maplewood Stables."

"Gen, it's me. Do you have a little time to give me good advice?"

She snorted. "When did you ever take my advice? But yes,
just not today. Do you want to come up or shall I call you back?"

He'd already cleared his schedule. They arranged to meet
the following day. McLean hunted for his old duffel before he
remembered it had taken its last trip in a San Francisco garbage
truck, then packed the new rolling one instead. At five o'clock
on Saturday, he wound up the long lane to his former home
in Connecticut.

Tall and lean, Genevieve McLean stood on the wide front
porch and watched his approach.

No fool like an old fool. McLean set the parking brake and
climbed out of the Jeep.

Gen hurried down the steps, hands extended in greeting.
She took his, looked him up and down, and wrapped her
arms around him, and he relaxed into her welcoming warmth.
They held each other for a long minute before she stepped
back and looked again. "My goodness, Chris, you've gotten
downright trim."

He laughed. "Hello to you, too, dearest one. You look won-
derfully happy. Thanks for letting me come."

"Of course. Can't wait to hear what advice the great Dr.
McLean needs from me."

"Ouch."

"Sorry, turning over a new leaf tomorrow. Hope you brought your bag, you'll stay the night."

Without waiting for his assent, she laughed, slung an arm around his waist, and walked her ex-husband into the house they had shared a very long time ago. Visible through the great room's wall of windows, the green meadow, the paddocks, and the grazing horses created a peaceful backdrop.

She offered scotch. He asked for water.

Eyebrow raised, no other comment, Genevieve filled her own stemmed crystal and brought his water before she settled at the end of the scarred leather sofa that faced the windows and the world she'd created.

McLean sank into the armchair that had long ago replaced his battered one, downed half a glass of water, and contemplated the woman he'd loved and married when all things had still seemed possible. They'd been separated for years, but only divorced after he'd proposed to DeMello in the early days post-9/11. She was a successful horsewoman, a canny business owner, and, once their divorce was final, a trusted friend. She did have a sharp tongue, however, and didn't let him forget the sins of his past.

"Okay, Chris, spill it. You're moving to Tahiti with the newest Miss America? You've discovered the cure for cancer? You're dying and you want me to tell the girls?"

He took a deep breath. "I'm thinking about retiring."

That shut her up. He grinned. "Close your mouth, dearest, you'll catch flies."

"Chris McLean, retire?"

He talked for an hour.

"So let me be sure I understand," she said when he finished. "You're afraid you'll no longer be the great cardiac surgeon H.

Christian McLean, MD; you're afraid that you won't be able to keep up with the rescue crowd; you're afraid that you'll make a fatal mistake and some mother's child will die; you're afraid that you'll die alone and lonely as Miss Havisham in your moldy Georgetown mansion. Is that about right?"

He grimaced. "Sounds pretty egoistic, grandiose even, when you put it like that."

She snorted. "Of course it is, but that's the deal. It *is* about you and what you want in your life. You're thinking about it for a change instead of just rushing into action half-cocked and probably half-snockered."

"Ouch again."

Her turn to smile. "All that's missing is the woman." A statement, not a question.

Heat rose up his neck.

"Aha. I knew it. I need to know that part, too, if I'm to give good advice." She waggled one finger at him. "No details though. Even at this late date, I do not need details."

His clenched fists rested on his thighs and for a moment took all his attention.

His ex-wife sipped her wine and waited.

"Her name's Eliza King."

Genevieve sputtered. "God, Chris, not *that* Eliza? Eliza K, YouTube diva?"

His head jerked up. "You've seen her?"

"Of course. Most of the civilized world has seen her. She's the nine-day wonder of the nightly news. She just doesn't seem your type."

A rumble deep in his chest, laughter or protest unclear.

"Sorry," she said. "Tell me."

He did.

Genevieve McLean was quiet for a long time.

Chris shifted in the suddenly uncomfortable chair. He drained his water glass, waited, crossed one knee over the other, fiddled with the empty glass while Gen stared out the window behind him and said nothing.

Maybe this hadn't been such a good idea after all.

He readjusted his butt and searched inwardly for patience. When that failed, he stood and poured himself some more water, refilled Gen's wine glass. Still she sat silent.

He stared out the window, and the pastoral scene blurred before his suddenly damp eyes. "Gen? Just tell me I'm a crazy old man and get it over with."

"Hush, Chris, that's a lot to dump on somebody all at once." She picked up her glass, seemed surprised to find it full. "I'm thinking. Go. Be busy. Find us something to eat."

McLean surged to his feet and strode into the kitchen. At least his hands would have something to do. The big room gleamed with efficiency and appliances he didn't recognize, but he did know a refrigerator when he saw one, even a giant economy-sized one, so he opened the door, rummaged around, and found enough to make a meal.

The salad was ready, and he'd just dumped shrimp into the garlic butter bubbling on the stove when Genevieve wandered in and sniffed the air. "Scampi? You can cook? My goodness, Dr. M, you really are in the throes of a remake." She patted his shoulder. "One thing for sure, you can still surprise me. Shall I toss the salad? Then we can eat while I tell you what I think."

They sat on her patio while citronella candles battled the mosquitoes and fireflies danced in the grass, and she spoke her mind.

"First of all, I don't think you need advice. I think you know what to do. So consider this just a push in the right direction." She sipped her wine, bit into a garlicky shrimp, and sighed.

"This is really good. If you can learn to cook like this, you can do anything."

He didn't know what to say, so he gulped his water, and he pushed his food around his plate the way he'd seen DeMello do when nerves took over, and he waited for the advice that he'd requested but now wasn't sure he wanted.

"Sorry, I digress." Gen put down her fork and reached out to cover his hand with her own. "Chris, you're not just a guy with a knife and a pretty face. You're a surgeon, and a brilliant one. You can always use those skills, any time, any place. Or," she bit into another shrimp and purred, "you can become a chef."

He managed a weak smile, not quite ready to laugh.

"Sorry. Probably even Maui can use another physician. And I know you've got enough put aside that you don't even need to work. Some people really retire and don't work at all. Just a thought."

He considered her words, nothing new but confirming. He couldn't just do nothing, he knew, but maybe the next step was discovering what something he wanted to do. And he already knew Maui could use another doctor.

"So now to the crux of the matter—the woman. Did she write that song she's singing?"

"I guess."

Gen's brow furrowed. "Did she write it for you?"

He stared at her. "For me? Why would she do that?"

"Close your mouth, dearest, you'll catch flies." She chuckled as she repeated his earlier admonition. "But oh my goodness, Chris, for a smart man you can be very stupid. Did you not listen to the words?"

Of course. Her words had filled his head and his heart for days. It just hadn't occurred to him. "Do you think?"

"I do. And if that's true, you'd better snatch her up before she changes her mind."

They finished the meal in silence, McLean deep in thought, his ex-wife chuckling and helping herself to the last of the shrimp.

DISHES DONE, THEY HEADED DOWN THE hall to the bedroom wing. McLean stepped into the guest room and was starting to close the door when Gen called his name. She sounded hesitant. He turned toward her.

"Dianne's fortieth is next week," she said.

Their oldest daughter, Dianne, had entered the world on one of the most demanding nights of his general surgery residency. She now lived with a husband and two sons in upstate New York. He knew all that. Her sister, Stephanie, two years younger, lived just up the lane and worked the farm with her mother.

"I know."

He remembered so well it hurt. Gen had called when her labor started, and he'd promised to try and get there. But he couldn't leave the operating room, so, while the attending cursed his big hands, he prayed for a quick delivery, and he cried at the news of his daughter's birth. His absence that night had created the first schism in their marriage and carved the first lines on Gen's smooth forehead.

Saying he was sorry one more time would do no more good now that it had then.

"I know," he repeated.

Her brow furrowed again and her eyes focused on his left shoulder, and he recognized her old *thinking hard* look. Wondering if she should speak her mind? Not like his Gen.

Her shoulders moved in a what-the-hell shrug. "The girls love you, you know. They've just adjusted to the fact that everything else comes first."

She held up a hand to ward off his protest, but he remained silent. She was right.

"It's up to you if you want that to change, but it would be a great start if you showed up for her party. Randy, you do remember her husband, Randy?"

She waited for his nod. "He and Steph are planning a surprise."

Emotions flitted across her face, the familiar defensiveness and a new, softer sadness. McLean sagged with his own loss and the distance he had created. Was it too late to make changes?

"You'll get an invitation. Just be there." She turned abruptly and disappeared into her bedroom.

McLean stepped back into the guest room and closed the door. In the dark, he thought about Gen's words, the ones about his daughters, the ones about Eliza, and the ones he understood but which hadn't been spoken. He thought as he undressed and climbed into the bed that was too big for this room and that he knew had been purchased with his large body in mind. Sleep was elusive, so he lay in the dark and thought some more until, finally, inner arguments depleted, he listened to his own heart.

In the morning, decisions made, he drove away before the household roused. The note he left said simply, "Mahalo, thank you."

CHAPTER 51
ELIZA

WHEN JAIME CALLED THE NEXT MORNING, he was furious. "What were you thinking? There's a restraining order, for God's sake. That means you can't get close to him either. Why, Lizzie? I don't get it."

Eliza made a face. Her brave charade had been for naught; Martin had already been escorted upstairs and all her pleading didn't get her close. So much for taking care of herself. Now she had to endure Jaime's thunder and brimstone. No, wait . . . she didn't.

"Jaime, just stop!"

He did.

Surprise. "I appreciate that you all want to protect me, and goodness knows you're all bigger than me, but I had to try and take care of things myself."

After a lot of rumbling and huffing and then a long silence, Jaime said, "Okay, I kind of get it. Rosie always tells me I'm too protective. 'Bossy,' she calls it." He waited while Eliza laughed. "You did what you needed to do and it didn't hurt anything."

She appreciated that he didn't add, "Didn't help either," although she knew it hadn't.

He went on. "And now I've got some good news, if you want to hear it. With your approval, we have a gig in Las Vegas. Rick and Derek are on board, already packing. What do you say?"

The *gig*, he told her, would be at a Station Casino managed by his brother-in-law, Matt, filling in for the regular band whose lead singer was in bed with a fever of one hundred and four and laryngitis. On doctor's orders, she couldn't sing for a week, maybe longer.

"We'll start day after tomorrow. Aloha Air cut us a good deal, native sons that we are. We can stay with Matt and my sister, Linda, and . . . drum roll . . . we'll get paid."

She didn't have to feign enthusiasm. Vegas, performing, dollars—a no-brainer. "That's terrific, Jaime. Really great. But can you leave your work, Rosie, the kids?"

Unlike the rest of them, Jaime had a real day job and responsibilities.

He didn't hesitate. "For this, I can. Thank God for Rosie; she gets it."

Eliza sucked in a big breath. This was what they'd been working toward, a chance for their music to find a wider audience. And, for her, there was another bright spot. In Las Vegas there would be no Martin polluting her days, no Harrison haunting her nights. Las Vegas would be new, and, when the gig was over, she could return and her apartment would again feel like home.

She smiled at the thought, didn't share it. "I'm in. Believe it or not, I've never been to Vegas."

"Really? Hawaiians love Vegas."

"So I will, too. Do we get top billing?"

His anger was gone and she could almost hear his grin. "We get the only billing."

So that was that, and four days later, wishing for a nap but settling for a Diet Coke and a twenty-minute break, Eliza tucked herself into a corner booth at the Palace Station in Las Vegas, Nevada.

Three days earlier, tired and cross, Eliza K and the Hawaiian Cowboys had arrived on a red-eye flight. They had dumped their stuff at the brother-in-law's and, loaded into a casino van with brother-in-law Matt as host and tour guide, trundled off to their first mainland appearance.

Apparently, the venue began life as The Casino in 1976, became the Bingo Palace in 1977, and in 1984, with a grand opening attended by then-governor Richard Bryan, transformed itself into The Palace Station Hotel and Casino. It targeted locals with giveaways, cheap buffets, and bingo. As Matt segued into Las Vegas history, she glazed over and didn't remember any more.

Tonight the noise level in the casino reached ear-splitting levels. The air was rank with cigarette smoke, and her feet hurt. Out of sight of the patrons, Eliza pulled off her right boot and spread her toes. *Ahh . . . better.* Whoever invented cowboy boots should take lessons from the flip-flop makers.

On the stage, the guys fiddled with equipment still not quite to their liking. On night three of the five-night gig they'd signed on for, she was already homesick. Born and raised in Carson City, she'd never been to Las Vegas, her father believing that Oregon and California were better venues for their infrequent family vacations. Turns out, he'd been right.

Both nights they'd played to a full house, with the audience—no tourist garb in evidence—half listening and half involved in their own lives. She had already decided there'd be no more casinos for this girl. But the whole room went quiet when they did "In His Arms." Vicariously soaking up YouTube celebrity? Odd. Really, just the oddest thing.

Eliza sipped her soda and wished she knew what Harrison was doing.

A woman approached her table. Thin, tall, with aqua-blue eyes and a hesitant smile. Levi's and a tank top branded her as local. "My name's Quinn DeMello," she said.

Uh-oh. Harrison's lover.

Eliza's heart pounded like Rick's drums, and she could hardly breathe. *What is she doing here?*

"Can we talk?" Quinn DeMello's hand rested on the back of the booth. She didn't look like she would take no for an answer.

Besides, schooled in polite behavior, Eliza really had no choice. She scooted over to make room and held out her hand. "Of course. My name's Eliza—"

Quinn laughed as she accepted Eliza's handshake. "I know. Eliza Grace."

Eliza froze. He'd talked about her. "You know me?"

"Barely. McLean's so smitten he can hardly say your name without getting all googly." The strange eyes twinkled. The voice was kind. "So I thought I'd better check you out, just in case you were—"

Eliza's turn to laugh. "A serial killer or a scam artist? I did that, too." She looked the other woman up and down, felt a little small and insignificant, and sucked air. "As you can see, I'm here and Harrison is not, so your visit is unnecessary, but go ahead. What can I say?"

Quinn looked thoughtful for a moment. "Nah, McLean has good taste in women. You're fine."

Eliza cocked her head, chewed her lower lip. "And you know that how? Not that it matters."

"Fair question. I was here last night, too. Came down after the five o'clock news. The news anchor called this," her voice deepened, took on a self-important note, "the next step for the newest YouTube sensation.'"

Quinn laughed at her own attempted impersonation, continued, "Anyway, I wanted to see for myself. Watched you in action, watched you sing that song." She made a face. "Wish I could do that. Now let me tell you some things you might not know about McLean."

Tension whooshed away. Whatever this inquisition was about, at least the woman wasn't yelling at her. If she just weren't so darned attractive. But Eliza King didn't need Quinn DeMello, attractive or not, to tell her one single thing.

From the stage, Jaime riffed their reminder. Eliza wiggled to the other side of the booth, realized she still had a red boot in her hand. So much for classy exits.

She shoved her foot into the boot and stood. "Gotta go," she said. "It's been nice."

Quinn stood too. "Can I buy you breakfast tomorrow?"

Looking up at the taller woman, Eliza consigned curiosity to the devil and straightened her spine. "I don't think so, Ms. DeMello. Whatever is between Harrison and me is our business, and, quite frankly, it would be awkward discussing it with you."

Quinn's laughter followed her onto the stage.

CHAPTER 52
McLean

I T TOOK TOO MANY DAYS TO set things in order.

Dianne's birthday arrived, and McLean stood at the door of his daughter's summer home. His son-in-law shook his hand with courtesy if not warmth. What did he expect? Of all people, Randy knew the damage of McLean's absence.

"Honey," Randy called into the backyard melee, "Dianne, another guest."

A statuesque blond woman looked up. Tall like her parents, with the wide shoulders and slender build of a water athlete, Dianne McLean turned toward the door.

Even from a distance, McLean could see her blink, blink again as though her eyes might deceive. "Daddy?" She glanced at her husband, then back at her father, and then launched herself across the grass and into McLean's arms.

Forgiven, whether he deserved it or not.

His preteen grandsons warmed enough to show him their dock, their small sailing craft, and, finally, the medals they'd won at the summer events.

His younger daughter watched from a distance. She'd greeted him so politely no one watching would know they were related, then slipped away without conversation. Again, what did he expect? But when he said his goodbyes, Stephanie hooked her arm through his and gave it a squeeze. "Good that you came, Dad. It means a lot to Di." Before he could respond, she squeezed his arm again and hurried into the house.

A start, more than he'd earned. He smiled as Gen slipped her arm around his waist and walked him to his car. "A good start," she said, echoing his thoughts, and hope was in his heart as he drove the long road home.

Before and after the party, he negotiated with the hospital administrators. By the time talking was done, he wasn't sure if they were reluctant or relieved as they sent him off to Human Resources to fill out the paperwork for retirement and the new adjunct status. He offered to clear out his office. They refused, as he'd been sure they would, assuring him that his place with George Washington University and its hospital was secure. He knew he'd be back, just not sure how or when. Through it all, the planning, the talking, the packing, the leaving, he searched inside for any sign that his decisions were unsound. Finding none, he locked his office door, pocketed the key, and left the campus where he'd lived his professional life.

Without a backward glance, he drove home and parked in his seldom-used garage. White coat over one arm, backpack on the opposite shoulder, briefcase in hand, he scanned the Jeep and the garage, then stepped into the late afternoon sunshine and pulled down the door. All good—his work, his home, the occasional roll in the hay with a compatible and willing companion—all good, but now he knew there could be more.

At last he was ready.

"Vacation?" the driver asked as he hefted McLean's bags into the trunk of a black stretch limo.

In the vehicle's window, McLean saw himself reflected—pressed khakis and Tommy Bahama shirt, grin permanently in place—obviously mistaken for a tourist. His smile widened as he climbed in and settled back against the worn leather seats for the long ride to Washington Dulles International Airport.

"Nope," he said, "headed home."

He arrived on island midday. All efficiency—gathering up his bags, renting a car, driving off to find the woman at whose side he would spend the rest of his life. Not one minute to waste.

On the second floor of the Waipuilani Apartments, a sturdy new screen door confronted him. Locked. The doorbell chimed. Unanswered.

A man wearing boxers, scowl, and bedhead stepped out of the adjacent apartment. "Lookin' for Eliza?"

"Yes, I am. Do you know—"

"She's gone, don't know where." Eliza's neighbor gestured toward the screen. "Had some trouble here. Lots of banging and crashing. Sirens even. Woke me out of a dead sleep." He scratched at his head, fingers trying to penetrate the hair mass. He seemed to have nothing more to say.

"And then?" Sweat trickled under McLean's shirt; icy fingers traced his spine.

"Oh, yeah." The man gave up on his head and started on his chest. "Sorry, not thinkin' too good. I work nights and you woke me up. Just like that other guy did."

McLean gritted his teeth, barely listening to the man's words. "Eliza?"

He peered at McLean, seemed to recognize the bigger man's distress, that or his own imminent danger, and he stepped back, face screwed up in concentration. "Eliza. Yeah. Great neighbor, music puts me to sleep."

McLean's fists clenched; another minute and this buffoon would be in his grasp.

"Doors crashed, slammed. Then that big guy, the guitar guy, pounded up the stairs, and police cars showed up, lights and sirens. Then the cops asked me questions and went away, and she put up that new ironclad door, and then she just wasn't there anymore. She's just gone, man. Sorry." He disappeared back into his own apartment and firmly closed the door, leaving McLean with panic rising and Eliza Grace missing.

He called Jaime Hokoana's office. Gone. Sorry, nobody knows nothing. He knew they were lying, but what could he do. The apartment manager was another dead end.

He got back in his car and brooded as the August sun beat down on visitor parking. What had happened? Where was she? She was not a figment of his imagination; she couldn't just vanish.

Deep breath, McLean, calm down. Women don't just disappear.

But he knew they did, and air couldn't find enough space in his chest.

Eventually his thoughts cleared and his heart steadied, and he drove upcountry to Makawao. His car was idling in front of the Hokoana home, and he'd checked the hospital and all the police stations by the time Rosie Hokoana pulled in with her truckload of kids.

Three small children jumped out and dispersed down the street. McLean stepped from his car.

"Homework," Rosie shouted, and the Hokoana twins waggled little fingers at him behind their mother's back before they were shooed into the house. Rosie was smiling, but her eyes held caution as she crossed the driveway to greet him. "Aloha, Harrison, good to see you."

Before he could ask his questions, she said, "But what are you doing here? Eliza and the guys are in Las Vegas, and I'm not sure when they're coming home."

"Huh?" Like air from punctured balloons, breath whooshed from his lungs. Without air, he could only squeak. "Las Vegas?"

"You didn't know? Didn't you call her?"

Another squeak. "Tried." He sucked in a breath and started over. "Of course I called, more than once, in fact." His voice was back and, with it, his frustration. "And when I tried to leave a message, voice mail was full. I didn't want to wait."

He'd been so excited, so anxious to hold her. And now this.

His confidence wavered, and he could imagine Gen's snort. "Again, Chris? Assumptions? When will you ever learn?"

Rosie looked up at him. "You thought she'd just be sitting around waiting for you?"

"No. Yes. No." Chris shook his head, but in fact that was just what he'd thought. He kicked one of the truck's tires. "What the fuck is a man supposed to do?"

Rosie raised an eyebrow and patted his arm, her expression not very sympathetic; in fact, wariness had been replaced with poorly suppressed mirth. "Just keep trying, I guess," she choked out. "Do you need a place to hang?"

Deflated, he shook his head. This was not going the way he'd planned.

Next morning, Chris McLean sat in the Maui Beach Hotel's coffee shop watching the tall palms bend in the wind, the waves crash on the rocks, the steam rise from his coffee—anything to keep despair at a distance. Even this early, people swarmed the beach like ants. He closed his eyes and imagined himself alone on that pristine stretch of sand.

Only me and the woman of my dreams.

In his mind's eye, he and Eliza strolled in the surf, laughing as they scurried up the packed sand just ahead of a ruffled wave.

Eliza Grace King, not at all the woman of my dreams, he thought, and yet she was. And until he'd found her gone, he hadn't realized how much he'd taken her welcome for granted. He scowled into his coffee, sure that all the gods were laughing.

Nene had greeted him like a long-lost friend, kept his coffee mug full, and plied him with enthusiastic details. Apparently all of Maui was following the rise of Eliza K and the Hawaiian Cowboys.

He'd just booked tonight's red eye to Las Vegas, Nevada— what else could he do?—when his phone rang.

Eliza.

With fingers suddenly shaky, he punched talk. "Goddammit, Eliza Grace, why don't you hold still so I can find you?"

She giggled. "Didn't your mother teach you how to answer a phone, Harrison Christian? Hello would be nice."

He sagged back in his chair and let out the breath he'd been holding.

"Hey, are you still there? Rosie told Jaime you were looking for me."

"I'm in Maui. Did she tell you that?" Angry, ill-used, more relieved that he wanted to admit, he growled out the words. "And what the hell are you doing in Vegas?"

Bitterness crept in, frosted her answer. "Thanks for asking. And thanks for all your calls and well wishes. The guys and Jaime and I are in Vegas playing at the Palace Station.

I'm singing, Harrison, doing what I thought I could never do. Again, thanks for asking. Anything else?"

Her sarcasm scorched him. A fist tightened in his chest. "Dear heart, I'm sorry. I'm catching the red eye tonight. I'll be there sometime tomorrow. Will you wait for me? Please."

Silence.

"Please."

Another beat. Her voice thawed a degree. "I can't. The gig's done. We leave tomorrow, early."

Another beat.

A hard swallow partially dislodged the lump in his throat. "Eliza Grace, I want to see you. I left things badly, dear heart. I know, and I'm sorry."

He forced himself to speak softly. She was not a nurse in his OR, she was the woman he'd flown miles to see, to be with . . . and obviously he'd assumed too much. Now was a time for reason, not rant. He could pitch a fit on his own time. In fact, he could almost imagine her saying those very words. That thought made him smile and the begging easier.

"Is there somewhere and some time we can get together?" He swallowed hard again. He was not used to being at fault. "And will you please leave your damn phone on so I can call you?"

He didn't understand the sigh that traveled the long distance between them. About him? About them? Or something else?

"No phone," she finally answered, "but I will check my messages. We've been invited to play in Reno, a little venue called Bartley Ranch—Emmylou Harris got sick, lucky for us—so that's our next stop. I'll save you a seat if you want to meet me there."

Before he could answer, just before she hung up, she added, "And then you can explain why you sent Ms. DeMello to check me out."

WHEN HE COULD THINK STRAIGHT, CHRIS canceled his Las Vegas flight and booked the soonest one he could get to Reno. All these changes must be helping the airline make its bottom line. Eliza didn't sound happy to hear from him, but she didn't tell him to go fly a kite either.

What did he expect? They'd made no promises. He'd left so abruptly they couldn't even decently say goodbye. And his ambivalence must have been neon bright. But she'd given no sign she was interested in a long-term commitment either. There had been no talk of love.

And now she was moving in on fame.

No doubt about it, he was going to be making a fool of himself. He considered this for a long time, sitting in the café and staring out at the clear blue water, before he decided she was worth it. No fool like an old fool.

He picked up his phone and called DeMello.

"Where are you?" If he could have snarled, he would have.

"And hello to you too." Amusement laced her voice.

God, more fucking telephone etiquette. He was not amused, but deep inside he did realize his behavior was out of line. "Sorry. Hello, DeMello. Where the hell are you?"

He visualized her lazy smile. "Why, I'm in Las Vegas, big guy, checking out your newest honey bun. I must say she's a talented eyeful."

He ground his teeth, and petulance crept into his voice. "Why?"

"Why? Because you don't have a mom to vet your girlfriends, and you sounded like you were going off the deep end. You're a nice man, McLean, and I love you and Owen loves you and the kids love you. Do I need any more reasons?"

Harrumph. "Okay. I get it. You were worried about me." His throat tightened, and for a moment he couldn't speak.

"Just not used to that."

Nene refilled his coffee, patted his shoulder as though his plight were obvious.

"So what did you say?" He knew he sounded anxious, didn't want to, couldn't help it.

Quinn chuckled. "Just what the other girls told me," she said, "that you had a woman in every disaster, that your nickname was—"

"Stop. You didn't?" He'd already told Eliza, but it would sound different coming from DeMello's lips. "Tell me you're kidding."

For what seemed an eternity, all he could hear was Quinn's laughter. Finally it dwindled to hiccups and snorts.

"Damn it, DeMello, this isn't funny."

She coughed and spluttered and started laughing again. He pictured her wiping her eyes and blowing her nose and having a good time at his expense. He waited—maybe he'd earned it.

Finally she continued, "Nah, just told her you were one of the good guys, and that she passed muster. She pretty much told me I could fuck off, not quite in those words, though, 'cause she's a lady."

He glared at the phone, wishing he could wring DeMello's neck but strangely touched by the lengths she'd go for him and by the gumption Eliza had shown.

"Where are you anyway, and are you coming to Reno? I know her band is playing at Bartley Ranch." Before he could ask, she said, "It's a sweet little outdoor theater in south Reno. Good folks play there, and the audiences are always happy. It'll be good. That place in Vegas was kind of crappy, and I don't think she liked it much. But that song she does solo, the one that went viral, is wow. Is it for you?"

He told her what he knew. She promised to pick him up at the airport in his red Mustang convertible, which she did not want to relinquish. "And we can have a barbecue at the house on Sunday. The band and all. Everybody likes barbecue."

The familiar air kiss and she was gone. Harrison Christian McLean sat over his coffee until it went cold, then left a big tip and went to get his things. Just time for a trip to Makawao. There was one little thing there that he needed.

CHAPTER 53
ELIZA

THE GIG AT THE PALACE STATION had been grueling but rewarding. They'd gotten a great review in the entertainment section of the local paper, and two more agents had tracked Jaime down. Not bad for a week of late nights and hair that smelled like an ashtray.

Now they were flying north. Eliza liked Bartley Ranch, had seen Michael Martin Murphy there and Emmylou Harris there years back. It was fun to sit under the stars, usually in a down jacket with a blanket around your knees because even summer nights were cold in Reno, to eat a picnic supper and drink wine and share good music with folks who, in those hours, were friends.

Jaime, next to her on the plane, interrupted her thoughts. "What about that guy? Grimes? You worried?"

It wasn't that she hadn't thought about Martin, especially when the chance to perform in Reno had come up. She remembered how he'd looked standing at her screen door, not quite as polished and professional as she remembered him, suit jacket unpressed, shirt collar unbuttoned and askew. His voice had been shrill, a little strident, and his eyes—what she remembered from seeing them across the room—a mixture of crazy and sad.

"I think it's okay, Jaime. The police escorted him off island. There are two restraining orders against him. He must realize now that I'm serious. I told him, and then the judge told him, that I wanted him to leave me alone." She patted her friend's arm. "I feel sad for him. Besides, you'll be there, so no worries."

He caught her hand. "Your man, he'll be there, too?" From Rosie, he'd heard the whole story.

Her voice quavered. "Not my man, but yes, I believe Harrison will be there, too."

"Good. We need all the help we can get."

His concern was so blatant that she deferred her don't-worry-about-me spiel. She was family, and families took care of each other.

One not-too-bumpy landing later, Eliza settled them all into her sparsely furnished house with its For Sale sign still out front, then stocked up on groceries for the weekend. Chores and excuses exhausted, she turned on her phone.

I'll be at the Atlantis tonight, Harrison's text said. Will you drive out with me in the morning?

"I'll be at the Atlantis"—*does he want me to be there? A drive in the morning—what, to give me more bad news?* Her thoughts careened. *Dear heavens, do I even want to see him?*

After that terrible morning, when he'd driven away and left her heart shattered, she'd been sure she'd never see him again. Heartbreak Harry, just living up to his nickname. Now, that same heart almost mended, she wondered—could she survive another leaving? A headache brewed. She was reading too much into his terse words, making herself miserable.

Besides, who was she fooling? She did want to see him again—very much. And he *had* called her "dear heart" when he apologized.

Conscience prickled. *I probably owe him an apology, too. After all, I didn't call him either. And I did leave my phone off and didn't check my messages.* She shuddered. *And then I was all huffy when he didn't call me. What a dunce.*

But the DeMello person had called Harrison "googly" and "smitten." Eliza smiled at that foolishness while anxiety and apprehension and excitement tap danced inside. She needed action. A phone call to his number sent her directly to voicemail; served her right, no help there. What to do?

She knew the Atlantis Casino Resort Spa. Since its humble beginnings as the Golden Road Motor Lodge, the hotel had been growing and expanding and changing its name until now it stood aloof from its casino brethren, its newest twenty-seven-story concierge tower lighting the south Reno sky.

Her family had celebrated special events at the Purple Parrot Buffet, Cal's particular favorite, and, until his illness had derailed her social activity, she'd been a member of Soroptimist International of Truckee Meadows and attended the service club's weekly lunch meetings in a second-floor conference room there.

She knew the Atlantis. More importantly, she'd become friends with Norma, whose daughter, Andrea, was the Atlantis's night concierge.

ANDREA HAD COME THROUGH. Now, CURLED into a leather armchair in Harrison's twenty-sixth-story suite, Eliza watched night descend and hotel lights brighten the sky. She'd used the plumeria soap he liked and let her hair dry curly around her face. She wore the orange wrap and nothing else. Brazen.

She laughed, thought she sounded a little happy but mostly crazy and scared. So many out-of-character things since Harrison McLean had entered her life, what was one more? She'd planned a nap, too, not sure when he'd arrive, but instead, wide awake and quivering with nerves, she sipped her second glass of chilled courage and struggled to keep from flying apart.

The door handle moved.

Time stopped.

Harrison stepped into the room and scanned his accommodations.

In the casino's flashing light, Eliza saw his eyes sweep over her, return, and widen.

"Eliza?"

She had planned to be nonchalant, a cool Grace Kelly to a suave Gary Grant, but she couldn't. The surprise and joy on his face undid her, and she burst from the chair and into his arms.

"Harrison," was all she could manage before he swept her up and found her mouth.

When they could talk, he said, "How?"

"I have friends." She giggled and shrugged. "Really, really good friends."

He cleared his throat. "We should talk."

Eliza laid her hand on his cheek. "Later. Right now, you're here and I'm here and there's a king-sized bed in the other room." Feeling young, sexy, beautiful, she fluttered her lashes. "For your information, I've never made love in a suite."

"God, another oversight." A grin spread across his face. "A tough job, but somebody has to do it."

Orange silk slithered to the floor as he lifted her into his arms. Hunger, needs. Bodies told their stories. Words could wait.

In the bedroom with windows open to the sky, her lips trailed kisses up his chest and over the scar while he struggled out of his clothes. Finally naked, he pulled her close, skin to skin. Her arms twined around his neck. He buried his face in her hair.

"My God, dear heart, I'm a stupid fool and I've missed you."

Her heart raced. For tonight, this was enough. She lay back and let him take her to the stars.

ELIZA WOKE IN THE DARK, HEAD still full of a familiar dream. A figure hovering just out of sight, dark and malevolent; her fingers keying in numbers, never right; help never coming. She shivered. It wasn't new, the dream, usually occurring when she was troubled. Never in Hawaii. A longing for home swept her, and she shook it aside. *Only a dream*, she reminded herself, *nothing new*. Just roll over, make it go away.

She completed the maneuver and bumped into a solid wall. *Harrison.*

Like a warm blanket, relief enfolded her. As she snuggled closer, he turned, drew her into the safety of his body, and mumbled what sounded like "love you" into her hair as he settled back into his deep sleep.

Wide awake now, Eliza surrendered to his warmth and her shivering stopped, but her mind raced. *I told myself this was enough, but is it? I told him I don't do one-night stands, but isn't that what I'm doing, just one-night stands with the same man?*

Her thoughts bounced like overstimulated children—lust and love and sex, commitment and independence, Grace and Eliza. She'd vowed never to submit her life to another's rules. How could she be with this man and not lose herself again?

And what did he want with her? He liked her. She was sure of that. And he wanted her, a fact she accepted in surprise—he'd traveled across the country to find her, hadn't he? But he'd been nicknamed Heartbreak Harry for a reason, even though the other woman had said he was one of the good guys and not into breaking hearts anymore.

I'm in love with him, and I can't keep acting like it's a game, a lark, fun while it lasts. I thought I could, but I can't.

Doubt and fear dug their harsh fingers into her gut, and her heart knew the wreckage of dreams she hadn't realized she was dreaming. *I love him and I have to let him go.*

She mourned even as his hands began to roam and his body searched for hers. A moan escaped her lips and she opened to him, surrounded him, felt him pour himself into her.

"*Aloha wau ia ʻoe,*" she whispered. *I love you.*

Just today, just one more day.

Chapter 54
McLean

McLean woke as his body searched for Eliza's in the dark. He pulled her to him, slid into her warmth, reveled in her velvety softness, the strength with which she held him. Slow and smooth, his thrusts deepened, and he felt her tighten, stiffen, then go limp beneath him, loved her whispered words even though he didn't understand them.

His hands moved over her body, damp with the sheen of that first orgasm, and he tasted the salt from her skin. Her aftershocks excited him. She trembled for him, just for him, and he thrilled in that knowledge. *I want this woman, her body, her heart.*

Her hands flew, touching, caressing, driving him crazy. She wrapped her legs around him and drew him deeper, holding him as if life depended on it, and he could barely maintain control. She arched, his name a tickle against his shoulder, then bucked again as he pushed her up and over. *Mine—she's mine.* He slowed his stroke, wanting the moment to last forever. *I need her in my life, my bed, like this.*

"Eliza, look at me."

In the dawn's light, he saw her eyelids flutter. "Open, dearest, let me see you."

Eyes soft and gray as morning mist met his, in them love and need and a desire to match his own. Not just lust but love, he knew then, an ocean of tenderness filling him even as he drove them higher, let them both hover on the peak before they fell together.

WHEN HE WOKE TWO HOURS LATER, the sun's rays penetrated the room and he was alone in the big bed. He'd slept hard. *Too old for back-to-back red eyes*, he thought, as the smell of coffee coaxed his eyes open, *but not too old for this welcome. Never too old for that.* Smile on his face, he dragged his weary body out of bed. This day promised to be the best of his life, and he didn't want to waste one second. Thirty minutes later, fresh from his shower, he left the bedroom.

Dressed in jeans and a blue-striped T-shirt, hair tamed severely at the nape of her neck, Eliza stood in the suite's kitchenette spreading cream cheese on a toasted bagel and looking cool and lovely as a breeze.

His breath caught, and he wanted to tear off her clothes and ravage her. Would it always be thus—the sight of her, the thought of her driving him mad? He'd find out soon enough, maybe in the next ten or twenty years. He'd tell her today that he loved her, wanted to be with her, and they could begin their life together.

She looked up and flashed a smile. "No shorts? No Hawaiian flowers?"

She laughed as he looked down and frowned at his khaki slacks and plain chambray shirt with its rolled-up sleeves. The ones with Hawaiian flowers, imbued with his own equivocating, were folded deep inside his travel bag.

"No worries. Come eat. No papaya, but I thought bagels and cream cheese and coffee would do for starters. Then, if your invite for a drive is still on, we could go up to Tahoe for breakfast." She offered him a cup of coffee and a kiss across the counter, then handed him the bagel. "I hope that's okay. I have to be back no later than four. We're on tonight."

Eat, walk on the beach, plan our new life. Chris McLean didn't need Hawaiian flowers or even Maui sunsets for that. "Sounds perfect." He bit into his bagel, chewed as she sipped her coffee, and said nothing more. He'd meant to ask her what *aloha wau ia 'oe* meant, but something felt off. "You okay?"

She didn't quite meet his eyes. "Sure. Why wouldn't I be, the world's best lover in my bed? Hope you weren't too upset, me being here last night and all."

He caught the glint of mischief and decided he'd been mistaken. "I'll stay at the Atlantis forever if that's the kind of service provided. Who did you have to bribe?"

"My friend's daughter is the night concierge. She has a romantic streak a mile wide so she was easy."

"I went by your apartment in Kihei."

"Figured."

"That's a sturdy new screen door. Your neighbor said there'd been some excitement?"

Color fled her cheeks. "Martin Grimes came by."

His head came up. "The stalker?"

Eliza nodded. "He saw the Azeka sign in the video and figured out where I was. Actually, he believed I'd sent the whole thing as a sign, a message that I was ready for him. Next best thing to a message from God, it sounded like. Said we belonged together and he'd come to bring me home."

Matter-of-fact voice, a glimmer of fear, quickly masked, in her eyes.

Chris reached for her hand, busy scrubbing an imaginary spot on the counter. "Eliza Grace, I'm so sorry." Owen's report had lulled him. He should have been there.

She kept scrubbing and didn't look up. "They picked him up, charged him with violating the restraining order and breaking an old screen door, then sent him home with his promise to leave me alone. Done and done. Let's talk about something else."

An awkward silence settled as they finished their coffee and she gathered up her things, and it hung like a storm cloud as they descended in the elevator and walked through the islands of slot machines to the parking lot.

"Harrison, your red beast," Eliza exclaimed when she saw the Mustang. "I should have brought my hat."

He opened her door, happy that she remembered, even happier that she sounded like herself again. After he put the top down, he tossed her a Washington Nationals baseball cap. "Here. Brought you a present." He didn't mention the small box tucked deep in his pocket. His visit to the jeweler in Makawao had been fruitful. But that was for later, after she'd agreed to his plan.

"Perfect. Thanks." She pulled her hair through the cap, settled into the seat, and stretched out her legs. "Ahh. This is nice. I can't tell you how crazy it's been. Emails, phone calls, texts, and then singing five nights in a row in Vegas." She made a face. "Not my favorite place, but it really was quite exciting. And agents, agents coming out of the woodwork, people that didn't have the time of day for us until that YouTube video. Thank goodness, Jaime's fielding the business stuff. I'd be tempted to tell them all to take a hike. Derek and Rick strut around like young gods, preening for their new fans. Hope that phase passes soon; it's not pretty."

He chuckled, decided not to worry about how he would fit into the picture. "Where there's a will, there's a way," his mother used to say, and there certainly was a will.

She turned toward him. "You didn't call."

Guilt rose, and his jaw clenched. He had tried, before he'd known the futility of it and stopped, but saying that right now didn't seem productive. "I didn't know, not until I heard you singing on the ten o'clock news. By then your mailbox was full." He should have tried harder, he knew, had been drowning his sorrows instead. His mother would *not* have been proud.

Eliza looked away. "No worries." She didn't sound like she meant it, and she didn't ask why he'd returned to Maui. "Turn left, we'll go up Mount Rose to Incline."

McLean turned left and followed her directions.

Silence took over and with it a sense of foreboding. His Eliza was talkative, quick-witted, funny, and there was plenty in her recent life to talk about. Today she just hummed and kept her eyes on the road.

The Mustang easily covered the miles up the Mount Rose Highway and into the Sierra Nevada. It was seven on a Saturday morning, and traffic was light, the air cool, and the sun still behind them. Chris forced his attention to the twists and turns of the mountain road, but anxiety prowled.

Act natural. This will sort itself out. She's peeved, rightly so. When he couldn't stand his thoughts anymore, he broke the silence. "What about your sons? How are they liking the famous mom thing?"

She laughed. "As expected. Jed and Caroline are pretty sure this will lead me down the path to sin and degradation. Jacob and Raul arrive tonight in time for the concert. Jacob's already making plans for my Kennedy Center debut, and Raul claims they're feeling left out and want to meet all my new friends." She glanced at him from under the brim of her hat. "You'll be there?"

"Wouldn't be anywhere else. The star promised me a ticket." He reached over and tugged at her ponytail, wanting to stop the car and take her in his arms and hold her until she told him what was wrong. A snarky voice in his head murmured "maybe you don't want to know."

Eliza resumed her humming, eyes once more on the road as it crested and dropped into the Tahoe basin, and the lake came into full view. He'd been here once before, visiting DeMello's family, mostly chasing the triplets in and out of the freezing-ass water. Still beautiful, but not enough to tamp down his worry as the silence lengthened. He knew she wanted him, that much was obvious, maybe even loved him—just this morning he'd seen love in her eyes, hadn't he?—but did she want him in her life?

And there was still another subject to broach. He cleared his throat, now as good a time as any. "DeMello and her husband will be there tonight, too, and they've invited everyone for barbecue on Sunday."

Humming stopped. Eliza shifted her gaze from the road to his face. "Why? Didn't she get a good enough look in Vegas?"

Before he could answer, they were at a stop sign and she pointed left. "That way, and then the next right onto Lakeshore."

Apologizing, proclaiming his innocence, McLean turned toward the village.

"Don't worry about it. She filled in a few details that you'd omitted, called you one of the good guys, and was smart enough to leave before I called the bouncer. What nerve." Her voice had risen an octave, and she stopped as though surprised by her own rage. "Sorry, not your fault."

Anxiety gnawed his insides.

"Turn here." She pointed toward the lake and a sign for the Lone Eagle Grille. McLean turned in and pulled into the first available parking spot.

She was out of the car before he could kill the engine. "Come on, let's walk. I'm not ready to eat yet."

Raw inside, he forced his legs to carry him to her side.

They had walked almost a mile before she spoke. "I'm sorry, Harrison. I didn't even know I was still mad. I thought we had something special, even if I couldn't go with you, but you didn't call so I figured I was being stupid and naive. Just the woman of the moment, I guessed. And you didn't acknowledge the video even when you must have known how important it was. And then you send your lover to check me out? What was I supposed to make of all that?"

His own temper flared. "If you'd turn your goddamned phone on and empty your fucking mailbox, maybe a man could call. Of course, I knew it was important. And I didn't send Quinn, who, as I've already told you, is no longer my lover, to check you out. I was trying to get my own fucking head together and my own fucking life under control so I could come back and convince you to make a life with me. If you weren't so—"

He stopped and turned around when he realized she was no longer beside him.

Sunshine peeked through the branches that lined the path and cast her in light and shadow. He couldn't read her expression as she stood, several steps back, head cocked, as though she hadn't heard him right. Who could blame her? It certainly wasn't the proposal he'd planned.

"Make a life with you?"

He remained where he was. "That's what I said. I want you, Eliza Grace. I want to sleep with you and wake up with you and laugh and cry and grow old with you. I was figuring how to make that happen when you sang that damned song."

Not quite true, he acknowledged inside, but she didn't need to know how close he'd been to crawling back into the bottle. *Truth be told, her song saved me.*

Fisted hands on hips, she scrunched up her face, considering. "I think maybe you've left out something important."

She sounded so much like herself that the fear in his belly loosened its grip. He stepped toward her, cupped her face in his hands, and looked into her eyes. "Eliza Grace King, I love you, and if you'll have my sorry self, I want to marry you."

They stood in the middle of the path, oblivious, as bikers whipped around them and a runner pushing a double-wide stroller had to ask them to move. Eliza slid her hand into his and tugged him out of harm's way as two skateboarders zoomed past.

Just when he thought repetition might be needed, she laid her free hand on his cheek. Nothing had ever felt better—that soft little hand with its callused finger pads and lingering scent of plumeria—and McLean knew his life was complete.

She shot him her cocky grin. "Well, why didn't you say so? As it happens, I love you, too, so let's go get something to eat and we'll see if there's a way to make your cockamamie idea work."

CHAPTER 55
ELIZA

JUST BEFORE FOUR O'CLOCK, FEELINGS JUMBLED, Eliza hurried into her Reno house. Staged for a quick sale, its rooms were sparsely furnished, impersonal. An arrangement of summer flowers sat on an entry table she didn't recognize. Like someone else's home.

Relief. *Nothing to do with me anymore.*

Equipment and men filled the living room where Jaime, Rick, and Derek fiddled with their instruments. She masked a smile knowing the men did not consider their single-minded concentration *fiddling.* She should be helping, or at least making sure her own guitar had survived the last plane ride, but surprise, frustration, and excitement vied for the top of her inner pile, and she bubbled over. "Got some news."

Good-natured groans met the announcement. No one looked up.

"Guys, Harrison's in love with me and asked me to marry him."

At that, Derek did look up, a disdainful expression on his tanned face. "Ahh, Eliza, that is *so* old news."

Stunned. "You're not surprised? You knew?"

Jaime's laugh was as big as the man himself. "Anyone with two brain cells to rub together knew it was just a matter of time." He made a mock bow to his friend. "Sorry, except you. More than two brain cells, all taking a nap."

She threw her new hat at him while the others laughed. Rick jumped up and gave her a quick hug. Derek said he didn't play weddings, but he did eat cake.

She turned to Jaime. "No hug from you?"

He smiled. It didn't touch his eyes. "You know I'm happy for you—"

"But you're worried." She picked up the hat, used it to bat his arm. "Let's go make coffee and you can tell me all about it."

"That's my line," he said but set aside the acoustic guitar he'd been tuning and followed her.

In the kitchen, Jaime filled the coffee pot. Eliza perched on the counter so she could watch his face and told him about the morning's conversation, leaving out the F-words and her petty remarks about Quinn DeMello. Even a very good best friend doesn't need all the details.

He listened without comment, his expression still grave.

"I'm not ready for marriage, Jaime, maybe never will be. No matter what Harrison says, living separate lives will be difficult, and I'm not sure he's as ready to retire as he thinks. But this is a step, a big step, and a commitment, and for now that's more than enough. I've got to practice being with someone and not turning into a doormat." *Or Grace*, she thought but didn't say.

This made him laugh. "No ring?"

She let out a big breath. "Oh, yes, there's a ring." She fished in her pocket, drew out the velvet box, and flipped it open.

He sucked air.

"Yeah. I think it cost more than my house."

She looked at the dark green stone glowing with its inner light. Diamond chips surrounded the emerald, winking in the afternoon sun. She lifted the wide, gold band from its box, slid it onto her finger, marveled again at the perfect fit, and grinned at her best friend. "It does look like me, doesn't it? The me that's rich and famous and can have anything she wants." She waved her hand, and the stones reflected her mood.

"I think you should wear it."

"Really?"

Jaime nodded. "That's not an I'm-taking-over-your-life ring—that ring would have a two- or three-caret diamond standing up like an erection."

She snorted coffee out her nose.

One eyebrow raised, he said, "Good that I don't get this response in court," and tossed her a towel.

At the commotion, Rick sauntered in. "Everybody okay?"

Between coughs and snorts, Eliza choked out, "Jaime thinks big diamond engagement rings are like erections."

"Sure," Rick nodded in agreement as he poured his own coffee, "everybody knows that."

When the hubbub died down, Jaime turned a solemn face to Eliza. "Honestly, little sister, I was worried, but that is one I-am-serious ring, and you didn't have to promise a single thing to get it. Wear it, enjoy it, learn how to live with the idea that someone can care about you just the way you are." He tapped her nose with his forefinger. "You wrote the song; listen to your own words."

He left before Eliza could think of a reply, so she sat at the kitchen table and drank her coffee and thought about what he'd said. After a while, ring still on her finger, she went upstairs to get ready.

Worries like butterflies flitted through her mind and took up residence in her stomach as Eliza drove across the covered bridge into the Bartley Ranch County Park. The Robert Z. Hawkins Amphitheater, product of a private gift and a belief in the arts, featured a garden atmosphere, permanent seating, lots of room for chairs and blankets on the grass, and a full performance stage—the source of her current worry. She'd never performed on a stage bigger than the truck bed at Fourth Friday. Even the Palace Station's stage had been handkerchief-sized. More worrisome yet, this event was a fundraiser for her old Soroptimist club; she'd never performed in front of people who knew her.

She thought about the band: her guys, her family. They were already inside setting up. Confidence fled. *What if I let them down? What if I fall down?* She wanted to laugh, couldn't quite manage it. She parked beside Harrison's red Mustang. *Dear Heaven, what if I mess up and Harrison is disappointed. What if I let him down?*

With dire imaginings like mean-girl voices in her head, Eliza climbed out of her sedan, straightened her shoulders, and walked toward the entrance where Harrison stood conversing with two women working the check-in table. The flash of jealousy didn't improve her mood.

She reached his side and slid her hand into his before she realized she knew the taller woman.

"Hello, Martha, good to see you again," Eliza said to her former coworker, surprised that she meant it. She'd become a stranger to her old life, but now here she was. "You've met my friend, Harrison."

"Grace, wonderful to see you. I was sorry to hear about your husband." Then the woman's lips formed an O as she looked Eliza up and down, the curls, the skintight jeans and western shirt, the red boots—then glanced at the picture on their quickly printed brochure. "Oh. You're Eliza K?"

Eyes wide, Martha paused as though she didn't know what to say next.

Eliza produced a brief explanation, then excused herself and tugged Harrison through the gate. Conflicting emotions—confusion, craziness. It seemed Grace had become a totally separate individual.

"Sorry, that was awkward." An urge to giggle, quickly stifled—she didn't have to act as nuts as she felt. "I worked with her at the hospital. I forget people know Grace."

Harrison stepped closer. "No worries. It's probably stranger for you than for anyone else." He glanced over his shoulder, and she followed his gaze. Martha was gesticulating wildly to the woman beside her at the table. "Except maybe a gossipy coworker." He laughed, and after a stiff moment, Eliza did too. "So let's give them something to really chatter about."

Before she could respond, he drew her in and kissed her.

She started to pull away, then dissolved against him as his lips molded to hers. Licks of fire rose in her belly, and her whole world became the man who held her.

A teasing voice brought her back. "Hello, Mom, remember us?"

On wobbly knees, glad for Harrison's supporting grip, Eliza turned to greet her son and was swept into a three-way hug that left her breathless.

Chapter 56
McLean

A JOYOUS LAUGH, THEN EMPTY ARMS, AND McLean watched his new fiancée sandwiched like the center of an Oreo cookie and laughing like a loon.

Ah, yes, the son and his partner. No mistaking which was which—one, in Levi's and a crisply pressed shirt, a curly-haired blond the image of his mother; the other, in black slacks and black shirt and sunglasses, dark and chiseled as a god. Jacob Dart and Raul Sanchez.

Jacob maneuvered the laughing trio so he faced McLean. "And this must be the man? Unless there's a cadre of suitors undisclosed?" He held out his hand. "Jacob Dart, son of the infamous Eliza. Let me look you over and make sure you're good enough for my mother."

Hard to feel nervous with such an impish smile directed at him. McLean grasped the proffered hand. "Chris McLean, unworthy suitor."

"Right answer." With a laugh, the younger man pulled him into the hug, and, just like that, he was family.

"Enough, I've got to work." After several minutes of laughing and chattering and happy tears, Eliza stepped out of their encircling arms. "How did you two get in here, anyway? I was going to leave your tickets but this one," she poked McLean's arm, "distracted me."

The impish grin again. "You forget, Mom, I look just like you. And I remember the ticket lady from the time I broke my arm, so sweet-talking was easy. Besides, she's famous by proxy right now—knowing the star and all." He dropped a kiss onto his mother's flaming cheek. "Better get used to it. My friends all want my autograph just because I know you."

McLean took in the happy banter, admiring the younger man's spirit and his obvious love for his mother. Eliza's untapped charisma radiated from this younger son like a sunbeam. He glanced at the darker man standing quietly beside him and was rewarded with a chuckle. "They're quite a pair, aren't they? Sure you know what you're getting yourself into?" He pushed his shades up, exposing startling green eyes, and extended his hand. "Raul Sanchez, prince consort."

Taken back by the man's tone, McLean held his tongue. If this man had adopted his Eliza as "mamacita," he must be all right.

Eliza must have read his confusion. "Raul, don't tease the man." She planted a kiss on his cheek, then turned her face to McLean. "Kiss me quick and wish me luck, Harrison. I'm off to earn my keep."

He complied, followed her with his eyes as she flew up the stairs and disappeared behind the stage curtain. Beside him, Jacob and Raul hummed "she's got me under her spell." Nothing he could do but grin like an idiot and agree before the couple moved away to find their seats.

At seven-fifteen sharp, Eliza K and the Hawaiian Cowboys settled onstage to a hearty welcome after the lengthy introduction made it clear Eliza was a hometown girl, new name notwithstanding.

Just as they started out hot with Eliza's rendition of "Queen of Hearts," Quinn DeMello and Owen Johnson slid into seats flanking McLean.

"Sorry we're late. Kids wouldn't give up the ghost." DeMello squeezed his hand. "She's marvelous, isn't she?"

McLean shook Owen's hand, returned DeMello's squeeze, but couldn't tear his eyes from the woman prowling the stage, a stalking lioness with her lithe body and mass of curls and voice that could call a jungle to attention. He'd seen her sing before—rehearsal, backyard luau, even that long-ago Fourth Friday before he'd recognized her and been struck dumb—but never like this. He pressed a hand to his chest to contain the thundering of his heart. Not just marvelous—magnificent.

The audience pulsed, tense and excited—one of their own was sounding mighty good—as the beat quickened and the volume increased. Chris had sat through enough practices to recognize the songs: Eddie Rabbitt's "I Love a Rainy Night," then Johnny Cash's "Ring of Fire," with Derek's rousing bass solo. For forty minutes people clapped, sang along, and danced on the concrete walkways as Eliza and her guys wove their magic.

Sure, he was biased, but even those people who had remained sitting and whispering to each other were on their feet humming and swaying as Eliza and Jaime finished the set with the Kenny Rogers-Dolly Parton duet "Islands in the Stream."

Silence, the words drifting into the night. Eliza bowed low. A burst of applause followed the performers off the stage. Intermission.

As his friends went off to get drinks, McLean stood and stretched, and in the dusk talk swirled around him. He perused the crowd, all of whom appeared intimately acquainted. Reno seemed a friendly enough town, maybe like the old sitcom *Cheers*, "where everybody knows your name." Is this what life on Maui would be? Would he ever get used to it?

Just as he finished a one-sided conversation with the woman behind him who claimed to have known Grace forever, a shiver ran up his back, and he stiffened, instantly alert. He'd felt this sensation before—in Mexico just before an aftershock, in Iran just before a ruined house tumbled down where he'd been standing, in the operating room just in time to locate a hidden bleed—and Chris didn't doubt it now.

His head came up, and he slowly scanned the crowd. Far to the left, three women conversed, their eyes flicking toward him as though he might be the topic of their conversation: nope. People moving past them, out the gate toward the bar, back to their seats: no one else paying him any mind. Directly in front of the stage, a man frowned into the crowd, but just when McLean thought the gaze centered on himself, the fellow waved and the frown disappeared as he rushed up the stairs toward the woman waving back: not him. Feeling foolish, almost doubting his senses, he kept looking, and then, with a jolt, he saw. To his far right, a slender man stood alone and stared back. Their eyes locked, but before McLean could move, the man turned away and disappeared into the line of people waiting for the bathroom.

What the hell?

DeMello slipped into her seat beside him and handed him a bottle of water. "Did you see that odd little man, McLean? He was at the end of the bathroom line, and I thought he was staring at you."

Not my imagination.

McLean started down the steps when a guitar riff recalled the audience, and the band returned to the stage. Frowning, he stood to one side and scanned the theater. No odd little man. No more tingle. What to do?

On his acoustic guitar, Jaime strummed a haunting melody. Derek's bass softly paced him. The audience stilled as Eliza walked onto the stage, her rich voice giving up the words: *"vaya con Dios*, my darling . . . ."

Even though he knew it was impossible, McLean felt his heart rise into his throat.

Skintight jeans and lioness attitude were gone. A layered white skirt flowed like water around her legs, a lacy white tee clung to her petite form, silver sparkled at her ears and in layers around her neck, and his emerald flashed on her finger.

How could he have doubted his love for this woman? Desire stirred and tenderness, the need to love, to protect, to share. How could he spend a day without her?

He had to find that stalking bastard and keep him away from Eliza forever.

Jacob came to stand beside him. "You look troubled?"

"Saw someone."

"The stalker?" Jacob's voice immediately hard, his eyes steely.

McLean shrugged. "Don't know. I felt someone staring, skinny guy, got this feeling. DeMello noticed him, too."

"Does Jaime know? Mom?"

Frowning, McLean shook his head. "No time."

Jacob turned to Raul, who had joined them. "I'll find security, just in case." He stepped to the gate, spoke with the woman there, and disappeared toward the back of the building. McLean scanned the crowd as Eliza crooned Juice Newton's "The Sweetest Thing" into her handheld mic.

No sign of a small man in gray. No more premonitory shiver. McLean felt his shoulders loosen, his fists unclench. Maybe it was just imagination after all. Or maybe he'd been here and now was gone.

Eliza moved gracefully across the stage, the layers of her skirt swirling, her jewel-encrusted boots twinkling like Dorothy's magic slippers. Far left, she held position for just a moment, then stepped forward as though reaching out to her listeners, and, before McLean could do anything but watch in horror, she wobbled and started to fall.

CHAPTER 57
ELIZA

*T*HEY'RE WITH ME, ELIZA THOUGHT AS the audience grew still. Exhilaration rising, wanting to give more, she moved to her right, stepped forward. She neared the edge of the stage just as an icy sensation crept down her back. *Intuition?*

She jerked her head up. *He's here?*

Vision diminished by the bright stage lights, Eliza stared into the audience, scanning, senses pushed outward as she searched for her stalker . . . one more step forward. She glimpsed a sudden movement far right just as the toe of her boot snagged the monitor's cord and she staggered, momentum carrying her forward . . . falling . . . .

The crowd gasped.

The concrete walkway loomed.

Twisting, straining, praying, Eliza regained her balance, forced laughter from a dry throat, and twirled until she was again center stage. "Sorry, folks, just wanted to make sure I wasn't putting you to sleep."

A collective sigh of relief before the crowd clapped and cheered, and the music continued as though nothing had happened.

Was it him? Is he here? Now afraid of what she might see, Eliza kept her eyes down, all her focus on the words she sang. Jaime slipped his arm around her waist, ready for their second duet, and mouthed, "What's wrong?"

She shook her head, turned to face him as though she were singing just for him. With a frown, he joined his voice with hers, and the moment passed. As the last notes faded, Jaime stepped forward and introduced Rick and Derek. He'd skipped two songs on the playlist, but the duo didn't bat an eyelash. Rick launched into his solo, and Jaime's words were masked by the pounding of the drums. "What?"

"Think he's here."

Jaime's expression didn't change, but he gripped her wrist and his eyes went cold as he scanned the crowd. "You're outta here."

She shook her head. "Nope, we finish what we start." She slipped away from his protective hand and danced to Rick's drums.

The audience applauded. She danced and hummed as the others sang. Two more songs, then the four stood together center stage, instruments behind them. Their closing number would be a cappella. Eliza held her mic close, her lips almost kissing its hot metal. Four voices blended as they hummed the melody. Eliza scanned the crowd—audience swaying, sensing something important. Up close, she could see her beaming son, Raul gripping his hand; Harrison to her left, his gaze unwavering; on stage, the rest of her family. Fear melted away.

Heart full, she began. "There are days when I am weary . . . ."

CHAPTER 58
McLEAN

BLINDED BY TEARS, McLEAN HEARD ALL of "In His Arms" for the first time, and he thought his heart would burst. The last notes clung for a moment in the cool night air, then dropped into silence. One beat, two. The audience erupted in applause.

Two encores later, McLean fought his way backstage, and Eliza fell into his arms, laughing and crying, triumph in her eyes. He had no words. He held her, his world complete.

Around them, the guys high-fived, accepted congratulations, and began packing up.

A uniformed security guard escorted two police officers into the melee. "Eliza, Ms. King?"

She turned to the woman. "Yes?"

"Jessica Brown," the young officer introduced herself, then indicated her partner, "Mark Dolan."

Jacob and Raul arrived just as Dolan nodded and said, "Your son said there was some kind of problem?"

McLean bristled as he heard doubt in the officer's voice.

Apparently Eliza's son did also. "Mom, I saw. Harrison saw. His friend saw. You tell them."

McLean felt her hesitation, knew she didn't want to soil this evening. He nudged her away from the crowd. "Just tell them, dear heart, and then you can get back to celebrating."

His arm stayed around her shoulders. Jaime stood at her other side. Succinctly, Eliza explained the situation. When she was finished, Dolan and Brown exchanged glances. They didn't ask him any questions, McLean noted, and in the man's eyes he read *overactive imagination*.

Dolan, older and clearly in charge, adjusted his equipment and fiddled with his shoulder-mounted radio before he turned his gaze on Eliza. "Ms. King, the security guard patrolled the area after your son spoke with him and found no one fitting this man's description. We'll file this report with the restraining order, of course, but there isn't really anything else we can do tonight."

Polite, correct, dismissive.

McLean wanted to punch the supercilious fuck. A quick glance at Jaime told him the other man shared the sentiment.

As though she could sense tempers fraying, Eliza slipped her hand in his and gave a reassuring squeeze. "Thanks, officers. We appreciate your time. Have a good evening."

Jessica Brown threw a sympathetic look over her shoulder as she followed her partner. No one said a word until they'd disappeared from sight.

"Assholes." Jacob's anger sizzled. "Who does that prick think he is?" Jaw clenched, McLean endured Jacob's rant. He couldn't fault the younger man for his anger. Raul kept a supportive hand on his partner's arm and listened, but finally he interrupted. "Stop, Jacob, just stop. We can do nothing more here. Let's go buy enough pizza and beer to make everyone happy."

Jacob's expression turned mulish. At any other time, McLean would have laughed, so much did the man's face resemble his mother's when her world was not cooperating.

In a firmer voice, Raul added, "Your mother needs to eat. We can do that for her. Besides," he cast a long look at McLean, "this one is staying."

For a second it appeared that Jacob wasn't listening, but then he gave his mother a quick hug, and the men disappeared toward the parking lot.

Chris scanned the now-empty theater. *Damn right I'm staying.* He'd left her alone once, and see what happened? Irrational, he knew, but Eliza was stuck with him.

He jumped when Jaime's hand settled on his shoulder. "Sorry, man. I've got no clout here."

"Yeah. Me neither." Nothing else to say.

Derek shouted, "Ready," as he and Rick hauled the last of the equipment toward the ramp. "Let's get outta here."

"You good?"

Nothing would be good until Eliza was safely back on Maui, but for now . . . Chris nodded. "All good. She's changing, but we'll be along in a minute. See you at the house."

The rental van's engine roared to life, then gradually disappeared into the night, and Chris waited alone. Watching. Listening. Then Eliza's hand slipped into his. "Ready when you are, dear man," she said, and he could breathe.

Hand in hand, they walked toward their cars. His Mustang and her sedate brown sedan sat side by side in an otherwise empty lot. Behind them, the lights winked out in the amphitheater and a chill ran up his spine. "You'll stay with me again tonight?"

Her full skirt swung seductively. "Why, kind sir, I thought you'd never ask."

Heartened by her playfulness, he squelched his fear, but his eyes kept moving as they walked alone in the dark.

She noticed.

"Harrison, I'm sorry you've been pulled into this craziness. I'll admit, Martin scares me, but I'm sure he won't hurt me. It's just unnerving to know that he might be watching, like tonight."

McLean ground his teeth and didn't reply, just kept walking, kept her hand tight in his. He wasn't so sure.

When he didn't reply, she continued, "I hate that you guys feel like you have to protect me, but I understand and I love that you want to." She stopped in the gravel lot, made him look at her. "Please understand. I won't live scared. I spent too many years doing what I was told, what was expected, what was safe. I'm not doing that again."

Since she reminded him of a fierce Chihuahua, he snorted and she batted his arm, only half playful.

"Sorry," he said. "I want you safe. I want to grind that fucking asshole into gristle." At his words, she looked so distressed that he tried to smooth the anger from his voice. "About tomorrow?" The band had volunteered to participate in Sunday afternoon's Concert in the Park, an end-of-summer fundraiser for the local food bank. "You know Jaime wants to cancel tomorrow's deal and take you home?"

Eliza stamped her foot, scattering the tiny stones and sending tinkling sounds into the dark. "Not going to run. Sooner or later, Martin will get tired of this and leave me alone. Meantime . . ." She raised her fisted hand and, one finger at a time, ticked off reasons to play, "One, people have paid good money to see us; two, the food bank needs the money for their kids' backpack program; three, the guys need their time in the sun; four . . ." She waggled her open hand under his nose. "If we don't play, can sex overdose be a cause of death?"

He spit out a laugh, drew her close.

"Besides, we don't really know that tonight was even him."

Before he could protest further, she flashed him her own impish grin. "And we still have a barbecue to attend."

She stood on tiptoes, planted a kiss, and the matter was settled.

CHAPTER 59
ELIZA

Eliza pulled into her driveway, and Harrison pulled in right beside her. He'd insisted on following. "Not necessary," she'd said, but truthfully she'd felt safer with the little red Mustang in her rearview mirror. *Dumb*, she decided as she got out of the car. She'd cried on Jaime's shoulder, clutched Harrison's hands, let her men close ranks around her, a quintessential damsel in distress. *Grace*. In the dark she felt her cheeks burn. *Dumb and embarrassing. Martin's not going to hurt me.*

"What's wrong?" Harrison stood beside her ready to draw his sword and vanquish her villain.

She stifled a sigh. Martin wouldn't hurt her, but he might do something nuts. *I should have confronted him when I had the chance. Next time, I'll just say I'm Eliza, you leave me alone.*

She slid her hand into Harrison's. "Nothing," she said, "just thinking," and turned her attention toward the house that had been her home.

Lights shone through open windows and the front door stood open. *I don't hate it anymore*, she realized. *It's just a plain*

*old house waiting for another nice family to move in and make
it home.* Before she could register surprise, another thought
popped in: *That's what we were—a nice family, no matter how
Cal and I ended up.*

Relief, happiness, understanding—permission to move on.
She felt her smile all the way to her toes. She must also have
clutched his hand, too, because Harrison tensed. "What?"

"Nothing."

Someday she'd tell him, someday when they sat on the beach
or waited for the sun to set, and he would tell her about his life,
about his children, about his dreams. Then the van full of guys
and equipment lumbered to the curb. *Someday soon, just not
tonight.* "Nothing wrong," she repeated. "Just happy." She nodded
toward the pearl-white SUV parked at the curb. "Looks like
my boys beat us home, but who knew you could rent BMWs?"

HALF AN HOUR LATER THEY WERE all sitting on the living room
floor guzzling beer and pizza and dissecting the night's performance. She'd changed into jeans and a red T-shirt and now
sat shoulder to shoulder with her man, their backs against the
sofa as they enjoyed pepperoni and cheese and Sierra Nevada
Pale Ale.

She had just started to say something when Jaime shoved the
last bite of crust into his mouth and said, "That guy is freaking
me out."

Conversation stopped. Everyone looked at the biggest man
in the room.

"I mean it. We need to change our plane reservations and
go home tomorrow."

Eliza frowned. Nothing scared Jaime—no judge in a courtroom, no wave in the Pacific Ocean, no shark prowling Makena

Beach—nothing except maybe facing his mother when she was angry. He was afraid for her.

Before anyone else could respond, she said, "I don't think so, my best friend. We need to stay and do our job."

He glared. "You're being stubborn. You don't know what this creep might do."

Out of the corner of her eye, she saw Harrison nod agreement. Across the room, Jacob looked like he wanted to shout "hallelujah!" Rick and Derek drank their beers and kept quiet.

She understood their concern. They didn't see Martin Grimes as she did, scary but basically harmless. *Just unsettling*, she'd told Harrison earlier, and she believed it. Besides, Jaime had his career and she could always write songs, but, in many ways, Derek and Rick were like boys just reaching manhood. They needed all the exposure the band could get so they, too, could achieve their dreams. It wasn't fair to let her problems get in their way.

She met Rick's eye. He gazed back, handsome face expressionless. Derek didn't look up, his attention all on the beer label he was trying to peel off the bottle in one piece. *They care about me, too*, she knew, *and they're trying*. She grinned. *If nothing else, they should get their day in the sun.*

"You're right," she agreed in a reasonable tone, "but we can't let fear drive us away."

Jaime's lawyer voice thundered his reasons for leaving, liberally interspersed with such epithets as "fuck all," and "shit on a shingle," and character references such as "foolish woman," "stubborn chit," and a few Hawaiian phrases she was sure were even less complimentary.

When she could get a word in, Eliza listed her reasons for staying. "Besides," she finished with an evil grin, "we don't want to miss the party Harrison's friends are throwing in our honor."

Silence. If she could be brave enough to meet Harrison's lover—ex or not—then they should shut up and deal. The guys didn't need a blueprint to figure that out.

Jaime just sighed. "I rest my case."

She crawled across the carpet, threw her arms around his neck, and kissed his cheek. "No worries. I promise to be careful. It will be fine."

Jaime didn't look convinced and neither did Harrison, but there was no more talk of leaving.

Just after two in the morning, Eliza and Harrison stepped into the cool of his suite. Earlier, she'd been too nervous to appreciate her surroundings, so now she looked around. It was all a suite was supposed to be: granite counters and stainless steel in the kitchenette; sumptuous, overstuffed couch and two plump chairs, reading lights at the ready; dark wood tables polished to a high gloss.

There'd been a time when she'd longed for just one night in a place like this. Now, missing sand and sea, it was a little much.

She stepped to the wall of windows, tugged back the heavy silk drapes. Harrison came to stand behind her, his arms loose around her, chin resting on the top of her head. In the distance, the casinos—Silver Legacy, Eldorado, Circus Circus—illuminated the sky and outshone the stars.

"Nice view."

She nodded. "I like it. I was born here, went to school here. Except for a few vacations when the boys were little and a trip or two to see Jacob in Washington, I never knew anything else until Maui."

She turned in his arms and snuggled against him. She'd already discovered that difficult things were easier said into his chest. "Harrison, I'm a homebody and Maui is my home." A protest rumbled under her cheek. "Don't get me wrong, this is fun, and the concert is fun, and I do want to travel and see a little of the world, but at the end of the day, I want to write my songs and watch the sun set into the ocean from my own backyard."

Harrison, the man she knew had been everywhere and done everything, shifted his hands to her shoulders and held her so they were face to face. Conviction, determination, belief—she saw these in his eyes, knew they would shine with the same light as he assessed a tiny heart, discovered a way to make it whole. Her own heart fluttered, almost ready to believe.

"I want to be with you," Harrison said, his voice as sure as his gaze. "A whole life, not just bits and pieces. We'll figure it out."

He captured her left hand, looked at the ring. "You're wearing it. I wasn't sure you would." He kissed her fingers, the ring, her mouth.

A delicious warmth filled her, and she surrendered to his lips. The conversation wasn't over, she knew, as well as she knew there would be days and months when they would be apart. His life was one of action, and loving her wouldn't change that forever. As long as they came back together, she could be content.

His lips moved to her eyes, her face, back to her mouth, and then trailed kisses downward. She hung breathless in his arms, head thrown back to give him room. Tonight was hers, and she'd take every bit of it.

Light streamed through open windows as she woke, stretched, and slowly opened her eyes. No birdsong, no scent of plumeria filling the room, but the sheets were silky on her body, the bed soft beneath her, and the man at her side thrumming with desire.

"Good morning, dear man." Her hand found him as she whispered his name.

With a groan he slid into her and drove her up. No foreplay here, just heat and need, hers and his, and her body surged to his pounding rhythm.

Moments later, wet with perspiration, he collapsed on top of her. "Sorry, couldn't wait."

Luxuriating in his desire, she laughed. "Guess I couldn't either."

The morning slid by on ball bearings—a long, lazy swim in the third-floor pool and then breakfast poolside before children swarmed in for their end-of-vacation water play—and then their play day was over.

Later, wearing only pink bikini panties and a no-nonsense bra, Eliza bent at the waist, letting her hair hang loose and the curls dry as they would, and her words were muffled as she outlined the rest of the day's agenda.

"It's called Concert in the Park," she told a fully dressed Harrison, who sat in a side chair drinking coffee and watching her get ready. "At Wingfield Park, right downtown on the Truckee River. We play for about twenty minutes and then switch in and out to perform with the other bands. Not sure how Jaime finagled this gig, but it should be fun, good exposure, and another good cause."

She liked that he watched, but right now she could almost feel his scowl. She peeked through her hair and saw she was right.

"I know you're worried, but please don't be. There will be so many people Martin could never get close. I will be watchful. I promise."

She flicked him a mischievous grin. "And when we are done, there's a barbecue to enjoy."

The scowl stayed put, but he didn't argue. Nothing more to say.

Frowning herself, Eliza shook her head to separate the damp

strands into Eliza K's signature ringlets and changed the subject. "Harder to get curls in this dry climate. Have to be patient."

She heard him put the mug down, sensed his movement, and shivered as his lips brushed her bare neck.

"Patience is overrated."

His touch sent sparks up and down her spine. "Not now. If it doesn't dry curly, I'll have to start over."

"No worries." His fingers slid under the elastic of her panties. "Just hold still, and I'll do all the work."

Instant heat followed his fingers, smooth and gentle and relentless, until they found her center, then slow delicious torture as they stroked. Throbbing, breathless. Would she ever become used to this instant desire, so new and so surprising?

Hair be damned.

His hand slipped away as she straightened and turned to face him.

Not scowling now, and somehow his clothes had disappeared.

She choked on a surprised laugh. *If this is makeup sex, I'll take it.* "Will we always be this horny?"

"God willing," he said and lowered them both to the floor.

She rode him then, her curls carefully uninvolved. His hands found her breasts, insistent thumbs rubbing her nipples until her whole body demanded release. Crazy with her own need, she tightened around him, held each thrust until she thought she would explode, then let him go and took him back, his pleasure her only goal.

Her heart leaped when he stiffened under her. One powerful thrust as he emptied himself into her and then he stilled, captured in her depths. Shaking, she held him tight against her body for a moment longer, then let herself fly.

Later, held against his sweaty chest, Eliza thought, *If I died right now, I would be happy.*

CHAPTER 60
McLEAN

TRYING TO LOOK HARMLESS, CHRIS McLEAN lounged against the wall at the edge of a modern-looking stage and scanned the crowd. While the band had been setting up, he'd scoped out the Wingfield Park venue as carefully as he would an earthquake site. The stage sat at the corner of First Street and Arlington Avenue in the heart of downtown Reno, and traffic flowed heavily these last days of summer. The park itself encompassed a wide expanse of lawn inhabited now by throngs of people. Nearby, families frolicked in the Truckee River, which bisected the grounds. Cars and pedestrians, skateboarders, walkers, runners, music lovers, and people just out for the day—all probably benign, maybe not.

Fear tightened his gut.

A high-desert day with a slight breeze carrying the promise of fall. The bands good, none quite as good as Eliza and the guys. *Prejudiced? Nah.* He grinned.

The men talked quietly about the pros and cons—mostly cons in Jaime's opinion—of being on the road, then made plans to meet at the DeMello-Johnson home at six. Lots of time for barbecue before their 12:05 flight home.

"Look." Jaime nodded to the other side of the stage where Eliza stood surrounded by women in animated conversation. "Friends from before. Looks like she's enjoying them, but hey, where were they when she needed them?"

McLean nodded, checked his watch. One more hour. "I'll just wander around the perimeter, make sure the fucker isn't here." Jaime nodded and McLean strolled off, trying to keep it casual so security wouldn't think he was the wrong one.

The bands joined on stage for one last tune. When the notes faded into the sunshine, the audience clapped wildly, then gathered up chairs and blankets and kids and disbursed for dinner, and McLean made his way to Eliza's side. "Time to go."

"Don't be bossy." Her smile removed the sting. "I'll help the guys pack up, and then I'll be ready." She patted his arm. "Easy, dear man. We're almost home."

He stayed close, chatted with a very small girl in pink cowboy boots who wanted Ms. Eliza to autograph her tiny guitar, and grinned with undeserved pride as Eliza did just that. Through it all, he struggled to keep her in view.

Suddenly she wasn't there.

"Relax, man," Jaime's voice behind him before panic took over. "She's just gone to change."

His heart rate was almost back to normal when Eliza emerged from behind the stage wearing one of her island dresses, a riot of colorful Hawaiian flowers on soft white cotton, a yellow sweater tied around her neck, white sandals on her little feet. She reached his side, stood on her tiptoes to kiss his cheek. "Ready when you are."

He didn't scold, just pulled her close and kept her there until she was safely tucked into the Mustang. She pulled the

Washington Nationals cap over her curls, stretched out her legs with an "ahh" of pure pleasure, and fell sound asleep before his seat belt was buckled. He settled his own hat on his head and headed south, one hand on the wheel, the other gently covering hers as it lay on the center console.

Will I ever get tired of this? he wondered. *Watching her, touching her, loving her?* His head spun with the wonder of it.

As he pulled into the DeMello-Johnson homestead, the weight dropped off his shoulders and the fist in his gut stopped squeezing. *We made it.* He brought the little car to a halt in the driveway. *All good.*

The ranch-style home occupied the right front corner of a five-acre property on Huffaker Lane. He had been surprised when they'd chosen it.

"Unionville is too far away," DeMello had explained on his first kids' birthday visit as she toured him through the ghost town where she and Owen had met.

"Winnemucca doesn't have the opportunities the kids need," Owen had told him later, clearly sorry that he couldn't raise his brood in his nearby hometown.

No matter. Today, bathed in afternoon sunlight, it looked just like what it was—a home. Chris felt a tug in his heart. Was it too late for him?

Eliza opened her eyes when he turned off the motor, and he wondered if she'd really been sleeping.

"We're here?" She removed her hat and fussed with her hair, the look on her face suggesting she'd rather be cleaning toilets than walking into his lover's home, however *ex* DeMello might be.

"Yep."

Before he could say more, three children swarmed the car.

"And here's the welcoming committee."

He opened his door and jumped out. Two squirming

girls—stringy blond hair, their mother's aqua eyes, all arms and legs like puppies—pounced, and he swept them high into the air. The third child, a tall, sturdy boy with dark hair and a smirk, remained just out of reach, legs braced, voice taunting. "Can't catch me, Papa Chris. Betcha can't catch me."

No time to reassure her, McLean thought as he feigned left and then hustled right to trap the boy between his knees, and the four fell giggling to the dirt. He heard her door open, saw white sandals and trim legs emerge from the car. Children climbing him like a jungle gym, he hauled himself to a seated position and watched.

Looking like she wanted to run, Eliza closed the door and smoothed imaginary wrinkles from her dress.

Quinn sauntered down the gravel drive to greet them. Only the exaggerated sway of her hips belied nervousness. That and the palm swipe down the legs of her jeans.

At that moment, Chris McLean was very happy to be surrounded by children.

Eliza stepped forward and held out her hand. "Ms. DeMello, it's nice to see you again. Thank you for inviting us."

Quinn paused as though reminding herself to be nice, then grinned and pulled the smaller woman into a hug. "It's Quinn, or DeMello if you must, and believe it or not, after my curiosity was sated, I just wanted to get to know you."

Better than expected. Chris let out the breath he'd been holding, stuffed Will into a headlock, and started to get to his feet. "DeMello—"

Still in their hug, both women looked down and frowned at him, then started toward the house.

Will wriggled out of the headlock, pushed him back on his butt, and climbed onto his shoulders while the girls stayed close enough for Papa Chris's tickles. At least the kids wanted him.

He was still sitting in the drive when Owen arrived with two beers and a sympathetic expression on his face.

"Come on. If you can get up, I can rescue you from the minions." He nodded toward the house. "The girls went inside so we'll be safe in the backyard, and one beer should be enough to drown your troubles."

McLean extricated himself from six little arms, and their father sent them off to feed the chickens, which, it seemed, were even more entertaining than Papa Chris. He took a deep pull at the bottle, made a face. *Yep, one beer will be just enough.*

Before they made it to the backyard patio, the rest of the guests arrived—Jaime, Rick, and Derek in the rented van; Jacob and Raul in the snazzy white BMW, Raul at the wheel. And in moments, the backyard was alive with talking, laughing, sweaty people all looking for cold beers and shade. Somehow everyone got introduced. Owen's sisters, Vivian and Victoria, brought out trays of food—chips, salsa, guac, and an array of meat-filled pasties.

Mouth full of crumbled meat and some fantastic spice, McLean reminded himself to thank Vivian again for her cooking advice and maybe get the recipe for this delicious bit.

Before he could reach for seconds, little hands tugged him away, and soon he was ensconced in a lounge chair with Will on his lap. While the boy read *Anatomy for Children* out loud, McLean sipped his beer and looked around. Besides the chickens—one of which had been paraded for his inspection by the girls, Makena and Megan, and deemed a very fine specimen—he'd noticed ducks on the pond and two medium-sized young dogs that mingled easily with the guests in their common quest for treats.

Will looked up from his reading. "That's Daphne and Daisy, Papa Chris, you remember I helped them get born." Without waiting for a comment, the boy returned to his book. McLean remembered. It had been on his visit last year for their fourth birthday when Owen's bitch Sadie had delivered her tiny pups into Will's waiting hands. That memory put a smile on his face—a budding physician, to be sure.

Air cooling, sun dipping toward the Sierra reminded him—time passing. He looked around, didn't see either Eliza or Quinn. Where were they? Had he been foolish to bring Eliza here? He loved Quinn dearly, but she was not always kind. Just because she was his friend didn't mean she had to be Eliza's. The meat was sizzling on the grill, almost ready. Should he go find them?

Thinking, *fool, this is all on you if things go south,* Chris sent Will off to find his sisters and hurried around the house. A shiny new-model black car—Cadillac? Buick?— hovered near the driveway, then sped away. Huh? Someone trying to find an address in this out-of-the-way part of Reno, he guessed, and forgot about it as he entered a large room full of comfortable-looking furniture, a doll house, Legos, a large dump truck, and books everywhere.

Quinn and Eliza sat at opposite ends of a shaggy sofa, legs tucked under them in an almost mirror pose, engrossed in an animated and, he noted, friendly sounding conversation. Both used wine glasses for punctuation, and their laughter rang like music. Happiness rose inside him.

Quinn looked up and noticed his presence. "Go away, McLean, we're talking about you."

He flushed.

Eliza took mercy. "No we're not." She extended her hand. "Come sit with me, I'm getting caught up on five years of life with triplets."

DeMello just grinned and rolled her eyes.

He felt like hanging his head, scuffing his toe, and mumbling, "It's all right, ma'am," but he mumbled, "Owen says dinner's ready," instead, and escaped back out the front door.

He was in the driveway when they flanked him, laughing and teasing and then falling silent as a black Cadillac careened into the driveway and screeched to a halt in a spray of gravel that had Owen and Jaime hurrying around from the back to see what was going on.

Martin Grimes stepped out of the car, his eyes fixed on McLean.

McLean took in the details as he would an emergency in the operating room— dark suit, clean and pressed; white shirt, neatly buttoned; blue-striped tie, carefully knotted; eyes wild and crazy. At his side, Eliza's startled inhalation.

"Steady now," he whispered to himself.

"Martin." Eliza's voice broke. "Martin, what are you doing here?"

McLean extended his arms, pushed the women behind him. Quinn pulled out her phone and keyed it on.

Without shifting his gaze, the man shouted, "Stop."

They froze.

Martin Grimes raised his right arm, and McLean saw the little pistol, a .22, his memory told him even as he moved forward, his body positioned between Eliza and the man. Behind him someone gasped.

"Easy," he cautioned as fear threatened to choke him.

"Don't move." The man's voice trembled. The hand holding the gun held rock solid.

No one moved. Nothing moved. Color seeped from the scene. Birdsong faded. Backyard chatter disappeared. As the black and white world shrank to the size of a very small gun in an unpredictable hand, all McLean could hear was the ragged breathing of the women at his back—that and the sound of his own heart pounding harder than it ever had before.

He stood still, hands down and open, mind busy.

In a conversational tone, Martin addressed him directly. "It's your own fault, you know. You shouldn't be here. You turned her against me. You want to take her away." He waved the gun wildly, emphasizing each word, then steadied it with both hands. "You should have left things alone. Grace doesn't understand yet, doesn't realize that we belong together, soul mates, but she will. I'll help her to know that she can't be with anyone else."

Eyes on the gun, McLean mouthed to Quinn. "Kids?"

"Owen."

He nodded, almost sagged with relief. "Step back. Take Eliza. He won't hurt you. It's me he's come for."

The little man, his eyes now blazing, raised the gun to a bull's-eye on the bigger man's chest.

Knowing he'd been saved for this moment, Chris McLean stepped forward.

CHAPTER 61
ELIZA

WHEN THE WINGFIELD PARK CONCERT WAS over and Eliza had settled into the Mustang, leaned back and closed her eyes, it wasn't to sleep, although she was exhausted from the excitement and the work of their last performance. She needed to think, and, since Harrison had been clinging like a burr, retreating into pretend sleep seemed the only reasonable way to get thinking time.

For whatever reason, and it wasn't hers to say, Quinn DeMello and her family were Harrison's family. She could be pissy about an ex-lover or she could get over it and see what happened, one barbecue at a time. That problem solved, she did doze a little before they arrived. Decision made, nerves still crackled—at least until the tall, skinny blond wrapped her in a hug warm as toast.

That was all it took. The two women curled into a sofa surrounded with the evidence of a life full of children and laughed as they drank sparkling water and learned about each other. By the time Harrison stuck his head in to say dinner was ready—really to make sure they hadn't offed one another—she'd forgotten to be nervous. But he'd looked so worried that when he escaped back out the front door, she'd jumped up to follow him, Quinn at her heels. They caught up with him in the driveway. She had just reached up for a kiss when brakes screeched, gravel peppered her legs, and Martin Grimes climbed out of the shiny black car.

"Martin." Her voice caught in her throat. "Martin, what are you doing here?"

Dumb question—she knew why he was here, and it was past time to set him straight. No more star-crossed lovers. No more romantic drivel. *Stupid man*, she thought but didn't say, *you are not going to spoil our party.* Heartily wishing she'd done it earlier, Eliza started toward him, extended her hand. "Martin, let's ta—"

Harrison's arm shot out, stopping her in her tracks, pushing her behind him. To one side she saw Quinn pull out her cell phone, heard Martin yell, "Stop." Harrison trembled as he held her back.

Darn, they don't get it. I'm the only one who can fix this mess.

Martin started talking. Eliza peeked around Harrison and her knees turned to water. *He has a gun?*

Sound faded, and she was in the black and white world of her worst nightmare, the world where she stood paralyzed and watched disaster strike. Head spinning, vision dimming, Martin sounding so normal, so everyday, it took a minute for his words to make sense. "It's your own fault, you know. You shouldn't be here. You turned her against me. You want to take her away."

Dear God, he's blaming Harrison.

Harrison stood between her and the gun, and from a great distance she heard him direct Quinn to take her away.

He's blaming Harrison, and he means to hurt him. She forced courage into her knees. *Not gonna happen!*

Martin raised the gun to the level of her big man's heart. Harrison stepped forward.

"Nooooo!" Eliza darted between them.

Her head snapped back. The rumble of a thousand trains filled her world. Everything went dark.

Chapter 62
McLean

McLean dropped to his knees. Blood gushed, already soaking the gravel around Eliza's head. *Nooooo! It was supposed to be me!*

He'd intended to protect, to give his life for hers if need be, yet it was Eliza who lay motionless, eyes closed, lifeless. He rocked beside her still form, barely aware of the gun dropping from Martin's hand, Martin's body forced to the ground under the weight of enraged men.

DeMello slugged his arm. "You're the goddamned doctor, McLean. Save her."

The earth resumed its turning. Of its own volition, his hand went to Eliza's throat. Pulse thready but present. When he leaned in, a tiny breath caressed his cheek.

Tears streaming, he looked up. "She's alive."

Quinn nodded. "Good, keep her that way. Help's on the way."

Someone tossed him a towel and he made a pad to staunch the blood. That done, Chris McLean did the only other thing he could do—he gathered the woman he loved into his arms and gave her the warmth of his body until the paramedics shoved him out of the way and took over.

EIGHT DAYS LATER, MCLEAN SAT BESIDE her hospital bed, her small hand motionless in his own, and listened as machines, like metronomes, ticked the beat of her life. Time since Eliza had crumpled to his feet was blurred, remembered in vivid patches punctuated with dismal gray fuzz. He knew he'd forced his way into the ambulance, a nuisance to the paramedics who were doing the work he could not. He remembered pacing outside the operating door, his presence inside having been denied, until DeMello's shocked, "Oh my God, McLean, you're bleeding," brought unwanted attention to the blood oozing from his own arm where the .22 slug had come to rest. Only the threat of involuntary sedation had convinced him to let the physician assistant from the emergency department tend his wound.

And always someone—DeMello, Owen, Jaime, Jacob, or Raul—at his side.

Jed Dart's arrival had provided a frenetic interruption as Eliza's elder son wielded his Health Care Power of Attorney and accomplished little—all that could be done was already done.

The bullet had creased her skull, its force and its noise concussing her. Surgery had relieved the pressure. The medically induced coma into which she'd been placed had been reversed as the swelling of her brain decreased. She breathed on her own. Her heart muscle contracted and released in a fifty-five-beat-per-minute rhythm, slow and regular. Her mind and spirit continued somewhere else, tucked safely into a place he couldn't reach.

He was a physician. He knew the odds. The longer she was away, the smaller the chance she would ever return. Pain wracked his chest. He lifted her hand to his lips, kissed her fingers. When he realized the calluses had already softened from disuse, he burrowed his face into the rumpled sheets and sobbed.

DeMello slipped into the room, followed a minute later by her husband. Owen placed a hand on his shoulder. DeMello was less sympathetic.

"Christ, McLean, you look a wreck. When the poor woman wakes up and sees you, she'll hustle right back into her safe coma."

He scrubbed at his eyes. The tears flowed anyway. "It should have been me."

"Yeah, yeah, we've been all over that. It shouldn't have been anyone. And it's no help to Eliza if you continue on this death-warmed-over path. We'll sit with her a while. I brought your clean clothes and a razor. Go find a shower. She saved your worthless hide. The least you can do is smell good."

McLean stood. DeMello was right, it shouldn't have been anyone. She shoved an overflowing grocery bag into his arms. Throwing one last glance at Eliza, he shuffled out to find a shower.

In the doctors' lounge, McLean stood under a scalding spray. There must be a way to lead her back. As the water sluiced off his body, he gathered his determination and his courage. Dried off, shaved, and dressed in clean khakis and a denim shirt, he blessed DeMello and went in search of coffee and a charger for his phone.

In the second floor Starbucks, he sipped his third latte while he waited for Raul's download to complete. Raul had made a video of the Bartley Ranch show; now the clever man had recreated the soundtrack and was sending it to McLean—maybe Eliza's own voice, her own music, the band that was her family could rouse her. A beep alerted him. Download complete. He unplugged the phone and picked up the coffee he'd ordered for the others. Then, with a speck of hope in his heart, he returned to her room.

Quinn sat on his vacated chair reading aloud—*Winnie the Pooh and the Blustery Day*, perfect. Owen sat in the corner working on his laptop. Both stopped what they were doing when he stepped in.

"I've got something new to try." He distributed the coffee and explained his idea.

"Let's run it through my laptop," Owen offered. "Sound will be better."

They did, and soon Eliza's voice filled the room. Between songs, clever Raul had interspersed narrative—McLean's voice, Jacob's, Jaime's—and McLean's heart thundered as he regained his chair and drew Eliza's flaccid hand back into his own.

This has to work. I won't let her die.

Knowing Eliza's life was not his to command, his fingers went to her emerald ring, safe on a chain around his neck. The fear that she'd never wear it, never strut her red boots across a stage, never trail make-it-better kisses down the scar on his chest hitched his breath.

"Come back to me, dear heart; please come back."

DeMello had come to stand behind him, her hand resting on his shoulder.

From Owen's laptop, Eliza's voice caressed the word "resting," ready with the others for the final refrain. Her eyelids fluttered.

The hand on his shoulder tightened. DeMello had seen it, too.

Tears filled his eyes. "It's time, Eliza Grace. Open your eyes."

Her lids fluttered again, then went still, and his heart plummeted. In the emptiness, he heard little Will's voice—"Dear Almost-Gran E, please don't die. I'm not a doctor yet so I can't save you. I love you. Sincerely, Will Johnson"—and McLean did what he thought he'd never do again: he laughed. He laughed until tears streamed down his face, and Quinn laughed with him and across the room, Owen chuckled, too, and the room was suddenly filled with hope.

Clinging to that thin thread, McLean bowed his head and raised Eliza's fingers to his lips, whispered, "You heard the boy, dear heart. Don't die yet," and he bit her finger as she had bitten his so many months earlier. Her hand jerked. "Wake up, dratted woman, it's time to come home."

DeMello's grip on his shoulder tightened again, and he raised his head.

Soft gray eyes looked into his, unfocused, confused. Then they cleared, and Eliza Grace looked back at him, mischief gleaming.

He sucked in a breath of wonder.

Her impish smile flashed. Her voice, raspy from disuse, filled his heart. "About time, Heartbreak Harry. Let's go home."

Epilogue

TODAY I MARRY MY DEAREST LOVE.

Hand in hand, we stand on the beach, the oranges and pinks and reds of the setting sun behind us, to make our promises before witnesses. I wear white slacks and a white shirt, Eliza a flowing white dress that leaves her shoulders bare. Our feet are bare in the warm Maui sand.

Jaime stands for Eliza and DeMello for me on this just-right day, and Mrs. Leilani Hokoana presides. In her paper-thin voice, she chants the Hawaiian ceremony that will bind us each to the other.

I marvel that we are here.

Eliza has no memory of that terrible day, and for that I am grateful. Once fully awake, she was released to heal at home. Just before we boarded the plane, she visited Martin Grimes, incarcerated and incompetent, and afterward she wept. Must admit, even I felt a twinge at the slack-jawed, vacant-eyed drooler he's become.

Three months later, thanks to a marvelous therapist and Eliza's own fierce determination, the only sign of the injury that nearly took her life is the scar almost hidden under her short curls, and she has a new song ready to record. When I proposed again, she laughed and said, "About time. I took a bullet for you, Harrison, the least you can do is marry me," and here we are. We will live in her house and mine, together as much as we can be, and create a life that fits, but most of that is unimportant. When I look in her eyes, I am home.

She tugs at me now, demanding my attention, as Mrs. Hokoana finishes her chant. "Harrison McLean," the old woman says, "now you speak to your woman."

Filled with so much emotion, I'm not sure I can, but I turn to face Eliza and she squeezes my hand. I clear my throat.

"Eliza Grace King, I give you my heart. I will cherish and protect you, love and adore you until the moon forgets to rise and the sun forgets to set, and whenever I can, I will hold you safe in my arms."

DeMello hands me a lei. I place it around Eliza's neck and kiss away the tear that trickles down her cheek.

"Eliza King," the old woman says, "you speak now."

A smile blossoms as Eliza turns to me, and love gleams in her eyes. "Harrison Christian McLean," she begins, "I'd give you my heart but you already have it, so hear this, my dear man: The sun and the moon *do* rise in your eyes. I will cherish and adore you for all the days of my life, and whenever I can, I will rest safely home in your arms. *Aloha wau ia 'oe.*"

Jaime hands her a lei, and I bend so she can place it around my neck. She lays her hand on my cheek in a gesture so familiar and dear it almost stops my heart, then she pokes me in the ribs and whispers, "Hurry up and kiss me, these people have come for the show."

What can I do? As our friends and relatives clap and call out *hana hou*, I lift her and take her mouth, and we are one.

ACKNOWLEDGEMENTS

THREE YEARS AGO, AS WE WERE eating a gourmet breakfast in the delightful McCloud Hotel, I said, "I really like McLean," and my sister said, "Maybe he needs his own story." From that moment, *McLean's Heart* seemed to write itself.

That doesn't mean no help was needed. I am indebted to my sister, Linda Doty, for that initial suggestion and then for the many reads as the story went from idea to completion. I wrote most of the first draft in Maui, where my friend, Dr. Lisa Caverhill, gave me a home away from home and made sure we researched each happy hour site and scoped out every beach. As if that weren't enough, she also listened to me read each word as my thoughts became sentences and then chapters and, finally, the novel you've just read. Thank you, Linda and Lisa, from the bottom of my heart.

My friend and promoter extraordinaire, Linda Fine Conaboy, has read this story almost as many times as I have, always with thoughtful comments and words of encouragement. *McLean's Heart* is better, and I am saner, because of her.

I truly appreciate Tutti Bailey's help with Hawaiian customs and language; Dr. Kamin Van Guilder's assistance with details on shooting-related head injury; and Brian, Russ, and Stephanie's fearless critique.

Once again, my team at Lucky Bat Books has taken my words and created this beautiful book. Without Jessica, Sarah, and Nuno, *McLean's Heart* would still be stuck on my laptop. McLean, Eliza, and I thank them all.

And always, always, always, I am grateful that my parents, Stan and Mabel Doty, made books essential in my life.

ABOUT THE AUTHOR

Patti Doty is a Nevada native. Although she won prizes for writing while she was a student, she chose a career in medicine as a physician assistant and marriage and family therapist. But she never abandoned her first love, and in 2013, she published her first Quinn DeMello novel, *Runaway*, and *Finding Home* followed soon thereafter.

Retired now, Patti travels widely—most recently spending time in Antarctica, Thailand, and Maui—always looking for new locations for her characters and their stories of love and change. When she's not circumnavigating the globe, Patti can be found at home in Northern Nevada, where she lives with her standard poodle, Izzy.